JOE

Carol Rose GoldenEagle

Published by
BookLand Press Inc.
15 Allstate Parkway, Suite 600
Markham, Ontario L3R 5B4
www.booklandpress.com

Printed in Canada

Library and Archives Canada Cataloguing in Publication

Title: Joe / Carol Rose GoldenEagle.
Names: GoldenEagle, Carol Rose, 1963- author
Series: Modern Indigenous voices.
Description: Series statement: Modern Indigenous voices
Identifiers: Canadiana (print) 2025012923X | Canadiana (ebook)
20250129264 | ISBN 9781772312461 (softcover) |
ISBN 9781772312478 (EPUB)
Subjects: LCGFT: Novels.
Classification: LCC PS8607.A5567 J64 2025 | DDC C813/.6—dc23

We acknowledge the support of the Government of Canada through the Canada Book Fund. We acknowledge the support of the Canada Council for the Arts. We acknowledge funding support from the Ontario Arts Council and the Government of Ontario.

This book is dedicated to my dear friend, Alice Marvin, who teaches me about plants and has great wisdom about life, in general.

Acknowledgements

For my Baby Bears: Jackson, Nahanni and Daniel.

To the memory of our Canadian gem, the late Gordon Lightfoot. For some reason, his passing inspired me to write this manuscript. He created such beauty, in sharing his music. I hope this manuscript does the same, inspiring imagination and creativity. RIP dear friend to so many. May your guitar be eternally tuned, and, we'll watch for you in the stars and hear you in the wind.

For the strong Ancestors who have allowed in me, the gift of genetic memory: Marie Tawipisim, Gertie Montgrand, Lydia Bighetty, Maggie Morin, Lily Daniels, Emily Meguinis, Lena Adams.

And for my dear friends and contributors of knowledge while writing this manuscript: Craig Davidson, Jay Semko, Alice Marvin, Joseph Kakwinokanasum, Kim Trynacity, Kenneth T. Williams, John Brady McDonald, Wen Paisley, Bevann Fox, Ryan Kiedrowski, Valerie Raye, Laura Davies, Jeannie Leblond, Chad Czako, Shane Czako, Bruce Rodger, Pamela Rodger, Carol Wright, Skye Domotor, Stacey Fayant, Larry Hall, Danny Kerslake, Lori Nieto, Tyler Nickolson, Quincy Grohs, Rod Gawley, Alex Bodnarchuk, Rachel Brimacombe, Chris Exner, Trevor Herriot, Crystal LaMontagne, Kelly-Anne Riess, Shari Braun, Cristian Moya, Duane Wright, Betty Tomasunos Sellers, R. James Misfeldt, Keestin Bear, Denny Joyal, Saffy and Pumpkin, and to the Angels, both light and dark, who travel alongside me, offering protection, through this journey we call life.

I gratefully acknowledge the financial support in creating this book, and give thanks to SK Arts.

Table of Contents

Earlier	9
Shadows	16
Morning or Mourning	22
Dusk	25
Hazel	29
Sunrise Sunset	35
Paying it Forward	39
In Search of a Drink	44
Recreation	48
Guess Who's Coming to Dinner?	55
Gathering Evidence	60
Miserable Moments	64
Transition	67
The Curse of Woman	71
Drinking Alone	75
Patience is a Virtue	81
Biding Time	88
Great Expectations	91
Baptism by Fire	96
Truth or Dare	100
Redemption	105
Ancestral Land	116

A Kindness   123
The Watchers   128
Rejuvenate   135
Out in Public   142
The First Kiss   151
Only Women Bleed   162
Second Time Around   168
Pondering   172
Slow Dancing   179
Into the Night   183
Reap What You Sow   187
Afterglow   191
A Little Misstep   195
On Weathering the Storm   200
His Mother's Ring   204
Tortured Beginnings   208
For Better or For Worse   213
Start Spreading the News   219
Undercurrents   223
When Love Outweighs the Pain   229
Night Moves   234
Good Night Sweet Prince   238

Joe never meant to become an alcoholic.
He never meant to become a vampire either.
Both happened. And it is because of drinking.

Earlier

He had gone out after his shift. Joe works as a fry cook in a local restaurant. The Bluebird Cafe is the oldest restaurant in Regina Beach, a family-owned business that's been open since 1928. Very little has changed with the facade of the building, since then. The white stucco exterior has the look of old architecture. Picnic tables are set up at the side of the cafe, although most visitors seem to prefer sitting on the giant concrete steps, that lead up to the take-out window. From the stairwell is an amazing view of the lake.

The cafe has been using the same recipe for battering its fish for over 90 years.

That is Joe's job. He spends his summer days, sweating beside a deep-fryer, in an old, vintage kitchen, that has high ceilings and black & white tiling on the floor.

There is a bit of an art to properly battering the fish. The mixture needs to be fluffy, being quickly whisked by a blender to the point that bubbles are created. Then, the half-frozen cod is generously coated, and immediately it goes into the fryer. The result is a hot, light and crunchy piece of fish, served with fresh potatoes that have been hand-cut, and are also deep fried.

The town is a resort community, quiet during winter months and bursting with activity in the summer. The influx of seasonal residents returning to their cottages, and day-visitors from the city, makes for good business. Summer is the time of year when cafes, which close during the off-season, can make enough of a profit to ensure that there'll be no need to work during the cold winter months. The Bluebird Cafe, famous on the Prairies for its fish & chips, is one of them.

The main street, where most of the businesses are located, runs along one big hill, that leads to the lake. And, that street is ornate during tourist season, with large flower pots, bursting with colour, and sculptures decorating the side of the main street. The look is celebratory as banners hang from above, welcoming visitors, and there's usually some type of sidewalk chalk art at one or more of the intersections. There are so many trees, right throughout the town, that a shady spot to rest is always to be found, when the day gets too hot, as summer temperatures rise. Then again, there's always that lovely, fresh-water lake in which to jump in, and cool down. Last Mountain Lake. Kinookimaw is what it's called by the Cree. The word means long lake, and it is, stretching for miles and miles throughout this part of the Qu'Appelle Valley in southern Saskatchewan.

The lake extends all the way from the Town of Southey through to an area around the Town of Dundurn, which is a community not far from the City of Saskatoon. 93 kilometres of beauty. That is Last Mountain Lake. It's a haven in this part of the southern Prairies. There are so few natural bodies of water in Southern Saskatchewan. It's why people, and pelicans, flock to this area in droves.

It's been a busy day for Joe, putting out order after order of fish and chips. He's grateful for closing time.

Stepping out of the cafe, at the end of his shift, Joe smells as he always does. Like a combination of grease and sweat. It's in sharp contrast to the serene setting of tonight's sun, and the scent of fresh lilacs blooming in early summer. The busy season has just begun, and Joe is already tired. He's not quite ready for the steady pace of tourist season, just yet.

It will be dark soon enough, and Joe knows that he should go home and shower, then maybe turn on an action movie that's streaming online, and go to bed early. There is always a break-fast rush, and for some reason, he agreed to work a double shift tomorrow, starting early in the morning. It should mean lights out for him now, at an early hour tonight.

But that isn't destined to happen. All day long, while standing in front of the fryer, he's been thinking about where he will get his next sip of alcohol. It's his first thought each day, and it's what he thinks about all day. How can he finally satisfy the urge and taste another sig of vodka?

He's thinking specifically about apricot brandy now, because he has a bottle of it back at his home. Joe has a cavity in his back, right molar and it's causing him pain. He remembers that his Mom once told him that she used to rub the high-alcohol content liquor on his gums, when Joe began to grow teeth, as a baby. It does work at momentarily. at soothing the pain, so it's a practice that he's doing today, rubbing his gums with brandy until he's able to get in to see a dentist.

But, all these years, Joe has always wondered about how responsible it is, or how safe it is, to give alcohol to an in-fant. His Mother rubbed the brandy on his gums to lessen the pain of teething. Had ingesting it at such a young age some-how made him more susceptible to craving alcohol, now as an adult?

Joe can't be sure, but he does begin to salivate, glanc-ing at the pub across the street and seeing an older gentle-man taking a mouthful of beer from a long neck bottle. The gent sits at the large deck, attached to Joe's favourite watering hole. The pub is an establishment that is always busy when the weather's good.

He checks his pockets. He figures he'll stop by the pub and order a shot of apricot brandy to rub on his gums, and then maybe he'll order a large draught beer to wash it down and call it a day. That's his intention as he makes his way across the street. Tip out for the kitchen staff happened today. It means an extra one hundred and twenty dollars which Joe considers play money. So he does.

The pub is not the fanciest place to drink and spend time. The decor includes old hub caps from vintage vehicles, hanging on the walls, instead of original artwork. Most of the other business establishments in town support local artists, allowing them to display their colourful paintings, for sale. The tables at the pub are a hodge podge of old garage sale finds, including a painted picnic table. It has nicks carved into it, probably made by some kid with a new jackknife. The paint is chipped along the window frames as well, looking like there might have been water damage at some point, that no one ever bothered to fix.

But, it isn't the ambience of the place that attracts Joe. It isn't even the booze they sell. It is the waitress. Her name is Hazel. The first time Joe met her, he joked that Hazel sounds like the name for a witch. Not a good first impression.

She isn't rude to him for saying it. She isn't polite either, just curtly taking his order, with a stern sounding voice, "Right. What do you want?"
"A double vodka and seven, Darling." He snickers, and slaps Hazel on the ass as she writes the order down on a yellow pad of paper. Joe has always crossed the line when it comes to, what he thinks, is flirting.

He is crass and offensive, without even realizing. That, and too many double vodka's, is why he sits in the pub, alone again, at the end of the night. He never did just order his one draught beer and then go home, as was his intention at the beginning of the night.

The local residents, who know Joe, are likely to sit down and engage in small talk with him for a while, until he's had too many. There is always some point where Joe's conversation turns from being slightly interesting to just being stupid, and hard to follow. It's not that he's a mean drunk. He just doesn't make any sense; muttering gibberish, sometimes even reciting familiar nursery rhymes, and he repeats himself. He also starts talking very loud, to the point of yelling, as though the alcohol has somehow caused him to be hard of hearing. It's at this point that anyone who may have sat down to say hello, politely gives an excuse, and leaves. Once he's had too many, Joe is uncomfortable to be around.

Joe can't be called a handsome man. He's plain to look at, easily blending into any crowd. He's got the features of some good-ole farm boy, with a square jawline, green eyes and a shock full of brown hair. But, he is tall, six footer, and with a slim build. Just some regular guy next door. Joe is first-generation Canadian-born. His family immigrated from Eastern Europe and settled in Saskatchewan in the 1950's. His Mom remained fluent in her Polish language right throughout her life, and continued to speak the language, fluently.

Every now and then, that Polish accent can be detected in Joe as well. It becomes more pronounced when he's drunk. Like now.

He's been perched on his bar stool at the counter all evening, and when the waitress brings out his fifth drink, she doesn't set it down in front of him. Hazel smashes the glass down at the edge of the table, a bit of it spills. She walks away not meeting Joe's eye, and without comment.

More hours pass. Too many of them, and Joe has spent all of his kitchen tip out money on double vodkas. He tries making small talk with Hazel, telling her that he's supposed to come in early, to the cafe, in the morning. The oil needs to be drained from the fryer once it has time to cool overnight. "Drain the dragon. That's what I need to do."

Hazel grimaces and rolls her eyes at the remark. Drain the dragon. It's how she's heard other drunken sods describe sexual encounters that they have had. She can't figure out if Joe's comment is a bad attempt to entice her, or if he's making some type of reference to his penis. She feels a little less uneasy with his next remark.

Joe says, "Yes, that oil in the deep-fryer gets dirty so fast, now that it's the busy season. It needs to be drained almost daily. Not a fun job. When I left tonight, it smelt like when you open the hood of an overheated vehicle." Joe thinks he's being clever, until Hazel tells him that the word is smelled.

"A person smelts metal. It bugs me when people mis-use words." Joe can't decide if Hazel is ridiculing him, or just giving a much-needed correction. The tone of her comment is not mean-spirited or sarcastic. Whatever the case, Joe's just happy that they're engaging in something that, to him, vaguely resembles engaging in discussion. It's short-lived.

Hazel adds, "We're closing, Joe. Time to go home. Do you need a ride?"

Hazel has been patient with her drunken patron all evening, enduring his inane comments. But when the final bill arrives, he does leave her a big tip. Her suggestion for offering Joe a ride home doesn't mean that she plans on driving him.

Hazel recalls, with disgust, how he was so drunk, once earlier this spring, that Joe wasn't even able to walk home. But, he couldn't stay at the pub either, and Hazel didn't feel right just leaving him to sleep it off on the sidewalk. So, she did what she could.

By chance, there is a wheelchair in the back storage shed. It's there for use when the pub owners' elderly father visits. He's got mobility problems, and having the chair available ensures that the old man is able to get out and take part in whatever may be happening in the community, rather than just sitting indoors. That wheelchair came in handy, when having to deal with Joe that night. Hazel, literally, wheeled him to his home. She was able to fish his house keys out of his pants pocket, and wheel him into his home. She covered him with a throw blanket that she spotted on the couch, and left him sitting in the chair. She wasn't worried about its return. Joe comes into the pub often enough that he'll figure out where the chair came from, and know that he'll need to wheel it back.

Tonight, it's the bartender who wants to know if Joe needs a ride. He feels guilty for not cutting him off some time ago. Both, the bartender and Joe live in the same area of town. It's close by. He'll drive him home.

"No, my Darling. I can walk. It's not far. It'll do me some good to get some fresh air," Joe says to Hazel, as he staggers towards the door. By this time, all other patrons have left. No bar staff asks him if they can take his keys, knowing, he doesn't carry car keys. They know, Joe lost his licence after receiving a DUI almost a year ago. It's a small town. People talk.

The last thing Joe remembers is the sound of the lock on the door clicking behind him, as Hazel closes up for the night.

Shadows

There is a slight hill that leads from the pub to the pathway beside the lake. Joe stumbles towards it as he begins his drunken walk back to his home. The pathway, today, is where the train used to run, back in the early history of the town. Decades ago, train travel was a usual way to get from the city to the Beach. The tracks have been long since removed. Now, the pathway is tree-covered and quiet. There is a bit of worn asphalt in some places, but most of the path is covered in gravel.

Joe has no way of knowing that he's being followed. By whom?

It is a Being, who has been watching Joe drinking his doubles all night long. He wasn't in the pub though. Instead, he could see Joe through the large glass windows, as he sits perched on the concrete steps of the cafe across the street.

The man is a stranger. He's got a face that has seemingly no features, or a face you don't want to know. A man who hides in darkness, waiting for his moment to strike. A man? Maybe, but maybe not.

Now, he's following Joe, and watches as he stops along the pathway. Joe is struggling to open the fly on his jeans. He needs to take a piss. He doesn't like using public toilets. Some urine escapes before he's able to grab his hose and point it towards the weeds, growing along the shoreline.

The sounds of crickets and frogs, by the lake front, are prominent, at this hour. But those sounds promptly stop, as Joe stumbles and falls, hearing only a voice that sounds like someone who's had too much whiskey, "Need any help?"

Where did this guy come from? Joe doesn't remember hearing footsteps behind him. The shadow is dressed in old garb, that looks like something from a flea market. He's wearing a fedora, even though there is no need to hide from the sun at this hour. He's got an oversized trench coat over his shoulders. He has no natural body scent, instead, he smells like dust. He's skinny and as tall as a giraffe.

Like an apparition, Joe realizes he is familiar with the scent of this man. The same smell was there when Joe was a little boy, and hurriedly riding his bike down a gravel road one night. Joe remembers.

It is dusk, and little Joe wants to get home before dark. He knows if he doesn't show up soon, his Mom will worry. Maybe she'll even cry and start calling the neighbours, or even the police. The fading daylight doesn't allow little Joe to notice a big pothole in the middle of the road. He hits it with a thud, and goes catapulting from his bicycle. The boy is ejected and flying through the air, as if in slow motion. But he never hits the rocky ground. That tall man is there, catching him from his fall. Where had he come from? Little Joe doesn't care. He is just grateful that he's not hurt.

"Whoa, little fella, you need to be more careful," Dust Man says, before gently placing the boy back on the grassy area at the side of the road. "You go home now, before it gets dark. It's not safe out here for a young child, at this hour. Or any hour after dark." Joe remembers the stranger hoisting his bicycle, from the rut in the road. The front wheel is bent a bit, from the hard impact. Dust Man straightens it with a hard twist of his hands, fixing it like new again, as if the accident never happened. Little Joe arrives home safely that night, just as his Mom has turned on the light which brightens the front door and veranda area. "Glad you're home, Sweetie," she says, ruffling up his hair, "go on inside. I made some pocorn. You can have a little snack before getting ready for bed." Joe's Mom grabs the handle bars of his banana bike. Before leaning it against the fence, she straightens her apron and blows the little boy a kiss.

Another fragment of memory travels back, as Joe again remembers the scent of the tall stranger.

That also happened at dusk, years later.

Joe is a young teenager, and walking home down this same pathway. He's just played a game of scrub baseball, which is an impromptu game that happens when local kids gather at the ball diamond near the church at the top of the hill.

The adolescent Joe is proud of himself, and reveling in the fact that he'd hit a home run.

It's during this diversion in thoughts that he feels that same baseball, hitting him squarely on his back. It hurts. When he turns to look and see who's thrown it, the town bully is there, shouting, "You little fucker," the kid was the pitcher of the scrub game, "you think you're a hero now, eh? Showing me up like that." That's when the freckled-face assailant balls up his right hand, making a fist, "I'll show you who's the boss now." For a moment, the adolescent Joe feels fright, which quickly turns to relief as Dust Man unexpectedly steps out of the bushes.

The strange man is the same dark figure that Joe remembers being present during other times of imminent peril. The presence of Dust Man causes the bully to turn and run. Joe is never bothered by the scraggy kid again, after that day.

That's all Joe remembers tonight, before familiar black out sets in.

But even, that loss of consciousness doesn't happen immediately.

Joe blankly recalls, first asking the dark stranger, "Hey man, do you have a beer?" The shadow gives an answer of yes. He casts a spell, hypnotizing Joe, then watches and waits.

The calm stranger slits his own wrist with a long, yellowed fingernail, "Here, drink this," he says. Joe should be appalled, but in his own drunken state, the image of what's happening transforms. Instead of seeing blood dripping from the stranger's slit wrist, Joe sees an opportunity for what's called shotgun. It's that drinking game he's played many times, during his life as an alcoholic.

Joe is mesmerized into believing it's what's happening again. Shotgun is something that's kept him a constant state of abuzzment for years.

That's what the game is called. Shotgun. It's where the bottom of a beer can is pierced, allowing the liquid to flow freely and rapidly. Like turning on water at a kitchen tap. The aim of shotgun is to see who can swallow the flowing brew most quickly. The prize is winning another beer, a tall boy can this time.

As Joe recalls the game, he drinks from the wrist of Dust Man.

Once he's done, Joe feels sharp fangs, pierce his jugular vein.

It should, but doesn't hurt. Instead, other fragments of harsh and painful memory come crashing back.

He remembers being yanked off the couch.
He is five, and his father is slapping him. It is Sunday morning. Joe's Mom is in the kitchen making toast.
Little Joe is watching cartoons on the television, when his dad tells him to get off the couch if he is going to eat toast. Little Joe doesn't respond immediately, so his dad violently throws him to the floor. He remembers his Mom saying she is going to call the police, if he

doesn't stop. He remembers his dad punching his Mom in the head, for standing up for her son. Joe remembers that. Within a moment, little Joe is slapped so hard again that he passes out.

Similar violent scenes play out so often in the memory of his childhood home.

He remembers waking up one night, just a few weeks later.

He hears crying down in the living room. His father is drunk again, and raping his Mom by thrusting a long necked beer bottle up and down in her vagina. The drunkard spits and slurs towards Joe, "Now, you'll get it too."

His Mom cries. Joe stands frozen in fear. How old is he? Maybe nine, too young for a child to witness. After that, he figures out a way to block out memory.

He does it by using alcohol.

The double vodkas today still follow the pattern. Blocking memory by blacking out.

Joe will never know that what the Dust Man just did, by forcing Joe to drink his blood, is an act of kindness.

The dark angel can smell that Joe's prolonged and excessive abuse of alcohol has made him sick. Dust Man can hear Joe's high blood pressure rising. He senses that an aneurysm will suddenly strike. And soon. Dust Man knows, because the same thing almost happened to him, centuries ago, before he was changed too.

He didn't want the same fate for this boy, who he's been following around, for most of Joe's life.

Dust Man.

He is the dark angel, send to intervene, to steer others away from entering the dark portal where he is destined to live.

It can happen so easily.

Dust Man knows that Joe has already reached that fork in the road. It's a place of no return. And, Joe's been choosing the wrong path for years. Did Dust Man act out of kindness, salvation or mercy?

It's difficult to say, if what he's just done has caused more harm than good. The morning sun will be the witness. Dust man stays around long enough to watch, and make sure that Joe reaches the dawn.

Morning or Mourning

Joe wakes up just before sunrise. The birds are already singing and the lake is calm. To his surprise, he feels calm as well.

There is no familiar hangover, despite drinking all those doubles the night before. Joe wonders.

But why am I here? He attempts to recall what happened last night. He remembers getting off shift at the kitchen, and going to the pub. He remembers flirting with Hazel and ordering drinks. He vaguely remembers walking home, but he can't figure out why he never got there. Then, he feels a slight pain on the side of his neck. There is a crust of dried blood. He feels a thirst that he's never felt before, and has nothing to do with double vodka.

Joe takes a deep breath then heaves himself off the well-used asphalt, on this part of the pathway, before heading home. His hair is disheveled, his clothing is torn and his skin is pale, as he walks slowly. He feels like he should be shivering, having spent the entire night out in the open. Instead, he's comfortable, like spending time in the night elements is second nature.

The dawn hasn't yet broken, and the air is silent. There are no familiar traffic sounds, nor a trace of any type of movement, except for the morning birds. It's early and the world is still asleep. Even though he's just woken up, alone on the pathway, Joe feels the need to join everyone who is still at home and resting in their beds.

He is experiencing an overwhelming lethargy that only sleep can cure.

It is both odd and frightening to Joe, when he gets back to his home. It's as though, not only he, but his very house has transformed as well. Spiders always spin their webs during the warmer months. But it's usually just a smattering of webbing, and somewhere off in a private corner, like near a window that rarely gets opened. Today though, Joe's front door looks like it's been covered in some type of knitted Afghan blanket that the church ladies might make. The doorway is blocked by webs. All of it, created by the spiders, like a netting to keep him out. What's it supposed to mean, he wonders, but is too tired to ponder it.

Joe clears the webbing and enters. He immediately draws the heavy blinds in his bedroom and then makes a call, with an old rotary-style telephone that's been on his bedside table ever since he can remember.

The phone call is to the kitchen. He leaves a voice mail, "I can't make it in today, for breakfast rush. From now on, schedule me only for late night rush. Something's come up. Can't explain."

Joe falls onto his bed, as his thoughts drift to places they've never gone before.

Somehow, he knows that he is being guided by genetic memory. Some call it blood memory. In this case, the reference is literal. He has an innate knowing that the morning sun is a danger to him. It's why he closed the heavy blinds, first thing.

The sun is the brightest upon rising, the Hand of God coaxing new life from plants and trees. A new beginning, but those early rays can spell the end for him now, burn him up. He knows he needs to stay indoors during the morning hours and until the sun shifts past the noon hour.

Joe runs his fingers through his dark hair. What happened last night?

He wonders if he had a dream, or maybe it was a nightmare. Perhaps a combination of both, with some type of foresight or warning attached.

He recalls meeting Dust Man, the one who he remembers being his saviour in the past. But what did Dust Man do to cause such disturbing confusion for Joe, in these moments right now?

In an effort to find some clarity, Joe hoists himself off the bed and walks to the bathroom. He figures that maybe splashing some cold water on his face might help him make some sense out of the gnawing feeling of doom, he's experiencing since waking up outside.

As he looks in the mirror, Joe is startled to the point of losing breath. And, he's got his answer. He no longer has a reflection.

No reflection. No past. No future.

Joe feels weak, the slight scent of Dust Man still clinging to his clothes.

He does the only thing that makes sense in this moment, which is to go back to his bedroom and lay down in the darkened room.

Sleep takes him immediately, like it never has before. Bereft of dreams and memories, it's a new type of black out, behind the safety of blackened window shades.

One he will have to learn to get used to.

Dusk

The next day, Joe makes it back to the restaurant kitchen, in plenty of time to get ready for the supper rush. "Hey pal, glad you are feeling better," the owner of the cafe says, patting Joe on the back, "you look different today. Like a weight has been lifted. But, it's just good to have you back." Joe's boss rubs some grease from his hands, on the apron he's wearing. "It's going to be a busy night. You need to get these ready for the fryer." The boss points to a 50-pound box of fresh potatoes.

As Joe lifts the heavy vegetables up on a sterile steel shelf, he wonders how he ended up here. He figures he should be more affluent and settled at this point in his life, instead of being in his mid-40's and working in a kitchen.

Yes, he needed a job. Can't buy booze without money. Can't drive without a driver's licence, and he lost his some time ago. The cafe is within walking distance from the house he inherited from his Mom after she passed away, five years ago.

That is the last time Joe felt fresh. He'd been nine months sober and was working as an advertising consultant in Regina, at the time.

He's spent years towards earning a Business Degree at the University of Regina. Joe remembers how proud his Mom is on the day that he graduates. He still feels her hands, pinning on a red rose corsage to his graduation gown. Her words, "I am so proud of you, baby boy," is the manna he needs, to believe he'll carry on and do good in this world.

Before joining the advertising firm, Joe starts out small, working for Arts organizations that want help to rebrand, for funding purposes, and prove their relevance. As if the Arts ever need to prove their importance. All genres are necessary. Always have been. Just look back on history. There can be no good quality of life without the Arts. Bold colour. Powerful words and music.

It touches the soul, and Joe knows this. Feels it. He spends a year being an Arts advocate, until money entices him towards advertising.

That job is good pay, until the day he comes up with bad ideas that backfire.

The city that never sleeps is something everyone knows. A brand, and a place where everyone wants to go. New York, of course.

It is his job, with the advertising agency, to come up with ideas to increase tourism in the City of Regina. Rhymes with vagina, which makes Joe snicker, "We can turn this place into something sexy." It's his thought. So, he comes up with slogans like - Show us your Regina, and The City that rhymes with fun.

Not everyone finds it funny, especially women, who protest over the campaign. It's never smart to encourage the belittling of, or causing harm to a woman's body. Needless to say, the campaign and ideas didn't go over well, and Joe ends up being fired. He's given a substantial severance, probably because he's the fall guy for the release of an advertising campaign that proved to be so vile.

It's why he stands here now. Battering fish in a cafe kitchen. But, it supports his drinking career. This cafe job, and severance money. helps keep him financially afloat.

He's also helped by the fact that he's inherited money and property.

Joe can never figure out, where or why, his dreams went awry. Maybe it is a combination of things.

The night of his dismissal from his advertising career is also the night he's delivered sad news from the seniors home where his Mother's been living. She's died, alone in her room.

With his sobriety now unprotected, he walks to the liquor store. The season is Autumn and Joe appreciates hearing the sounds of geese as they migrate. He buys a 40-ounce bottle of vodka and drinks half of it, straight up, on the walk back to his home. By the time he gets to his house, the sounds of geese fall silent. Maybe it's because they've stopped their flight for the night, but it's more likely the vodka has canceled their voices out. His sense of hearing is so muted that he just can't hear them anymore.

Once home, he sits alone, finishing the rest of the bottle, in his living room that night. Or so he thinks. He's not alone.

Along with the night breeze that streams through the window, comes the scent of old dust and painful old memories. Dust Man is somewhere close by, watching again. Joe knows it. Instinct, and some form of unspoken connection, is the reason.

By morning, he wakes up outside, in a hammock that he's strung between two trees in his front yard. Joe doesn't remember how he got there. He's shivering but unharmed, like it's always been. He's guided by dark luck that holds him up and protects, so that even if he stumbles, he never falls because he's got no place to go. His hangover is pronounced though, to the point where Joe wonders if his heart might stop. And if that happened, that he died while being drunk and passed out, would he even know he was dead? Or would it be a case of aimlessly wandering around in some underworld, constantly searching for purpose, but finding none? He figures that's where ghosts come from. It leaves him wondering, there a place in Heaven for drunks?

He's been working at the cafe since.

There is no shame in having a hands-on job, Joe thinks, as he cleans up from the last of his fry cook duties tonight. He takes off his apron and says good night to the rest of the kitchen staff. But, he still craves a drink of alcohol and glances at the large window of the pub across the street.

That's where Hazel works and she's on shift tonight again. He can see her through the large windows. She's wearing a lowcut black dress. She knows the sultry look will bring her a great deal of tip money.

Joe has always hoped that, someday, giving her a big tip might also lead to a meaningful kiss from her. It never has, but it is still his wish.

Hazel

Hers is a story that is sad. A wound that never healed. She gave up a promising career to hold onto memory, and to take care of someone she loved most in the world, Kohkum.

Hazel was a pretty girl, with her long brown hair blowing in the wind.

She's a pretty lady now, who has kept up her lovely figure, not by going to a gym, but by walking, each day along the miles and miles of pathway by the lake. The soft wind blowing, the sounds of birds singing and waves hitting the lake shore keep her company. Anyone could refer to her as svelte, with rounded, perky breasts that catch the eye, each time she wears a sundress. It's a good look for someone in her late 30's. But, Hazel has never dwelt on her appearance. She knows that looks fade.

She's always only rejoiced in the things she knows will stay and grow, like love. Especially the love that she held for her Grandmother. She desperately misses Kohkum. Even though Hazel had a Mother, it's Kohkum who Hazel credits as the one who raised her, and taught her life lessons. Kohkum always taught about the Land, about humanity and about what's important.

Kohkum is the Cree word for Grandmother. But for Hazel, it's a word that really means, a special place in the heart.

She was a matriarch to Hazel, but really, she was everybody's Kohkum, always making the time to give a greeting, say a nice word, or share a story or advice. She is loved and remembered by generations of people in this Town. And when she passed away, Kohkum left behind rich teachings and wisdom. Hazel is determined to keep her memory and those stories alive.

As Joe finishes up shutting down the cafe for the night, he notices Hazel attending to a customer. The pub windows allow for seeing what's going on indoors, especially at this time of day, when the lights are on inside the pub, and there is darkness outdoors.

Hazel looks very pretty this evening, Joe muses. Her soft hair is arranged in a loose bun, and held in place by a pink chip clip. Joe knows that she has a hobby of making her own jewellery, and he's amazed at how precise his eyesight has become, since the night Dust Man followed him down the pathway by the lake. Joe can see details, like a pair of earrings, from this far distance across the street, as intricately as viewing something up close.

Hazel's earrings are made from polymer clay. She told Joe that she makes them herself, a hobby. The conversation happened once, during a slow time at the pub, when Joe was the only patron. Hazel felt like engaging in small talk with him. These types of interactions didn't happen often though because Joe was so often too hammered to enter into any type of conversation that might border on being intellectual or interesting.

But yes, she told him about the earrings.

He remembers Hazel's description of how she makes them.

As he studies them, from afar, Joe is impressed by the intricate detail of the design. In his minds' eye, he sees her shaping the soft clay, carefully painting the design and then putting it in the oven to harden, at a low heat. Tonight's earring design is that of Saskatoon berries, which, since childhood, has always been Joe's favourite fruit.

A gift of the Prairies. The wild berry grows in abundance in Saskatchewan. Joe's been picking and eating them since childhood. It startles Joe to realize that he can, now, actually smell the berry bushes that grow along the waters' edge. That's a block away from the cafe. Joe realizes that his sense of smell has heightened too, since the encounter with Dust Man.

Instead of immediately walking across the street though, he sits on the concrete stairwell for a bit. He enjoys watching Hazel. And, listening to the goings-on where she works. His sense of hearing is now heightened as well.

The sound of Hazel's voice is clear and distinct, as though she's standing right in front of him. "Here are your nachos," Joe hears her say to a customer, "if you need more salsa, just flag me down." Hazel also sets down a couple more half pints with the order, "Enjoy."

As Hazel walks away from her customers, Joe hears the young men making comments about her, "A milf, if you ask me. I'd tap that anytime." His friend snickers, before grabbing a nacho chip which crunches like the sound of kettle drums. Joe doesn't like what they've said about Hazel. Referring to her with the acronym for - Mom I'd like to fuck - is no compliment. A milf. To Joe, what they've said sounds more like a veiled threat. He worries about Hazel's safety, knowing that she walks home, alone, from work at the end of her pub shift. Joe hopes they don't have any plans to stay and harass her, for the remainder of the evening.

They don't.

After finishing their nachos and a few more pints, the young men leave the pub. They are polite to Hazel as they say goodnight, even leaving her a decent-sized tip. Joe is relieved, as he continues to listen to their conversation. The taller one, wearing a Hawaiian pineapple-design on his shirt, says he's going to drive. The other, with a brush cut, says he'll walk home, "It's not far. The walk might sober me up. Besides, I have work early in the morning. Need to clear my head."

It is during this exchange that Joe begins to salivate. The very smell of alcohol running through their veins is triggering him, just as it's been happening for years. And, he wants to drink.

He begins to follow the one walking home.

Joe can smell the liquor ingested, through the young man's body odour and his breath, as he walks away from the pub, then turns down a darkened side street. Joe follows, happy in knowing that no harm will come to Hazel, with the milf comment that the young men made earlier.

Joe is still attracted to the smell of liquor, but more so, he finds that he's lured by the heartbeat of this young man. He can hear the beating. He sees the blood pulsing.

Like when Dust Man approached him, Joe closes in on the space between him and the wandering patron. Stinging him with teeth on jugular, the man is not able to move. But, Joe does not drain him of his life's blood. Joe has always been basically a good guy, the type who would slap you in the face, but never stab you in the back. Even now, he takes only what he needs to serve his hunger, for alcohol in the blood and the blood itself.

It surprises him that he's feeding two needs now. The human addiction for alcohol still lingers, and he has the vampire need for blood. He lived as an alcoholic for a long time during his human years. Joe just never imagined that it would follow him into the afterlife. He also finds it upsetting that he knows how to be so precise, when making the incision into someone's jugular. He doesn't like that it seems to come naturally to him, like he doesn't need any training.

Even baby birds are taught by their mother how to use their wings. She teaches them how to catch their own food and hunt, before they disperse, leaving the nest and flying out on their own.

Joe doesn't consider it to be an asset that he seems to have a natural instinct to kill, as though being turned into a vampire is something that would have happened at any rate, like some type of birthright. It's too much for him to deal with, so he won't make a kill, as he promised himself, before sinking in his fangs. Instead, he releases his teeth from the young man's neck, before the heart stops. He lets go of the man's body.

The man collapses and falls into a hunch on the ground. The short t-shirt he's wearing doesn't provide any protection for the fall, and he skins his elbow on the pavement on the way down. Joe's thirst is satisfied. There has been no death, only a tasting. He knows the young man will wake up with the sunrise, feeling dehydrated and tired, but otherwise it would feel like it's nothing more than a bad hangover. He'll believe that he blacked-out on his way back home from the pub, and that he spent his night passed out on the sidewalk. For this young man, Joe figures it likely is not the first time that something like blacking out and passing out might have happened. And, he doubts that anyone will think anything sinister about finding marks on his neck. It is mosquito season afterall and those little bloodsuckers are far more troublesome than Joe imagines he'll ever be.

Over the years, and as part of Joe's alcohol abuse, he developed a bad habit. He has a hollow need to collect trophies.

Back in the day, after a night of drunken sex, he'd make a point of finding something to keep, as a way of proving his manhood and evidence that the night really happened. It started off innocently. One of his sex partners had removed her dangling earrings and left them on his bedside table, before she shamefully scurried off in the morning. After that night, Joe made a point of collecting trophies, and removing things from the purses of the women that he slept with. While they were passed out, he would root around looking for something like an interesting key chain or coin. He keeps the collected items in a small wooden box, beside his bed. It's a sick reminder, but on nights when he's feeling randy, and there is no woman handy, he opens the box, and studies the stolen items. The memory of how they came to be, helps him to masturbate.

His need to collect and steal became an affliction, which carries over even now.

Joe searches the young man's pockets, finding a roll of cash that is fastened together with an ornate, silver money clip. He removes the clip and tucks it into his own pocket, but puts the paper bills back into the man's jeans pocket. What he's doing is highly illegal, pilfering through the pockets of someone passed out on the street. Regardless, he doesn't feel the need to act suspiciously, nor hide in darkness and skulk in the shadows. People know Joe in this town. He's always been reckless. Year-round residents have seen Joe for years, stumbling in the night. Sometimes causing a ruckus. So, anything he is doing right now, can be done in plain sight. If anyone happens to be driving by, they will give Joe a wave, but they won't even bat an eye.

Once his trophy is removed, Joe returns to the stairwell across the street from the pub. He wants to follow Hazel home, as well, to make sure she gets where she is going, safely.

He watches as Hazel counts the money she made in tips that evening, before hiding the cash in her bra, just before her short walk home.

The hustle and bustle of tourist season in this resort town has quieted for the night.

Joe's night has just begun. He'll go out hunting one more time before dawn.

Sunrise Sunset

Routine. It is a built-in genetic code. We all have one. Vampires follow routine as well.

For Joe, it means following his nose, now that he's got a keen sense of smell. Science says that a dog's sense of smell is 10,000 to 100,000 times more acute than a human's ability to smell. For every scent receptor a human has, a dog has 50 more. Multiply that by 10, and that is how Joe's ability has evolved.

When his hunger sets in, Joe can smell a victim who's walking down the street, a full block away. He hears them too. Again with dogs, who have an elevated sense of hearing, four times greater than that of a human, Joe knows his surroundings without having to see with his eyes.

Joe has no appetite for food anymore. After his encounter with Dust Man, he cleaned out his cupboards and pantry, emptied his fridge and freezer, and donated all that food to a local charity. He packs up the food items, but not before pouring his half-finished bottle of apricot brandy down the sink. He no longer needs it. The tooth pain that he was experiencing before being turned into a vampire, is now gone. There is still an unopened six-pack of beer in his fridge, though. Joe figures, there is no point in wasting it too. He decides he will pack that up as a donation, as well. Someone else might be needing it today, to take off the edge of a hangover or to begin anew, at using drink to forget whatever it is that might be troubling them. He knows from experience that this, can also be seen as an act of charity. Leveling out.

The Regina Community Fridge Project in the Cathedral District of the city enjoyed boxes and boxes of food delivery from Joe.

He felt good, asking one of his neighbours to drive him, in order to drop off the donation.

That cherished acquaintance is named September Rust. He lives just down the street from Joe, and September has been Joe's ride, since he lost his driver's licence. Joe loves the sound of his name and figures it suits him perfectly, because he is an old man. September is the twilight month of any year, and he's 80 years old and proudly covered with well-earned rust.

September is retired. Many a day, Joe sees him sitting out on his deck, watering his colourful geranium flowers, and always with a glass of vodka and 7, somewhere close by.

September has that gleeful look of someone who's always been, just a little bit mischievous. His wrinkled face is mostly filled with smile lines, with prominent crows-feet to the side of his eyes. September has a playful childhood exuberance, that's followed him into his senior years. He tells bad jokes, and laughs at his own words, like a little boy who thinks he's being clever. Joe always finds it adorable. The old neighbour is easy to spend time with, never having a bad word to say about anything, or anyone. And, he never hesitates to offer his help, whether it be offering to pick up the mail or giving Joe a ride to the grocery store. Today, it's taking Joe to the city.

Joe thinks, there ought to be more people like him in this world. It would be a better place. September is in good health, which Joe finds himself to be grateful to know. Joe's already decided that he doesn't want to drain anyone who keeps themselves well, and who celebrates life each and every day, as September does.

Some stories just need to be told, and retold, even if they are old. September is one of those stories.

He seems to be timeless. That's the dream. To be content and happy with what you have, and where you are in life. That's how Joe always wanted his own human life to turn out, until addiction came in and took control. For Joe it's been a frenzied and uncontrollable ride that no one wants to be a part of. Not even himself. How did Joe allow that to happen? How does anyone allow addiction to call the shots, and take over? He's said to himself so many times, if I could only go back to that place and time where it all began, I would, and I would kick it in the ass.

Ironic.

He makes the wish too late. Too late is now. He's no longer human, and can only dwell on things that should have been.

There were so many chances to find a way out: family, friends, support groups. He reached out a few times, and was able to cope as a sober person for a period of time. Quitting never stuck. Anytime something bothered him, it was easy to just go to the store to pick up another 40-of something to numb the pain of remembering his past.

Childhood beatings from his estranged father.

Witnessing abuse.

Not having enough faith to find ways to fly away and change things.

For Joe, struggle has not been a path towards finding something to make him stronger. It's just a way to hang in there and carry on with the status quo.

Joe wishes he'd been more like September. That is, someone who drinks some vodka, but not to excess, then enjoys the day accordingly. No matter what it may bring.

September doesn't play music, from the radio or from a CD, when he sits outdoors, except for Sunday afternoons. That's the day he listens to CKUA Radio, online, for the program called Roy's Record Room. The host spins obscure oldies, mostly vinyls that are 45's and 78's. It's music from September's youth, and the type of songs that you wouldn't hear anywhere else. Other than that exception, he generally enjoys the sounds of the life around him. Bird songs, dogs barking greetings, the breeze that coaxes tree leaves to dance. It's a simple life, and Joe appreciates that September takes the time to take it in, and enjoy.

Paying it Forward

For today though, and once in the city, Joe finds joy in seeing the reaction of his delivery to the Community Fridge. Within seconds, people appear out of nowhere, carrying cloth bags. The six-pack of beer is the first item to be claimed, by a woman who looks to be in her 20's. Joe wonders about her story and why she's here. She looks to be healthy and doesn't exhibit any of the telltale signs of being hungover. Joe knows the look. He thinks, maybe she's a university student and that she's taking it because she's getting together with a friend later in the day. Maybe they plan to enjoy a couple of cold ones out on her deck, assuming she has one. It's a hot day. It could be as simple as that, finding free beer and taking advantage. Not everyone who drinks is an alcoholic.

Joe appreciates the friendly chatter, as folks sift through what's been donated, before deciding what to take. There's a quiet dignity within their interactions, like some type of unwritten code-of-the-street here.

Joe is heartened to see, people taking only what they need. There is no hoarding of the free food. Items are left for others, who are hungry as well.

One example is an unopened carton of strawberry yogurt. The carton holds 12 little plastic cups of yogurt, packaged in a cardboard shell. Joe witnesses an act of caring, as a young man, no older than 18 years, rips open the cardboard casing. He takes out four of the plastic yogurt cups, then leaves the rest for someone else, who is in need as well.

Joe has also donated an entire case of Pedialyte, which is an electrolyte replenishing drink. It's generally used to help children, who aren't feeling well and suffering from flu-like symptoms, or other ailments. Joe's been using the drink to help him with lessening the effects of a hangover. He's been taking his day-after shot of Pedialyte for years, and he swears that it helps.

Now though, there will no longer be a need to nurse a hangover, so the unopened case goes as a donation, where it'll likely be used for its intended purpose.

Similarly, he puts a couple of jars of unopened dill pickles on the shelf. It isn't so much that Joe is a pickle lover. He heard that drinking pickle juice also helps to curb the effects of a bad hangover, so he's tried it. Whether it works is not known. So often, his hangovers didn't last too long anyway. It's because he'd start drinking again, first thing upon waking. Hair of the dog.

He finds himself feeling just a little melancholy, placing a couple of packages of bacon in the freezer area. Not only has bacon always been one of his favourites, just in general, but it's always been a way for him to deal with negative effects of the night before. Maybe it's the salt. Somehow frying bacon to an extra crispy, and forcing down a few bites, always seems to have helped. He often felt so weak, that nothing short of a comfort food helped.

Joe hopes that whoever takes the bacon today isn't cooking it for the same reason.

On the day of the food delivery, Joe pulls some gas money from his wallet. He holds it up as an offering of gratitude, for his neighbour taking the time to help him out and drive him into the city. But September declines the offer. So, Joe makes another suggestion, that they make a pit stop in Lumsden instead, while driving back to the Beach down Highway #11.

Once stopped at the big warehouse, which is right at the edge of the Town, Joe follows through on his plan to meet kindness with kindness.

The destination is Last Mountain Distillery. Joe unbuckles his seatbelt, once in the parking lot, and leaves September's white 3/4 ton truck, which has seen a lot of miles. Joe runs his fingers through his thick hair, adjusts the suspenders on the overalls that he wears, then walks into the establishment to buy a bottle of their signature Distillery Dill Pickle Vodka. When he returns to the vehicle, Joe presents the vodka as a gift to September, for helping out with making the food delivery. This, September accepts. It makes Joe smile, knowing that he'll see the old man out on his deck again soon, watering his plants, and enjoying his dill pickle vodka, as it makes a sound of clinking ice in a hand-fashioned pottery mug.

It's no more than a 15-minute drive between Lumsden and the Beach, and as the two continue their trek home, Joe admits to himself that he misses drinking vodka. He can't ingest it anymore, now that he's a vampire. He knows this but he still has the craving for it.

As they drive, Joe silently recites a creed from Alcoholics Anonymous. AA is the support group that he's turned to a number of times, in trying to rid himself of the alcohol addiction. He's marked the words - Day One - on his calendar more often than he's able to count.

Day One. The first day of being sober. He'd be so proud of himself when he was able to stop drinking for 30 days, 60 days, 90 days. Then something would happen and Joe would revert directly back to where he started. Day One. It's why the creed sticks with him.

It's a teaching that recognizes, not all alcoholics can be rehabilitated and stop drinking, even though they may want to. They are referred to as, the unfortunates. Joe makes a silent admission to God. He knows that he is one of the unfortunates, in more ways than one.

*There are such unfortunates. They are not
at fault; they seem to have been born that way.
They are naturally incapable of grasping and
developing a manner of living which demands
rigorous honesty. Their chances are less than average.*

Born that way? Joe can't attest to that, but he does admit to allowing the dark force of alcohol, to become a destructive and dangerous part of his previous human life. Who knows how that happened?

Alcoholics anonymous helped Joe get off the booze, for a time. It was the encouragement of AA members as well, who helped him quit smoking. It was easier than he expected, getting off the nicotine. After that, a replacement addiction surfaced. He just couldn't stop drinking caffeine.

With that, Joe does hold a secret. It's a thought that he never uttered nor admitted for discussion during AA meetings. He has watched, as some people are able to quit drinking alcohol but they don't really abandon their addictive behaviour, at all.

He remembers one young lady, who was very proud of quitting drinking. It's true, she stopped imbibing a bottle of wine, or more, each day, as was her routine. Then, she began another bad habit, replacing the drink with food. Within a year, she'd gained more than a hundred pounds. She'd become uncomfortably obese, even just to see her. Overeating took over. It wasn't long thereafter that she stopped coming to meetings entirely. At that point, Joe often wondered if she simply joined another group, like Overeaters Anonymous, or maybe something more gentle, like joining Weight Watchers.

Whatever the case, he wishes her success, in facing and overcoming the problems that are at the core of what's troubling her. Still, Joe can't figure out which is worse, being drunk or switching to a food addiction and the possibility of being obese.

Turning one addiction to something else doesn't seem like a solution.

Joe supposes that he should have known better, during those healthy times when he was able to achieve sobriety for a while. He has no control over alcohol, and he is not capable of having "just one." That knowledge was there long before his drinking grew into overtaking his life. It's because his own dad was a drunk. Joe is likely predisposed.

His father had passed down his sins. And, when you come from a seed like that, Joe wonders if it is really possible to be born bad?

He can't remember a day, a month or a year when he realized, alcohol was taking over. The catalyst wasn't loosing his job. While heart-breaking, nor was it the death of his Mom. The abuse started long before then. He just didn't admit it. He still can't face it, so he buries it instead. Joe refers to himself as a storm chaser. He can see impending destruction approach but doesn't know how to safely find a way around it.

So here he is, still standing in a corner of darkness with an added layer. He's a vampire now.

Joe still needs to feed another uncontrollable hunger. The sun is setting, and the sky is the colour of bright pink tonight because of the haze of forest fires burning up North. The smoke has travelled this far.

Before September drops Joe at his home, he suggests that Joe come over for a drink, "Let's test out this dill pickle vodka, and see if it lives up to all the hype."

Joe tells a lie, because that is what alcoholics do. They lie. Joe says, "I think I'll go for a walk. It's a nice night, maybe I'll head to the pub for a pint. Thanks again. We did good today." He steps out of September's truck, closing the door and bidding farewell.

In Search of a Drink

Joe knows that he isn't going for a walk. He's going out hunting. The influx of seasonal residents and tourists means, he won't have to prey on anyone he knows.

Joe heads down the pathway beside the lake. As he approaches, the sounds of frogs and crickets go silent again, like they know that a danger is near. Him. As darkness slowly lowers her blanket, Joe can feel his hunger grow. But not for long.

There is someone else on the pathway. A drunken teenager, staggering aimlessly. He wears a black t-shirt with an AC/DC logo, and oversized shorts. There is also a small crucifix on a chain around his neck. It was given to him by his Grandmother for his 16th birthday, but it can't protect the boy tonight.

Joe surveys the area. There is no one else on the pathway, and no one out in their yards or on their decks. No one to witness.

"Oh, hey man," the drunk lad gives a crooked smile, as he sees Joe approaching, "I don't suppose you have a smoke on you, eh?" Joe doesn't smoke anymore. It's one bad habit that he was able to give up. But funnily enough, he does happen to have a couple of cigarettes stashed in the upper pocket of the plaid shirt that he's wearing.

The darts are in there because, a while back he was out doing the same thing, of wandering aimlessly and in a drunken stupor with a drinking buddy. His friend handed the smokes over, saying, "Here. Hold these for me. My last two. I'm going to jump in the lake to cool down, and I don't want them to get wet or get crushed."

The tobacco is old now, and it makes a sizzling sound, as Joe takes the cigarette from his upper pocket and lights it up for the boy. As the youth inhales, he gives a nod of gratitude, saying, "Thanks man. I really need to quit smoking."

Joe suggests the two of them sit down on one of the memorial benches that dot the pathway. They are benches placed in memory for loved ones who have passed away. They are sturdy and hand-built wooden structures with the names, of those deceased, carved in memory.

This teenager could be meeting the same fate of death. Joe's hunger is peaking.

But as he studies the young man's face, it comes to him that he cannot take his life either. He'll only take what he needs again. Joe crosses his boney fingers that he'll be able to keep his word this time. It hasn't worked in the past, when he'd quit drinking for a time, then promise that he'd have just one beer. It always resulted in guzzling down a 24, with no intention of doing so at the start. He hopes, for the sake of this young man, that his thirst for blood doesn't have the same effect, and that he'll be unable to stop before traveling into a point of no return.

Without the smoker even realizing what is happening, Joe's fangs protrude and he sinks them in to the large vein, pulsing, on the kids' neck. Sucking until he knows it's time to stop. Joe senses the teens' heartbeat getting slower. He removes his teeth from his prey before that beating stops.

The blood is tainted with the taste of alcohol, a combination of beer and several shots of Grey Goose vodka.

Two of Joe's needs being satisfied, he leaves the boy, spreading out his body on the wooden bench, but not before removing his necklace. The boy can sleep it off, Joe thinks, he'll wake up feeling weak and sick, but there's been no other harm. Once he makes it back to his Grandma's house, he's pretty sure she'll make him something like chicken soup to replenish his fluids. This boy is lucky that I can't kill, Joe thinks. Never could.

As Joe leaves the boy, he recalls the first time he was forced to choose between mercy and death.

> Joe is just a kid, maybe six years old. He's outside playing in puddles because of an afternoon rain storm. It was a deluge that struck quickly, leaving pools of water standing everywhere. The parched earth has little capacity to absorb the flash flooding. But, the sun is out now, so little Joe finds a stick that he wants to use to find the worms that make their way to the surface, to prevent drowning.
>
> As always, Joe's dog is by his side. The dog is little, but fierce, being part Jack Russel Terrier, and who knows what else, maybe part Labrador Retriever. That's Joe's Mom's best guess. She picked up the dog at the local dog pound earlier in the year.
>
> Joe doesn't think of the pup as aggressive, but on this day, the dog is a menace.
>
> Somehow, during the storm, a baby bird has fallen from its nest and is chirping with fright behind a bush at the edge of the yard. The dog notices, running over to where the bird is faltering on the ground.
>
> The dog grabs it by the neck and chomps. Little Joe watches, aghast, wondering how to stop the assault. Joe calls out to the dog, who keeps biting the baby bird. Joe tries throwing the stick he's carrying. A game of fetch. The dog finally lets go of the injured bird.
>
> Little Joe drops to his knees beside the struggling winged-one. Its beak is moving, like it's gasping for breath. But, what Joe recalls the most is the wretched sound the bird is making. Like screaming.

Joe knows the baby bird has been injured to the point that it needs to be put out of its misery, end its suffering. So he does the only thing that he can think to do. He stomps as hard as he's able, on the bird's head.

Instead of killing it, the bird's head is only pressed further into the soft, wet ground. It wails in agony, even louder.

Little Joe runs away with tears in his eyes. He's unable to kill it.

Recreation

There are wooden art deco signs all around the town, with painted sayings like, Life Is Better At The Lake. The saying is displayed on peoples' homes and outside of local businesses.

Joe is apt to agree. Even though he doesn't eat food anymore, he still enjoys the smell of barbeque. The summer months at the Beach means there are all types of unique foods offered. Seasonal businesses offer things like taco-in-a-bag, fancy helpings of poutine with bacon, and of course, hot dogs, even messy footlongs served with fried onions and sauerkraut.

He has to admit, he does miss taking a big bite of a mustard-laden hot dog, but now he's just an observer who enjoys watching others savour their summer treats. They laugh, and walk around the streets eating, or they find a shady spot on a grassy hill near the lake.

They live and enjoy.

Joe figures it's time for him to stop merely observing and become more of a participant. He's wasted so much time, not going out fishing, not swimming or hiking; instead, he'd always sit in the pub, sometimes nursing a beer but more likely chugging it.

Now, he wants to relish in the frenzy of summer fun, like everyone else that he sees doing the same, today. Joe figures he'll use his next tip out from the cafe to buy his first-ever longboard.

It's similar to a skateboard, which Joe never did as an adolescent, except a longboard is faster. Its design is, well, longer. Its wheels are wider which allows for easy turning, or for better maneuverability, if there is a need for a sudden stop. Little kids on bicycles are the main concern for longboarders, especially if those children are new to riding a bike. Even though they have been told, and told again by their parents, to look both ways before crossing the street, they don't always. Joe figures it's angels who have the big job of watching over them at times like this, ensuring their safety, and he's glad for it.

There is a group of youth who Joe has been watching for weeks now. They travel in pairs, standing gracefully on their longboards. They are focused and aware of their surroundings at all times, and they are both skilled and fearless. They easily dodge pedestrians, dogs and cars, as they race so quickly from the top of Centre Street to the bottom of the hill, which kisses the lake front. Once there, they pull out water bottles from the small backpacks they each wear. They squeal with joy, give each other high-fives, then grab their boards, walking back up the hill. They do it all over again. If anyone doesn't like it, there isn't much they can do. The main street is a public place where anyone can travel. Besides, if anyone wanted to stop them, they'd have to catch them first. With a town speed limit of 40 kilometres, it's easy to say this group of boarders travels faster than vehicles on that street. But they are cautious, respectful and aware.

Joe can feel their intentions. They are having fun and celebrating their youth.

Their antics have given Joe a bug.

He wants to feel that type of excitement as well, so he goes online late that night, after feasting on another drunken tourist.

He's looking for a business called 306SHOP. It's where Joe overheard the kids saying they buy their gear. The shop is near the McDonald's at edge of city, off 9th Avenue North in Regina.

He saw the actual place once, on one of the rare occasions that he'd travel to the city to attend AA meetings. That's before he lost his drivers licence.

Joe can't help but appreciate how insightful AA discussion can be. There's one particular warning that he remembers. It sticks in his mind, even now, the words that someone once said,

"If you don't stop, alcohol is going to kill you someday. One way or the other. It might be a car accident, it could be your heart stopping, but be sure, it will kill you."

There is no way anyone at those meetings could have guessed that being turned into a vampire might also be the result. It is a death. His.

He's fallen off the sober train, many times. Little by little, he allowed alcohol to strip him of his basic personality until there was almost nothing left.

It can happen so innocently, with no premeditated decision to start drinking again. For Joe, he would walk towards sobriety, wanting to find hope. But, it's where he'd meet the enemy instead. Joe recalls how easily falling can happen.

> The question - what to do when everyday is a bad hair day?
> This time, falling off the wagon happens with no intention of traveling in that direction. It's been three months for Joe now, without a drop of alcohol, and he is feeling good. His energy level is back up. He's fallen into a healthy, regular sleeping pattern again. He is more productive, in general. But, what he's most happy about is that when he wakes up each morning, there is no hangover, and coffee is the first thing he ingests instead of a bottle of Bud.
> How did it all come to a screeching halt?
> It's because of a gift that someone has given him for his birthday. It's also the reason why some at AA advise

that it is important to let others know that there is a battle going on with the disease called alcoholism.

In making the admission, friends can help, by supporting and, not doing things, as simple as like not offering a glass of wine at dinner. Joe didn't tell his friends. His decision not to could have been because of pride. Maybe due to shame. Whatever the case, a close friend of his could never have know that the birthday gift given to him would prove to be more like unleashing a dragon. It's a box, filled with spices and a gadget for roasting, as well as instructions on how to bake, what's called a beer-can chicken.

That gift becomes Joe's undoing.

Early one evening, Joe figures he'll try out the recipe, so he goes down to the off sale to pick up a tallboy can of beer. That's what the recipe calls for.

But, once home, having beer in the house proves to be too much of a temptation. The chicken never does get cooked.

Instead of using the beer to add to the chicken recipe, Joe drinks it. Within minutes, he finds himself back at the liquor store. This time he picks up a 6-pack of beer. Those cans are drained within an hour, and it is still early in the evening. Joe decides to make the drive once again, figuring this time he may as well get a 24-pack, instead of another 6-pack.

His logic is that if he has a lot of booze in his refrigerator, it'll prevent him from further drinking-and-driving. He makes at all too familiar promise that, this will be his last time. It isn't and it's a downward spiral from there.

Next morning, he wakes up scratching hives on his neck and chest. Joe knows the condition is caused because of his allergy to alcohol. His body has warned him with hives many times before. He doesn't heed the warning and goes to his fridge to grab another beer. It's the familiar start to the beginning of each day, after that.

What starts with Joe kidding himself into believing that he can have "just one" quickly turns into getting trapped in another quagmire from which he isn't able to exit this time. Joe's lament for past decisions ends with something he remembers hearing as a boy.

It's a Bible quote, from those long-ago days when he used to attend church services.

The spirit is willing but the flesh is weak.

That was then. Again, Joe can't help but think about trauma in his life. It explains his behaviour, but it does not excuse the behaviour.

But now, it is a new day, and Joe does his best to shake off that sad memory and aching realization of defeat. Although he does still carry feelings of embarrassment at not finding enough strength to have been able to quit for good. It's the reason that he never did return to attending AA meetings. He's faltered so many times. Now is the time to make another new start.

Joe pulls out his credit card from his wallet, proud of himself for deciding to purchase his first-ever longboard. The card isn't maxed-out for once, now that he no longer buys alcohol. He orders a starter longboard and some protective gear. It'll take a few days to arrive in the mail, and while he waits, Joe watches. He studies the movements of the longboard kids, how they use their bodies to control the movements of the board. It is intense and disciplined. Although, Joe does have to admit that it bothers him that not all the boarders are wearing helmets.

Safety first.

Joe figures the same mantra ought to apply to those who drink alcohol to excess here at the Beach, then try walking home each night. They don't necessarily need to worry about the police. But, they do need to worry about him.

Another reason Joe is so keen on taking up the new sport of longboard is because, he can do it now.

Before being changed, he suffers from diagnosed osteoarthritis in his knee. The condition developed as a result of a long-ago sports injury, that happened when Joe was a teenager.

The arthritis causes him to limp and lament, and hurts the most when weather changes are in the forecast. He's like a human barometer, who can predict rain is coming even better than Environment Canada. He doesn't have to listen to the radio to know when a storm is coming.

Some days, the joint pain is excruciating, even to the point where Joe wonders if he'll have to start using a cane just to walk. He would like to think that, on days like this, drinking to excess numbs the arthritis pain better than self-medicating with over-the-counter drugs from the pharmacy. The pain can sometimes be debilitating, and it causes Joe to swear a lot because it hurts so much just to move. So, he drinks even harder, numbing everything. Most of all, his sense of self.

Dust Man's not-so-sweet kiss changed all of that. The joint pain has disappeared.

Adding longboarding to his activities is one change to Joe's habits. There's another.

Joe has been further inspired by his neighbour down the street. September tends to his flowers and his garden each and every day, no matter the weather. He can feel the senior friend's intention as well, and knows how blissfully happy September is, watching the flowers bloom. He hums as he weeds, which will help the soil give nutrients to the vegetables he's got growing in a raised garden in his backyard. There is good sunlight there.

It is the reason why Joe takes out his credit card again, and heads to the Home Hardware Store, which is a prominent business on the main street in town. There's a unique greenhouse at the back of the property, which sells plants grown with care by Sweet Peas Greenhouse. That's a business located at an acreage not far from the Beach. Its proprietor, Alice, is a University-trained botanist, who knows all the varieties of flowers or vegetables which are most suited to growing, and harvesting, in the moist mixed grassland region, in this part of the province.

Joe has never gardened before. He was always too drunk to care about what his yard looked like. And, he didn't want to spend the money on plants when, back then, it seemed better spent on rounds of vodka and 7-Up, or beer. The thought causes Joe to ponder on a memory.

One time, he's so short of cash that he ends up eating plain spaghetti noodles, without any sauce or even butter. He doesn't even have any ketchup in his fridge, to add as a bit of flavour. He chows down on the meagre meal offering for three days, because while he has enough cash to buy some food, he'd rather drink. He'll use what little money he has, to instead spend it on buying beer.
He's getting paid at the end of the week, so a few days on a bland diet is something he'll just endure.

Now, he's a changed man, so to speak.

Once at the greenhouse, he loads up on buying tomato plants, and peppers, cucumbers and kale, while he waits for his longboard and gear to arrive in the mail.

Guess Who's Coming to Dinner?

There are those people who believe that a feral cat can never be tamed, and that they never show affection towards humans. Well, that might be true. Except, Joe is no longer human, and there has been a feral cat who shows up on his deck every night lately. Maybe that's what attracted this feline.

They now share a similar wild energy.

They are outsiders, doing what they must to survive.

The feline is a large, short-haired gray cat, who looks to be in a bit of distress. There is a small bald patch near the base of his tail, which Joe has watched the cat picking at. These past days, that constant excessive grooming has caused a bald spot, as the cat picks at its fur. Joe has seen it before, thinking back to something similar that happened when he was a kid. It wasn't his cat. It was the old woman's. She lived just down the street.

> One summer, when it is particularly hot and dry, her cat got fleas. Apparently, fleas flourish under extreme hot conditions. As part of their genetic cat routine, her tabby tries grooming itself, excessively licking in an effort to get rid of the pests that are, no doubt, causing the cat distress.

Joe remembers that the lady went to a pet store in the city, to purchase some type of spray. It is billed as a natural remedy to repel fleas and ticks. It's free of a drug called permethrins, which can be used to treat dogs suffering the same, but it's toxic for cats. Some of the ingredients within the natural repellent are safe, like the essence of cedar chips and lemons. Fleas are repelled by citric acid.

It doesn't harm the cat.

Joe figures he'll try making a concoction of his own, and that he'll do his best to spray the gray cat, who for some reason is quickly becoming a regular guest in his yard.

But first, Joe goes out and buys a can of tuna. He, personally, has never liked the smell of the canned fish, but he figures the feral will go crazy for it. He rightfully assumes that maybe the cat will even come close enough, so that Joe can hold its small body and spray on the homemade remedy that he's made.

Before getting that intimate though, Joe figures he ought to name the cat.

He thinks the little dude looks like an Xavier, with his large face and multitude of whiskers. He looks wise. The tips of his ears are missing, most likely from frostbite. The poor guy has to weather the harsh Saskatchewan winters, outdoors.

The smell of tuna attracts Xavier immediately. Even though he's a feral and not used to human touch, or vampire touch in this case, the cat's hunger exceeds his natural fear. Maybe the cat is not feral after all. Joe wonders if maybe he's just a stray who has joined the feral pack. Whatever the case, Joe is able to spray the infected area without any trouble. Xavier even purrs as he scarfs down the offering of tuna fish. It is a scene played out for more than a week, before Joe notices that the bald spots that had been troubling him are healing, and that Xavier is no longer tending to the area.

Fleas be gone.

It's for this reason that Joe is appalled, even outraged, as he overhears a conversation that's happening on the stairwell, as Joe takes his nightly perch on the cafe steps, after his shift that night.

Some old dude is sitting within earshot and bragging, about how he kills cats.

"I even sprayed gasoline on one of those rotten things one night. It came out of the bushes to watch as I was burning leaves," the fat man lets out a guffaw, "I watched it as it ran back into the bush. It was lit up like a firecracker. I followed it and took out my watering can to extinguish any of the underbrush that the burning cat might have ignited."

Joe can't remember the man's name, although he remembers that they have been introduced, and he's seen him around town. Joe still exhibits traits of having the alcoholic brain. That kind of stuff used to happen to him all the time when he was drinking, forgetting details almost as soon as they are learned. Like someone's name.

The man is older and always wears a ball cap. He smokes cigarettes, and snuffs out his used butts on the steps of the cafe, for someone else to clean up. The arrogant man is overweight, and the buttons on his shirt, where his belly protrudes, have popped off.

"I got another today," the asshole seems proud to proclaim, "a damn orange cat this time." He goes on to describe to the person, unlucky enough to be seated beside him, how the cat died.

He says that he killed the cat, because he thought it had been pissing in his garden. Despite his unnerving description, the louse does have some skill. He's one of those do-it-yourself mechanics. That's how the orange cat died. Joe continues to eavesdrop, listening to what the fat man is saying.

"I was going to buy some rat poison," the man lights up another smoke, "then, I remembered that I just did some preventative maintenance on my old Chevy. After popping the radiator cap and draining the reservoir, I realized the old antifreeze that collected is still in the drain bucket, in my garage," he sneers, "I call it cat juice now, because those stupid, little bastards are dumb enough to drink it. Isn't that funny?

I didn't have to spend a dime to kill off those mangy things. Just saving my old fluid did the job."

Antifreeze contains ethylene glycol, which tastes sweet and can be mixed in with food. The scumbag brags that he used tuna as a bait, to mix with the antifreeze. It causes death within mere hours, as oxalate crystals form in the kidneys, causing malfunction and a painful death.

Fat man laughs as he says that he found the cat's petrified body the next morning. The little corpse was laying amongst a petunia patch.

The man gives a sneer and seems proud to say, "Good thing is was garbage collection day. I put that stiff in a black bag and set it out to go to the dump, where it belongs. I bagged it up, right next to some damn birds that have been waking me up, too early in the morning. Stupid birds, they eat anything, so I put out some uncooked rice for them. It expands, once in their small stomachs, and they implode. Found five of those this morning, as well. Hee, hee, that'll teach them to stop singing by my bedroom window at 4 a.m. They are out there, making noise, even before the sun comes up. It's just too much."

With Joe's heightened sense of smell, he knows the man has already been drinking earlier that afternoon. Probably some cheap wine, like Royal White, that's sold by the gallon, or maybe even the cheap bubbly called Baby Duck wine. The heat of the day provokes the stench of his excess to exit through his pours. That, along with a greasy, puffy face equals proof of ingesting too much alcohol.

Joe follows him home that night, not attacking him in public. Joe stays outside, watching the man through his curtainless kitchen window, the smell of dead cat still emanating from the patch of flowers. Joe isn't surprised to see that the fat man has many prairie lily plants dotting his yard. While the flower is beautiful to look at, it's toxic for cats, who'll sometimes chew on plant leaves.

Joe waits, knowing the man's drinking spree is likely to start up again, once alone at home. It does. Joe can see the dim light of the refrigerator door opening. He hears the pouring of liquid. Not too long thereafter, it is quiet.

Once he knows the man has passed out on his couch. Joe goes into the small, wooden house. Viewing the lump of flesh laying still, Joe can smell that the dude has pissed himself.

Who's the vile creature now?

There will be no mercy here tonight.

Joe sinks his fangs in, past a mound of fat tissue, stopping only when he hears the heart stop beating. It seems inevitable that, one day, there'd be a first kill.

Joe feels no remorse with this one. Killers need to be killed.

Joe supposed it shouldn't surprise him that he wasn't able to keep his own promise of not killing, and just feeding instead. He is still a creature of habit, remembering the many, many times that he made vows to himself, that he'd quit drinking - tomorrow. He never kept that promise either.

Joe predicts town gossip will say, the man died from a heart attack. It will be repeated and repeated, until it's accepted as truth.

Before leaving, Joe grabs a fishing lure that's on the kitchen table. It looks to have been hand-made, and is a bent bottle cap with a hook attached. As he heads outside, Joe leaves the door slightly ajar, knowing there is to be a final irony. Once the body starts decomposing, the scent will attract the hungry ferals who will feed on the fat man's flesh. Payback.

That old fellow is not seen around town again. And his cat killing days are over. It's like removing a stain from the fabric of the town. Joe figures, the man won't be missed.

Gathering Evidence

With his heightened sense of hearing, Joe spends his nights lurking, hiding in the shadows, and eavesdropping on Hazel. He wants to better get the know the things she likes. Now that he's no longer a drunkard, and more lucid than he's ever been, Joe can pay attention enough to retain detail. It's a change from his old days of sitting at the pub until closing time, while he was slowly tuning out and later blacking out.

He still, sometimes, goes into the pub though, just to keep face. Tonight is one of those nights.

Joe enters under the guise of getting a night cap and reading Prairie Dog Magazine, which is a local Arts magazine. There's a copy of the free publication at the front entrance. It sits alongside a flyer that provides listings of upcoming events in the Town, and what local service clubs are offering, like this past weekend.

The elementary school holds its annual bottle drive. Residents are encouraged to leave their cans and bottles at the edge of their driveway, for pick up. The recyclables get cashed in, with the money going to extra-curricular school activities, like field trips to places like the Science Centre in Regina.

Strategically, the bottle drive is held at the beginning of tourist season, when it is for certain that seasonal cottagers will also contribute, making for more donations and more cash.

In the past, Joe could always be counted on to donate bags and bags, filled with empty liquor containers. Now that he doesn't drink anymore, the only thing at edge of his driveway on this bottle drive, is a large, blue flower pot. He's planted marigolds in it. The plant has a strong, pungent scent. It's a turn off for deer, which have no interest in eating that type of flower, so Joe doesn't have to worry about monitoring the animals when they do stop to graze on the cedar shrubs that line his property. Although, Joe wonders if he even needed to pay attention to planting something that repels deer.

Since his change, he's noticed that the animals now steer clear of his property. They avoid it, bolting when approaching his home. Joe has read somewhere that the Indigenous animal totem of the deer has a meaning of gentleness. Deer touch the heart and minds of wounded souls. Maybe he's beyond repair now, and they know it. Instead, they rightfully see him as a danger.

The peaceful horned creatures calm down, exhibiting their usual, graceful gait, once away from Joe's place. They resume their grazing in the neighbours' yard.

As Joe enters the pub, he takes his seat, on the tall chairs near the bar taps. Those are the shiny levers that serve different kinds of draught beer from a keg instead of being contained in a can or bottle. He hears the lowly sound of a train whistle, traveling on the tracks across the lake. The glass door to the pub is propped open again, enticing customers to come in. It's mild for early summer, and the fresh air coming in gives the place a feel of adventure and freedom.

As he hoped, Hazel is on shift and she is the first to greet Joe, as he arrives, "Hey stranger, haven't seen you in a while," she sets a coaster down in front of him, "the usual?" Joe nods, as Hazel starts mixing a tall double vodka and 7-Up, with plenty of ice.

He notices that she looks tired tonight, or maybe worried. Her energy is low and clouded. She does her best to hide her mood, with a smile, handing Joe the glass. "You look pretty with your hair up like that," he tells her.

Hazel is used to customers hitting on her, and her hurried response is just to say thank you. She gives Joe his vodka, then grabs her serving tray. An older couple has just walked in. Joe knows that, her abruptly leaving, is just a defence mechanism, so he doesn't take it personally.

Besides, he cringes when remembering all those times when he was downright rude to Hazel. He made so many disrespectful, and sexual comments in the past, thinking of himself as being debonair and cool with comments towards her. That was back then.

He knows all too well now, that what he's said in the past to her, was insulting. He's glad she seems to have put those comments and ass grabbing out of her mind. He can't help but think that maybe Hazel is guided by Deer spirit. She exhibits grace and benevolence. Although, he has to admit that he's just grateful that she no longer seems to bolt when she sees him, like she's done in the past.

Joe can hear the conversation made by the couple, as Hazel takes their order. They tell Hazel that they are celebrating their 30th wedding anniversary, as they take a seat at the back of the pub, beside a large window.

"We will celebrate by ordering a big plate of nachos, with extra jalapenos and cheese. We hear this place is famous for its nachos. But, more importantly, that was the first dish that the two of us shared on our first date, all those years ago," the man says with a smile, as he moves his arm across the table, so that he can hold his wife's hand, "and what else, Dear? Strawberry margaritas?"

The woman nods in agreement.

As Hazel takes the order to the kitchen staff and bartender, she finds herself feeling sadness welling. The couples' outward show of happiness is causing her melancholy, when it is joy that she should be feeling for them. They've been committed to each other for decades.

It's because Hazel has always longed to find that kind of love.

The kind that lasts, weathering storms through good times and bad. She is willing and has tried, but she has never found what she desires most. A real love that lasts.

At this point in her life, she's less than hopeful it might ever happen. Now, in her late 30's, all the good ones seem to already be taken. They are moving on without her, raising a family and planning towards a retirement together.

It's been a sad reality for Hazel to realize that children are not likely to ever be a part of her life. She's always wanted to be a Mom. The time left for that on her biological clock is quickly running out. Meantime, her greatest hope of seeing growth now is watching her garden grow, which holds its own joy, but it's a pale comparison to raising a family and moving through life with a partner.

That's been her prayer, to live a life with a loving partner, the way she observed the kind of happiness and belonging that her Kohkum and Mooshum shared. Hazel is saddened to think that time has passed, and that she might never find someone.

But, she's never been desperate enough to settle for something less, nor getting married for the sake of saying she's married. It's what Kohkum taught her. That finding true love is more important than feeding the stereotype of societal norm of having a ring on her finger, because at a certain age it is expected.

Hazel can still hear her words, "There is no such thing as an old maid, my Dear. We women only get better with age. You wait until it happens for real, my girl, love will find you."

Miserable Moments

It is with regret that Hazel recalls her last failed relationship. She held so much hope when they first came together. His name was Dirk.

He was as ruggedly handsome as the Marlborough Man, except he was wearing a long, black braid. They met at a Round Dance in the city. The first of these types of celebration dances is hosted every spring by the Regina City Police Service, and it's always well-attended. After months of a cold winter, bereft of community gatherings, springtime signals, it's time to get out and dance together again.

Hazel remembers feeling a spark.

As she is holding hands with others and stepping to the beat of the drum, the handsome guest at the Round Dance butts-in. He takes Hazel's hand, and when the drum beat ends, he introduces himself, "Tansi. My name is Dirk," he invites her to come sit with him, "I haven't see you at celebrations like this before. You new to the pow-wow circuit?"

Hazel explains that she's just moved back to the province, after being away to study broadcasting at a Tech School in Alberta. She's just taken a job writing for a local publication, Prairie Dog Magazine, and that she is at the Round Dance that night because her Kohkum likes to attend. The Old Woman has grown frail over the years, and now needs to use a cane for walking. But she still enjoys her Round Dances, and visiting with other Elders, who are most likely to be seated near the table where tea and bannock are being served.

Originally, Hazel had considered not attending the Round Dance. She's had a long day, covering an Arts Festival hosted at a local high school. Now, meeting Dirk, she is glad to have reconsidered. He seems like a dream come true.

The two of them dance together for the remainder of the evening, then they go to Smitty's restaurant on Albert Street North. Dirk orders a loaded burger with a side of onion rings. Hazel gets a club sandwich, but only eats half because she's already had her fair share of bannock at the Round Dance. Just as the waitress is wrapping what remains of her sandwich, so Hazel can take it home and have it for lunch the next day, Dirk suggests they meet up again, tomorrow. He walks her to the parking lot, holds her face and gives her a sweet kiss on the lips. It's a kiss that takes Hazel's breath away. After that, they are inseparable. They take long walks around Wascana Lake in Regina, they visit art galleries, and attend poetry readings, because those are Hazel's interests. Dirk is a non-drinker, so going to bar is out of the question, which suits Hazel just fine.

He seems like the perfect gentleman, until they decide to move in together.

It is almost immediately that Hazel watches something change in Dirk. He is no longer attentive and he rarely does anything but sit in front of the television every night, watching re-run after re-run of the sitcom, The Big Bang Theory. He comes home from work and doesn't inquire about her day. He offers no hugs to greet her. Instead, he asks, 'What's for dinner?" Like that's Hazel purpose in life, to serve him.

Taking long walks together, stop. There are no more visits to Artist performances. Hazel figures, now that Dirk thinks that he "has her", he no longer needs to put in the effort. Like she is some sort of possession to him. He treats Hazel more like a servant than a partner, and she can't figure out what it is that she has done to allow this to happen. What signal was she putting out, to suggest that she is content to be treated as a servant? When what she wants to say is, "Hey, I am not your door mat."

It is emotional abuse that goes on for almost a year, with Hazel holding on to hope that the magic the two had shared when they first met, will somehow be renewed. It never happens. She faces a hard reality. Some men always do this type of thing, of pretending to be something wonderful at the beginning of a relationship, then never feeling the need to put in the same effort later on.

Hazel grows tired of being alone, even though he is always right there, in the same room with her. Ignoring her. She's become invisible. Dirk becomes a jerk.

And Hazel grows tired of loving, half a man.

She moves out on her own, eventually, finding her own apartment in Regina's Heritage District.

It's an old brick building, right beside Maple Leaf Park on 14th Avenue. Hazel is grateful for her job as an arts reporter with Prairie Dog Magazine. It keeps her busy. But in those moments, when she finds herself alone at home, she figures she needs a hobby. Hazel saw an ad in the paper that Canadian Tire is having a sale on bicycles. She buys one, and is out on the bike trails as often as possible, after that.

Then, one morning at the office, Hazel is assigned to write a story about a local athlete, who is training to compete in an Iron Man Competition, in late summer in British Columbia. The athlete is also a well-known musician.

Hearing the details of the race, Hazel wonders why anyone would take part in something like this. It's grueling.

A full Iron Man race is a triathlon of three sports, including a 2.4 mile swim, a 112 mile bike race and ending with a full 26 mile marathon. The focus of Hazel's story centres on the amount of discipline anyone needs, especially balancing a musical career alongside training.

After finishing up a telephone interview with one of the Iron Man competition organizers, Hazel considers training for a similar event, herself. She's been feeling stronger, with the routine of cycling each day, now part of her life. That plan doesn't happen though.

Transition

Kohkum's health quickly starts to fail. The family considers putting her in a nursing home, because she's now to the point where she needs constant help with basic things, like taking a bath or cooking. She needs to use a walker now, too, just to get from room to room. And, she finds it difficult to dress herself, even tying her own shoes is laboured.

But, Hazel will have none of the talk of subjecting Kohkum to assisted living. There is no way that she'll entrust strangers to provide the care she needs.

Kohkum has always been there for her. Now, it is time for her to return that love and commitment. Hazel moves in with her Grandmother, who lives at the Beach. Hazel cares for her until Kohkum dies, peacefully in her sleep not long thereafter.

It is raining on the night that Kohkum passes., Hazel remembers the stories Kohkum has told her about how rain is an indication of a blessing from the Universe. She said, "When a person is either born or when they die, during a storm, rain or snow, it's Creator washing them clean. Taking the rust out of their lives and allowing for a new beginning. Our lives don't end," she says, "they just change. Spirit lives on, and I will always be with you, no matter what."

Hazel sits by the bedside of her now-departed Grandmother. It is important to her that Kohkum is not alone, as she prepares to make her way to the Ancestors. Hazel softly hums one of Kohkum's favourite drum songs. She holds her hand, and starts recalling memories of so many of things they've done together. Hazel brushes Kohkum's thin, gray hair and fashions it into a braid before kissing her on the cheek. It's time to make telephone calls to others to let them know what has happened, although her death was not unexpected.

Kohkum is making her journey back to the Spirit World.

In her will, Hazel learns that Kohkum has left her home to her favourite Granddaughter. Her. She's been living out at the Beach ever since.

The pace of life is slower at the Beach, rather than living in the city, and Hazel loves the fact that, each time she steps out her door each morning, it is the smell of lilacs that greets her instead of inhaling exhaust fumes from vehicles in the city. She still writes the occasional article for the magazine, but she does that work from home now. Hazel took the job at the pub, to get her out of the house and to be interacting with people. Living a solitary life as a writer has its perks, but it can get lonely.

She likes that her neighbours look out for, and care for each other here in this small town.

Like last Fall, after she raked her leaves. Hazel's yard has many trees, and there are more than a dozen bags filled with yard waste. She plans to hire someone to take them to the local landfill for her. There's no way all those bags will fit into her little Nissan. But, she doesn't have to hire anyone.

A neighbour who lives down the street happens to be taking his own yard waste to the dump. While he is on his way there, and driving by Hazel's home, he stops to say hello. Without being asked to do so, he voluntarily starts throwing the bags of fallen leaves onto the back of his pick-up. When Hazel suggests that she pay him, he says, "Keep your money, and pay it forward, help somebody else, somewhere down the road. I'm happy to help out with these. And, it's no trouble, I am heading to the dump anyway." These are the types things people do for each other in this community, which is why it's been easy for Hazel to make the transition from city life.

She appreciates the folks she meets each day at the pub, too. Even old drunks like Joe.

And she did pay it forward, by contacting the local elementary school and offering to teach a class, for free, on how to create beadwork for the grades 7 & 8 classes, sometime during the early winter season. That's a good time for this type of activity, working with the hands, participating in a cultural practice and connecting with another group of people who live in the community.

Now, here at the pub, Hazel puts in another kitchen order, and surveys the customers' needs. The couple celebrating their anniversary are laughing, sipping their drinks and still holding hands. She doesn't need to wander over and ask if they want another. Let them enjoy each others' company, she figures. But, there is a table of four of customers, who look to be people in their 20's. They each ordered a draught, the most popular brand at the bar, during summer months, is always Coors Light. Hazel can see there are no more suds at the top of their heavy glasses. They will likely need a top up soon. She makes a note to keep an eye on them. When she glances at Joe's vodka and 7-Up, she can tell that he isn't chugging tonight, like he did the last time he was in. He still has half a glass, and it's clear that he's nursing the drink, sipping slowly, because all the ice has melted.

Hazel begins to see Joe, tonight, in a different light. She thinks of him as being handsome and respectful. Whereas, he'd always exhibited crude behaviour in the past, he seems different now. Gentler and more refined. There is no more groping, which always made Hazel more than uncomfortable around him. She decides that, whatever he's been doing lately is likely a good thing.

If she only knew the reality of why he sits here now, sober and finally acting like a gentleman. It's how Joe always wanted to be regarded. He just didn't know how to do it, and he wasn't capable of gentle behaviour after swilling back way more than one too many, in the past.

What Hazel doesn't know is that Joe hasn't touched a drop of his vodka and 7-Up. He can't.

He waited until she was away from the bar top, tending to the couple. That's when he poured half of his drink down the spill bucket, which is at the back edge of the bar top. It's there to catch any leaks, drips or spills, and cleaned regularly throughout each shift. That's where Joe emptied half his glass, so that it looks like he's been drinking. He doesn't want to call attention to himself, sitting at the bar but not drinking something that has alcohol in it. It would be suspicious, considering that Joe may very probably have been Hazel's best customer, before everything changed.

It's his secret desire that things will change again, this time with Hazel, and gaining her affection.

The Curse of Woman

It's getting late, and Joe secretly pours the remainder of his drink into the spill bucket, before heading towards the door. He leaves a sizeable tip, and says good night to Hazel, before leaving the bar.

He has no intention of going home, though. There is no wind tonight, as is characteristic on the Saskatchewan Plains. Although, wind can offer a small reprieve from being bothered by mosquitoes. The pests, though, no longer agitate Joe anymore, so it's not a concern.

It's dark out. Only a sliver of Grandmother Moon shines in the sky tonight. Joe walks across the street, taking his perch on the concrete stairs of the cafe. Sitting in the shadows, Joe can see Hazel through the windows of the brightly lit pub. He is shrouded in darkness, so she has no way of knowing that she's being watched by him. The place has now emptied, and Hazel grabs a clean, wet cloth to start wiping down the tables. Moments before she locks up for the night, someone arrives. Joe recognizes the visitor. He knows that she is a friend of Hazel's because he's seen them together before. Indeed, he's heard her name before. He reaches to recall what it is, and just can't remember. It surprises Joe that he still has a case of brain fog, which was common for him during his drinking days. No matter. He continues to eavesdrop on the conversation.

"Hey, girlfriend, I hope you are just about ready to leave?"

There is an easy familiarity between the women. Joe makes the assumption, they've probably known each other for quite a long time because of the very personal conversation that follows.

"So, how was your night?" Hazel's friend wants to know.

"Oh, it was okay. Steady, but not terribly busy. I'm just glad I made it through. Shit! My cramps were extreme tonight. I almost felt like going home," she pauses, "and with that, I know you always carry extra tampons in your purse. I'm hoping you will pass one over. I brought protection, but Auntie Flo seems angry today, and I used up all of mine."

Auntie Flo is the code name women often use when referring to their menstrual cycle. The curse that has arrived every month, since adolescence.

"I've never bled this heavy before. I'm just glad I decided not to wear my white sundress, this shift." The friend takes a look at the black jumper that Hazel's wearing, telling her, "It's always smart to wear dark colours at that time of the month. You look great tonight. But, come on, quit dawdling, there's karaoke to croak."

Joe can hear the conversation from this far distance like he's sitting down and listening, right in front of the women. He didn't need to guess why her mood tonight was so low, already knowing that Hazel is having her period, again. He caught a whiff of menstrual blood the moment he arrived at the pub. As Hazel moves closer towards him, asking for his order, he knows the pheromone is emanating from her.

For a split second, Joe worried he'll react. He's secretly concerned that his hunger might overcome any common sense, of which he still might have control. He leveled out that possibility by taking in a long sniff of the vodka, in the glass that Hazel served him.

The pub closes earlier than the bar. That's where these two friends are heading.

When the two women turn out the lights, locking up for the night, they are still talking about feminine trouble, "You know, if you are really worried about irregular heavy flow, you should go see a doctor. We're getting older, girl-friend, and every single one of us will go through the meno-pause. It's a damn inconvenience but it can't be avoided. We're getting older and our bodies are changing. But, you know, we still look awesome. So go through the change, but don't let it wipe you out, my friend." At this point, Hazel's friend digs into her purse, looking for something that will of-fer a solution. She finds it, "Here, take this card. It's got the address of the Broad Street Medical Clinic in Regina, that's where I go. Promise me that you will make an appointment. They can help, or refer you to a specialist who can help. Do it. No sense in going through something that's knocking you out, to the point where you feel like you can't work. I know. Modern medicine is great, and they'll even guide you towards alternatives for care, like books on yoga and diet. Call them." Hazel accepts the business card, saying, "Okay, I'll call. I promise," she changes the subject, "Now, let's see who else has stumbled from here over to the Waterfront." That's the name of another place to gather and drink in Town. It's just around the corner.

Everyone is entitled to their own fifteen minutes of fame, so karaoke night on Saturdays usually draws a big crowd at the bar, especially in the summer. People get on stage and strut their stuff for a short period of time. It doesn't mat-ter that most sing off key. And while there are no food specials offered on weekends, Hazel has observed that it is popular for patrons at this bar to order, what's called the Sunday Funday special. That includes, 5 Corona beer, surrounded by ice, and served in a shiny, metal gardening bucket. Ordering it goes over especially well with the younger crowd, who are out looking for fun, and a bucket of beer.

As the women round the corner, heading towards the bar, they have no way of knowing they are being followed. Joe's footsteps are silent now. Like the quiet wings of an owl out on the hunt, he's evolved into being a silent killer.

But as he follows, he has no intention of taking their lives. He just wants to make sure they stay safe. No one is allowed to cause harm to Hazel. He's made it his task to ensure that she never has to worry about feeling scared.

It is a girl's night out, and these two have each other. Hazel won't require his protection tonight. Once he observes them, taking their place on the outdoor patio at the bar, Joe knows they are in for an evening of camaraderie and socializing. They will order appetizers, engage in gossip and maybe even have a Corona bucket. Joe continues to listen in on their conversation, and they are happy to be able to spend this time together. When he learns that Hazel's friend plans to spend the night, at Hazel's home at the Beach, he realizes that there is no need to watch any longer. He won't need to follow Hazel home. They have each other, and there is safety in being a pair.

It's a warm summer's night and Joe guesses that there will be many others, also out tonight and enjoying the season. One of them is destined for a visit from him. Joe is hungry.

Drinking Alone

Joe has access to people's lives and habits, even when they have no idea that he's lurking. He has the ability to become invisible, by mesmerizing people into thinking that he's not present. There is no safe place. Being inside of a building is no sanctuary, even if it's your home, and he realizes that it is a myth that vampires need to be invited in, if they wish to enter. He finds that he is able to go anywhere he wants. And what he wants and needs right now is blood. He hasn't fed yet this evening.

It's too early in the evening for Joe to expect anyone to be out stumbling around because they are stricken by the drink. He figures he can wait until closing time, as others make their way back to their cabins. But maybe he won't have to wait. He can always count on the day-drinkers, who are people who prefer to hide their addiction by drinking at home, alone.

It's in this moment that a practical thought hits him. Joe won't always be able to count on satisfying his lust for blood on cabin owners or visitors to the Beach. Their presence here, too, is seasonal. They are people who Joe doesn't know or live with as friends and neighbours. When autumn arrives, he'll need to find a food source, here at home. He won't be able to feed on strangers, by driving to the city or another town that is close by. He can't do this right now because he has no drivers licence and, contrary to popular belief, vampires don't fly. At least, it isn't something that he is capable of doing.

Those seasonal residents will be gone within a few short weeks.

He'll need to figure out a long-term plan for feeding. And, it is easy for Joe to come up with one.

The home alone.

They are a crafty bunch, making their own wine or beer. Home brewers who no one knows about. But they are here and, they drink too much, but they drink alone in their homes. The only difference with their malady is that there is no need to go to the liquor store. They make their own, so no one knows. And, they sit at home and drink alone.

Joe knows the dance.

It will be easy for him to figure out who in town makes it their practice to open a bottle of home-made wine, then sit down on the couch to watch a movie. Statistics say that one in five people are problem drinkers, so he'll have his pick. Because the Beach is so well-treed, many year-round residents don't bother to cover their windows with curtains. Generally, there are no prowlers and no one is out wandering around in their woodlot. And, this time of year, they leave their windows open too. That's how Joe will be able to ascertain who is at home and drinking alone. He'll be able to smell it.

As he makes his rounds, peeking into windows that are not covered, Joe wonders why more folks are not paying better attention to their own safety.

He remembers when he was a child and closing the curtains was always the first thing that his Mom did, the moment the sun started to fade. Joe's bedroom, back then and even today, faces east. There are nothing but trees out in that part of the back yard. There is no view from the street. Anyone would have to make a real effort to be a Peeping Tom. Plus, Joe would hear their footsteps because there are so many fallen twigs that would snap. Still, his Mom insists that the drapes need to be closed tight at night. After years of this, what he considers peculiar behaviour, Joe has to ask - why?

His Mom tells a story that sticks to this day.

She talks about creatures of the night, and she doesn't mean skunks, raccoons or porcupine. She's referring to monsters. The young Joe, can't figure out if what she's saying is for real or if she is trying to scare him into making sure he gets home each night before it gets dark. He remembers her speaking about a horned creature that she saw one night, as she was getting out of her car and coming home after a late shift at the hospital. Joe's Mom was a nurse. He remembers her saying.

At first, I thought it was a deer because there are so many of them in town. But when I looked closer, I realized that it had human features. Scared the hell out of me. Its eyes were fixated on the house next door to ours, just right outside your bedroom. Next, I heard a tussle, like a big fight was going on. I was too scared to check and see what was happening, so I immediately ran indoors. To this day, I have no idea what that thing was nor what it attacked in the yard next door. And, I don't want to know. I immediately checked on you, and you were safe and fast asleep, but your curtains were open. I closed them, first thing. Never let them see you, Joe, while you are resting and vulnerable. It's like they are looking for opportunity. For what? None of us wants to know. I realize it sounds crazy, but I saw what I saw, and I heard what I heard. So now you will ask, are monsters real? I have no idea, and I don't want to find out. Close your drapes, Joe. Because you don't want to know the answer either.

Joe isn't sure how to feel, now that he is that type of lurking monster that his Mom warned him about. And she was absolutely correct. As he gauges his thirst for blood, Joe knows it's time to go in, not to kill but to feed.

He does his rounds, walking and making note of homes where he knows he can count on feeding during the winter months. He'll even befriend those lone drinkers, once he knows who they are. That way, he can use his power of persuasion to find out where they hide their outdoor key. Everyone has one. It's a place where the house key is hidden, in case someone ever needs to use it, like visitors who have arrived early and the home-owner isn't there, or their dog walker has come to exercise the pooch. They can let themselves in with the hidden key. Joe will do the same, once he knows where the key is and that the home-alone drinker has passed out, after having one too many from their bottles of home-made brew. He has no super-power of being able to turn to smoke and drift in through the key hole, like he's seen vampires do in the movies. His plan is simple, he'll have a constant food source, without causing any real harm. Joe won't drain them and take their lives. He'll only feed, stopping from sucking their blood when he knows it's time and before their heart stops beating. He can do a rotation. The home alone drinkers can be counted on. They will be overly tired the next morning, after his visit. They will probably not feel well for several days, after Joe has feasted on their blood. But, they will never know the reason why. Maybe feeling horrible, after Joe has fed, might even convince one or two of them to stop drinking entirely.

It takes no time for Joe to find one of those places tonight. He locates his first such victim.

Her home is just a couple blocks from the bar. Joe takes notice of the property because her dog is out in the yard. It is a fenced enclosure, but the dog barks, as though it's in some kind of distress, like he's calling out that he wants to be let back in the house. But, no one hears him. He wonders how long the mutt has been left alone, like this. Abandoned in the night.

Through her screen door, Joe can smell a pronounced scent of red wine. He lets himself in, but not before making sure that the dog gets in the house first.

Joe has seen this woman before. She always waves a greeting, when she's out and about around town, picking up her mail or getting some groceries. When Joe checks on her tonight though, she is passed out on the couch and inside her home. Her door was left unlocked.

And, funnily enough, she's lucky that Joe arrived when he did. She's still holding a lit cigarette in her hand. If it were to drop onto the couch, the possibility is real that there would be a house fire. Joe removes the butt from her hand and snuffs it out in the ashtray, that's on a side table. The ashtray is already filled with old cigarette butts but there is room for one more. It leaves Joe wondering how many times this woman has been in this type of peril, and was just lucky enough that it didn't amount to disaster, and a fire, tonight.

The television is still on, and Joe can't help but smile. She's been watching an old movie called *Fright Night*, which is a movie he remembers watching in his youth. It's a story about a vampire who lives next door, and he just seems like such a regular guy that no one suspects that he's really a monster. Chris Sarandon is the main actor. Joe knows, that he too is the guy next door, but he knows that he isn't as handsome as Chris. Joe turns off the TV.

He glances around to see how this woman lives. Except for the over-loaded ashtray, her home is impeccably clean with a sense of order. She's relatively young, and someone who has done well in her life. Joe glances at a copy of her framed degree, Faculty of Kinesiology, University of Regina, that's prominently displayed in her living room.

Joe can't make a guess at the reason that she secretly drinks alone at home, but he hopes for her that she figures it out. He knows how something like this can happen, when drinking stops being a social activity and it stops being fun, and it becomes a shameful habit that needs to be hidden. This is no kind of life, checking out and using booze as a way to erase.

He makes a point to keep an eye on her, but for now, Joe drinks. While doing so, he can taste the home-made wine. It won't be his last visit to this address, as winter eventually approaches, he'll visit this woman periodically.

When he's finished feeding, he covers her up with a light throw blanket that's fallen to the floor. While doing so,

Joe spots an interesting coin, that's nestled in with a large, prickly cactus that sits on the coffee table. He removes the object from the planter. Glancing at it, Joe immediately recognizes it as an AA recovery chip. It's given to those who regularly come to meetings and have successfully stopped drinking for a full year. There is engravement on the chip, that says:

To Thine Own Self Be True

It's clear, this woman has been on the sober train before, but obviously she's slipped off for now. Joe hopes, for her sake, that she finds her way back.

Before leaving, Joe tucks the coin into his pocket.

Patience is a Virtue

How does someone capture the interest of a person who isn't interested?

It's been weeks of Joe sitting on the concrete steps across from the pub, watching Hazel through the window, while he sits in dark shadows. Only watching.

Joe has no idea how to successfully attract the attention of a good woman. He realizes that he's never known. In this aspect of his adult life, Joe feels like he's been cast out in the rip tide, so far away, that he never figures out how to safely swim back to shore. Or like he's tethered to the end of a kite string that's been caught in a storm.

He thinks back to a time, when he thought he was being sly and appealing.

The scenario.

A young lady has come into the cafe. She is likely in her late 20's, and is flirting with Joe, by giving him a smile and a wink when he brings out her order. Even though he's not a server, it is near to closing time and there is only one waitress still shifted at this late hour. She's just received news of a family emergency and is on the telephone, so when Joe readies the food order, he takes it out instead.

The pretty, blonde customer asked for a house salad with a side of vinaigrette dressing, which sparks a conversation, as Joe sets down her plate, "Here's your order, Miss," he says with a smile, "but we're famous for our fish & chips. You'll need to come back, sometime soon, and try them out." She tells him that she's a fitness instructor, living in Regina, and that she never eats fried food. There is a little flirting going on, amongst other banal banter about the weather.

Because she came in to the cafe near closing time, Joe suggests the two of them head across the street for a drink after his shift. She agrees to meet up with him.

Her body is slim and fit, and her complexion is clear, so wonderfully so that she could be a model for a company that produces a skin care regime, if she wanted. Once seated on the deck, at the pub across the street, it shouldn't have surprised Joe when she tells him that she wants to order a soda water with cranberry juice, instead of something with alcohol. "I don't drink," she says, "and I'd never be with anybody who drinks alcohol."

Well, that's a dilemma.

Joe tells her that he'll go inside, and let the waitress know what they wish to order.

But, he gives special instructions, "She wants a soda and cranberry, and I will have my special water." The waitress, not Hazel at that time, knows what it means. For Joe, "a special water" means, a tall glass, filled with 3 shots of vodka and topped up with tap water. He's ordered it before. Joe figures his date will never know. He'll tell her that he is drinking Perrier. They are both a clear liquids, surrounded by ice. Joe thinks he can fake it by being sneaky. But after ordering 3 of his "special water", he starts slurring and talking gibberish. At this point, his date tells him that she needs to get something from her car.

She never comes back.

He wakes up the following morning with a hangover so extreme, Joe worries about whether he might die of a heart attack. He's got the shakes and needs to run to the toilet every few minutes, not to throw up, but to relieve himself of foul-smelling and runny diarrhea. The colour of his excrement is black. Joe's done enough reading to know that a black stool can be a sign of internal bleeding, caused by long-term alcohol abuse. It's something that should be checked by a medical professional, but Joe never bothers to make the call. It would most likely indicate that he's nearing the point of no return, and he doesn't want to quit drinking.

He'd drained a whole bottle of vodka at the pub that night, then kept on drinking once he'd found his way home. He doesn't remember passing out.

Joe figures that's where ghosts come from, and that if a person dies while blacked out, they don't even realize they are dead, so they just keep hanging around. The thought is maudlin, with Joe feeling sorry for himself again, and continuing to place blame on everyone else for his predicament.

As rough as the alcohol left him that time, Joe continues to poison himself.

It is less than a week later, when he finds himself at it again, with another, sort of, love interest.

She is more like a drinking buddy, really, and Joe can't remember her name. But he does remember how she managed to save him from a DUI though, before the week that he actually did lose his licence.

The quick-thinking woman did it by pretending to be pregnant.

He so easily recalls how the RCMP are out patrolling that night. Joe's car is swerving, and not to avoid pot holes. He gets stopped, and is asked to step out of his vehicle.

"Good evening Roger Rabbit," Joe giggles, then corrects himself, "I mean, Officer, sorry. I'm still half asleep. That was the name of the movie I was watching before going to bed. I was fast asleep when my wife woke me up and said we need to go for a ride. My wife is expecting any day now." At this point the young constable looks in the vehicle and sees what looks to be a pregnant woman. Joe continues talking, "For the last few days, the baby has been kicking up a storm. And, it seems the only way baby settles down is if we drive around for a bit, it seems to soothe him." Joe couldn't have known that the young constable who stopped him, is also a new Dad.

His son turned two years old, earlier this month. Because of this, the cop already has a soft spot for new parents, so he lets Joe pass, without even asking to see his driver's licence.

The officer couldn't have known that the woman has been cunning enough to cram all of the beer cans under her large shirt, hiding the evidence, and making it appear as though she is pregnant.

The two drunken sods continue their drunken drive towards their destination, Joe's home. Once there, they immediately drink all of that beer that the woman hid under her clothing.

After Joe passes out from the excess, the woman goes rooting through his wallet, stealing his bank card. She then goes on a spree, tapping under-$100-purchases at businesses all across the city, over the next couple of days.

Normally, Joe would realize that his bank card is missing, because it is an almost-daily routine, ever since he's fallen off the sober train, yet again. Going to the off-sale is an everyday occurrence, to buy some more booze, pretty much each and every day.

That is something that requires a bank card.

The next morning, and through an alcoholic haze, Joe notices that the woman is gone. There are plenty of empty beer cans strewn across both the kitchen and living room floors, as evidence that he'd slobbered through another one-nighter.

Did they have sex? Joe figures, probably so. That's the way these nights go. But he can't remember.

The empty cans are a testimony to sin. They are the ones that the woman hid under her over-sized shirt, in an effort to dupe the police. She may have stayed longer, carrying on in this unhealthy and feigned relationship, instead of disappearing come morning light. Joe didn't tell her, so she has no way of knowing, there is plenty of beer still to be had.

He is recently a winner, after entering a raffle, which was held down at the bar.

The prize is a keg of draught beer. A keg. That is like 165 tall glass servings of beer. And, Joe won it about a week ago. The keg is still half full. He'd cleared out all of the shelves in the second refrigerator that he has out in his garage. It's how he keeps the keg chilled, and the beer inside of it, frosty.

Again, he doesn't need money right now, so he doesn't notice the missing bank card.

He still has his keg, and some food in the freezer. Joe remembers buying some breaded chicken strips and a bag of frozen fries, a few days ago. That will hold him until the keg is empty.

It is three days later when he checks his wallet, and realizes that he's been robbed. By this time, his bank account has been emptied. One tap at a time.

It empties Joe as well. Who can you trust? Can't even believe in a drinking buddy.

It should have been one of many signals that it is time to stop with abusing alcohol. That, and the fact that Joe shit himself again the night after draining the beer keg, by himself.

That should have been the precursor to the impending aneurysm, which the kiss of Dust Man prevented. And, it should have been a solid clue to Joe that his excessive abuse of alcohol was wearing down his body, to the point that his internal organs were already starting to fail.

He needs to clean the up his shit, figuratively and literally.

Joe wipes himself as best he can, before jumping into the shower for a quick rinse.

It isn't too long after the encounter with the fake pregnant woman that Joe ends up with a case of infectious mononucleosis. It leaves him feeling weak.

Joe can never be sure if his thief of a drinking buddy is the source of this infection, or whether the ailment came from somewhere else. Regardless, he is forced to bed rest and taking it easy for more than a week. Joe cannot rule out that he brought on this condition, all on his own, because of bad hygiene and bad decisions.

> The two didn't go directly to Joe's home after being stopped by police.
>
> Instead, they visited the off-sale. The woman wanted to pick up some potato chips and another 6-pack. While waiting outside, Joe goes to light-up, but he notices that his pack of smokes is empty. He knows there is an extra package at his home, but he wants one now. It's then he sees opportunity.
>
> A cement garden planter sits outside the side door by the off-sale. The flowering plant in it, somehow still manages to grow, despite the ground surrounding it is also being used as an ashtray.
>
> Joe sifts through the used cigarette butts, without a thought to possible health risk. Mono is passed through saliva.
>
> He finds a chipper that still has a decent amount of tobacco. It's a half-smoked cigarette. It is a discarded butt that someone has thrown away, but it still has a good amount of tobacco left on the filter. It is possible that's where Joe picked up his funk.
>
> One bad habit leading to more than a week of being sick, and sickening thoughts about the kind of lifestyle that he leads.
>
> He quits smoking after that. But the excess of drinking

is something that he just can't seem to get a hold of and stop doing that as well.

It's where this story ends and many others begin.

Joe counts his blessings that he doesn't have a tale to tell about contracting chlamydia, syphilis or even HIV, and that contracting mononucleosis is the worst that's ever happened to him, as a result of his wham-bam-thank you ma'am, and otherwise reckless, way of life.

Although, being infected with the blood of Dust Man is, without question, the ultimate. And, something for which there is no cure.

No going back.

Biding Time

Popular folklore suggests that vampires are incapable of having feelings, but that's like saying cats and dogs don't feel love. Those memories of Joe's last failed attempts at gaining the attention of a woman makes him cringe, now that he's been forced to be sober. He's ashamed that he even acted that way, in the past.

Hazel deserves better. Joe commits to start making a real effort. He's always felt a tenderness for her, despite that she's never shown interest nor reciprocated. No matter. Joe vows to make it his destination, to find a way into her heart.

Xavier can help.

In his quiet moments lately, Joe has been watching YouTube videos, instead of streaming action films. It makes him giggle to come across videos of cats on skateboards.

Since he started feeding the little gray feline, Xavier's become a regular visitor. He's fattened up, now that Joe has switched from feeding the cat canned tuna, to a proper diet of kibble. Xavier's bald spot is growing in as well, and he no longer licks the area near his tail. Joe's home-made remedy got rid of the flea fiasco. Now, the little furry dude has made another stride.

Xavier is warming up to Joe, even though experts say wild cats cannot be socialized to human touch. It doesn't apply here. Joe isn't human.

After seeing the cat videos, Joe decides he'll do what he can to train Xavier to do the same. He'll teach him to ride on a board.

He starts slowly, by propping his longboard up against the apple tree in the middle of his front lawn. Xavier is curious, so he climbs up the longboard and onto a low-hanging branch. When it's clear that the cat wants to come down, Joe takes the equipment and holds it up to where Xavier rests on a higher branch, softly mewling. He's delightfully surprised when the cat gingerly steps onto the board, allowing Joe to balance it, then lower it to the ground. With that accomplished, Joe rigs up some fishing line, looping it around the front of the board. He's surprised that Xavier makes no fuss as Joe gently picks him up and places him on the treated wood. He slowly pulls the cat up and down his paved driveway. Joe gets the idea to affix a cat bed to the back of his longboard, a place where Xavier can travel, feeling relatively secured. Repetition, repetition, repetition.

That's the start of how Joe becomes a spectacle down Centre Street. No longer brandishing the stigma of being the town drunk, he's become "the guy with the cat." It hurts his skin to be out sometimes, when there is no cloud cover during the late hours of the afternoon, but the sunlight is not as intense as it is during the morning and early afternoon, so he tolerates it. Joe can suffer being in sunlight, depending on the time of day.

Because Joe has been studying Hazel's routine and movements, he knows that she'll soon be walking up the street to start her shift at the pub. Joe steps on his longboard and starts what's called parachuting. He wears an unbuttoned flannel shirt to catch the slight breeze, so that he doesn't reach excessive speed, hollering a greeting as Hazel walks by.

She giggles, then quickly reaches inside her bra, grabs her cell phone and snaps a photo.

Joe finds it amusing and unusual that she uses her unmentionables as a place for storage. He wonders why she isn't carrying a purse. But one thing is for sure. He knows they will have something substantial to chat about next time he visits the pub, which he plans to do tonight.

In preparation, he starts rehearsing a conversation, figuring that Hazel may be likely to ask about Xavier, and how Joe managed to train him to ride on a longboard.

Great Expectations

Joe finds himself feeling like a teenage girl, going out on a first date, right now. He can't decide what to wear.

How he looked never bothered him before, which is why, in his human form, he'd just pull on a t-shirt. It didn't matter if it was dirty or clean. Joe goes to his closet. His work clothes are still hanging there, it's what he used to wear to the office before getting fired as a business executive. He chooses a fresh dress shirt that's a vibrant colour of blue. He even puts on a proper pair of dress pants, topping it off with a black leather belt.

Feeling nervousness, walking towards the pub, Joe tries to think of what he'll say to Hazel. He knows that women like her appreciate clever conversation. It's not something he's ever been good at, either.

He enters the pub, feeling hopeful and confident. He tinkered with the idea of bringing Hazel some flowers tonight. They sell mixed bouquets up at the grocery store. They're mostly arrangements of carnations and daisies, but sensible reason takes over and Joe decides against the idea. He can't know for sure if the gesture would be a bit too much, at this point. He doesn't want Hazel to think it's a come-on, and that he expects something in return, like eventually having sex.

That is one of Joe's concerns as well. He can't remember the last time that he was fully aware during intimate moments. But that's being kind. To be frank, there is nothing intimate and tender about having drunken sex, and that's been his only experience for as long as he can remember now. It is empty, and not even really physical pleasure, even though moderately satisfying. It really is just going through the motions of what we truly desire, and an attempt at trying to fill something that is already empty.

He knows that his feelings towards Hazel will mark an end towards this conundrum, should they engage in these special moments. He wants to say "when" they feel that touch. Even though Joe no longer lives as a human, the feelings and longing for love remain. She is a mystery that he longs to explore.

The moment he takes a seat at the bar top, he's glad for not doing anything that might be considered, over-the-top. Like bringing flowers. It's clear that Hazel is in distress. She is shaking, and her breathing is irregular. In her left hand, she holds a manila envelope.

"Hazel, what's wrong?" Joe wants to reach out and give her a comforting hug, but he senses that that, too, is not the right thing to do at this moment in time.

Hazel shakes her head, looks Joe square in the eye, then states with disdain, "Men can be such pigs." Joe is puzzled. He can't think of anything he might have done to have caused her dark mood.

"Oh, I'm sorry, Joe. It's not you. It's this." Hazel hands over the envelope and nods a gesture that she's giving him permission to see what's inside. It's a photograph that looks like it might have been taken with a cell phone, and likely developed by a wireless photo printer.

The picture shows an image of someone's erect penis. There's also a one-hundred-dollar bill attached to it, with a paper clip.

"Who did this?" Joe wants to show outrage but he's more inclined towards being startled, seeing the photo and the money. Who would do such a thing, and think it is appropriate or enticing? What! Does this person think of Hazel as nothing more than a call girl? How fucking disrespectful. I am putting an end to this right now, Joe vows.

He feels a frightening anger welling, wondering if this perpetrator might still be on the premises. If he is, Joe thinks, even God cannot help him now, I will get him.

Hazel does her best to regain composure, and begins to tell the story.

A seasonal resident from across the lake has been coming in regularly, to play during the twilight tee-times up at the local golf course. That means, a reduced rate for any games played after 4 pm. A couple of weeks ago, this man stopped in at the pub to grab a beer and a quesadilla. A little snack before jumping back on his pontoon boat, which has a spot at the yacht club, and before heading back to his cottage across the lake. Instead, he was smitten by Hazel and ended up staying until closing time.

Before leaving, he set out on an ego trip, making a point of grabbing her wrist with his left hand. His skin was sweaty, but the oversized golden rings had retained a chill from the cold beer, that also seemed a part of his hand. Hazel couldn't tell if it was the unexpected chill of precious metal touching her skin, or that this guy generally gave her the creeps, that made the hair stand up on her forearms.

He tried to impress, telling her how much money he's made during his lifetime. The guy was obviously in his 70's now, judging by the looks of him, but not a healthy 70-year-old. He has a gut full of sin, and breath that smells of too many sad stories. He tells Hazel that he owns 3 vehicles; a Dodge Ram truck, a sensible Honda Civic for road trips, and a sporty Ford Mustang, "I'd like to take you for a drive sometime." Hazel recalls being repulsed by the thought of some fat, sweaty, bald guy seated beside her in an enclosed space.

"He's a citidiot," Hazels tells Joe, "You know the type, seasonal residents who come in to our community, with a sense of privilege, like it's okay if they take over, or take whatever they want. I like our visitors, in general, but some of them are hard to tolerate. Especially this guy."

She says, the man further tried to impress by talking about the real estate that he owns. A completely renovated 2400 square foot character home, in Regina's Cathedral Neighbourhood, a rustic two-storey wooden cabin across the lake, and he talked about a condo that he owns in Mexico. He joked saying, it's in one of the gated communities, to keep out the riff raff, and near Puerta Vallarta. He said, he wants to take her there, too.

He made a point to telling her that he owns a helicopter, "I have a landing pad right near my house, across the lake.

Hazel watched a documentary lately, and knows that one thing that most people don't understand about helicopters is that helicopters are violent and they are not meant to fly. The amount of overhead and cost that needs to go into obtaining and maintaining a helicopter is astronomical.

A landing pad, indeed! Hazel figures this guy is likely to be both, violent and high maintenance, as well.

His parting words before the pub closed last night, were:

"I can give you anything you want, Baby. One of these nights, you need to come back with me to the other side of the lake, on my pontoon boat. I bought it with some spare cash that I had laying around earlier this spring. Come on over," he winked, "We can swim in the buff, and we'll have a fire by the lake."

Hazel isn't impressed, although she is intrigued at how someone so boring clings to such a high sense of self-worth.

The guy has been coming to the pub every night since. And, he came in again earlier this afternoon, before heading up to the golf course.

Joe is stunned by what Hazel's told him. The gall! Thinking he can buy Hazel, like she's some store shelf item. The lout has left Hazel many good tips, enough to pay her power bill. But now, giving her a photo and this one-hundred-dollar bill. It's too much. Joe balls-up his right fist, glancing around the room, "Where is he? That fucking guy! I'm gonna smash him."

"He's not here," Hazel says, "he left to play 9 holes about a half hour ago," she checks her watch, "which means he's likely to come back here in about 3 hours, just as dusk is setting in. I dread seeing him again."

She won't have to.

Joe has no intention of allowing this slime bag to come back and harass Hazel again. Joe orders his usual vodka and 7-Up, pouring it down the spill bucket when Hazel is not looking, and he plots, making a promise to himself,

"There will be a fire tonight, indeed. And you, ya damn asshole, will provide the kindling."

Baptism by Fire

Joe doesn't know what the pompous, perverted clod looks like. The details of his appearance are never discussed in detail. Hazel only mentions an approximate age. Judging by the penis photo, Joe knows he's an old white guy. Hazel did comment that he wears giant golden rings. That's enough of a description for Joe to find him.

As he walks up the Centre Street hill towards the golf course, he muses, that money has a lot more strength than metal, in the sense of binding people in shackles. Money today is our ultimate cage. This man's, for sure. He is a monster who hides behind his money.

Because Joe has inherited the gift of hypnosis from Dust Man, it's easy for him to walk about the golf club house, and on the greens, without anyone taking notice. He also has the power of intention, the ability to cast a spell so that others follow his will, without question. Joe knows that both are legacies to be used only sparingly.

Joe walks around the diner and bar area of the clubhouse. Vampire among us.

No one has a clue. No one sees him.

He's using his nose to see if he'll catch any familiar scent. Back at the pub, Joe made a point of sniffing the manila envelope, and the photograph, which would have been handled by the foul man who's been harassing Hazel. He recognizes no whiff of him in the restaurant, so he decides to go out for a walk on the greens.

The sun is setting, and at this hour, most of the golf carts are already returned. Only the arrogant will have enough guile to expect that clubhouse staff won't mind being forced to stay longer than what's shifted on their time sheets, waiting for lollygaggers to figure out, it's time to go home.

It's near the 9th hole, which is closest to the clubhouse and beside a pond, that Joe smells the man. His body odour is mixed in with a combination of sweat and whiskey emanating from his pours.

"Hey, hey, hey. Good game, old bugger," the partner who's been playing with the man bids goodnight, "time for me to get on home now. But, meet you, same place, same time tomorrow?"

They are the last ones on the greens.

"Yea, yea. So, you got lucky here today on the greens, you old sod. Now, run off home to the old ball and chain. I plan to get lucky where it counts. There is a nice piece at the pub down the hill, and I plan on tapping her tonight." His partner gives a nod and a thumbs up, driving off to head home, in a golf cart that he owns.

The man with the golden ring stands for a moment, checking the score sheet. Unaware that he's being watched by Joe. The man grabs a pack of cigarettes from the top pocket of his golf shirt and lights up a smoke. It's to be his last movement. Joe lunges, ripping into his flesh, saying, "Your money can't save you now." The shock of being suddenly grabbed causes the man's jaw to lock. The lit cigarette still hanging from his lips.

Again, Joe feasts, satisfying two needs. Blood and alcohol. He drains him to the point of unconsciousness, but doesn't kill him. He wants this guy to feel pain, no doubt not so different from the mental and emotional anguish he's been inflicting upon women, like Hazel, for years, causing them to be afraid for their own safety.

Joe wants this guy to experience terror and anguish.

He opens the lid at the front of the golf cart. The gas tank is on the passenger side. That's where Joe slumps the man's body, making it look as though he may have been checking for some mechanical problem, but not before Joe takes the package of cigarettes out of the man's pocket and tosses a couple of them on the ground.

Joe wants to make this look like an accident, knowing that, shit happens. It's why they invented toilet paper. He forces the lit cigarette from the man's mouth and tosses it into the gas tank, but not before removing the man's golden ring and placing it on his own middle finger. Within a fraction of a second Joe moves away. The explosion is almost immediate, and the golf cart goes up in flames so quickly that even he is surprised. It's a fire ball. The smell of burning flesh, mixed with gasoline, is sickening.

Joe watches from the nearby bush as fire crews quickly arrive. As a crowd gathers, he heads for home. As Joe walks slowly down the hill, he ponders. On the day of my judgement, what will I say to St. Christopher?

Xavier is sitting on the veranda, right beside a couple of plants that Joe hasn't gotten around to putting in soil yet. There's a grand-looking King Tut grass plant and a flower that's part of the petunia family. Funnily enough, it's called Calibrachoa Dracula. It is a flower with vibrant pink outer petals, with the inside of the bloom coloured black. Joe figures that is the likely colouring of the insides of his victims, once they are drained. A flower named after Dracula. Coincidence? Maybe not. Joe bought the flowers because he was attracted to its unusual colouring. It isn't every day that a greenhouse carries black flowers. Both plants are still in their small containers.

Joe picks them up, then heads over to where Hazel lives.

He knows that she has one empty, large pot, still waiting for transplanted flowers, right beside her door. Earlier this week, she painted the door the colour of blue. Joe overheard because he was spying on her. She was on the telephone, and he remembers her saying that a blue door is symbolic. It represents prosperity and abundance, as well as God's protection and guidance.

Joe thinks the pink and black flowers will make a nice contrast beside the blue-coloured door. He hopes it brings her joy, when she sees them, coming home after her shift tonight. He also hopes that the gesture doesn't make him appear, like he's being too forward.

Truth or Dare

Joe has acted on impulse, in planting those flowers and grass for Hazel, but this time it's being spontaneous in a good way.

Upon walking back to his home, and carrying the spade that he used to transplant the foliage, Joe's memory travels back to another time that he acted in the spur of the moment. Although, a more apt description is to call what he did, plain and simple stupidity. Again, alcohol is the culprit for where this story begins.

It happened just this past spring, as nighttime temperatures are starting to stay warm well into the evening. He finds that, how he acted that night is now an embarrassing memory for him, and something he'd just as well bury and forget.

Joe recalls drinking vodka & jello shots, as well as swilling beer, with a friend. They are in his backyard, and sitting around the fire pit. They've started to slur, while sharing stories that aren't really that interesting, but typical of drunken conversation. Joe's brought out his CD player, so they can listen while they drink. *The Devil went down to Georgia* by Charlie Daniels is playing on - repeat.

It seems an appropriate tune, as the two listen to the loud music and begin shouting even louder, as they continue to talk.

"I lost my cell phone while canoeing out on the lake, the other day," Joe's friend says.

"How'd that happen, bro?"

"Ah, we went out fishing and took along a 40. The sun was hot that day, so I guess the booze set in more quickly than either of us expected. Before I knew it, I felt hammered but we stayed out there anyway,"buddy takes another vodka shot before continuing, "and, you know, it wasn't their usual time for biting, but just as I was checking a text message, I feel this tug on my fishing line. As I start reeling her in, my phone just pops out of my hand and I watch as it slowly gurgles down towards the bottom of the lake. I can still see the screen saver as it disappeared, shit."

Joe's friend stops talking for a few seconds, which gives him just enough time to dip his index finger in to a big jar of peanut butter. He sucks it off as though it's a lolly-pop. Peanut butter. Who knew it was a snack food? It's what these two seem to think, as they continue to sit around campfire. But, their habits aren't that adorable. The only reason it's a jar of peanut butter, instead of chips and pretzels, is because Joe didn't have any other suitable snack food in his patry.

"That's a bummer, man," Joe laughs.

"Hey," his friend interrupts, "talking about bummers, that reminds me of a funny song I heard on the radio the other day."

He goes on to recall the lyrics of a popular song from the 1970's, called *The Streak*. Running naked through a public place defines what became known as streaking. People did it as a form of protest, or as their way of condoning the sexual revolution and the growing women's movement.

"Ever heard of it? Streaking?"

"Of course, I've heard of it," Joe says, "but we weren't even born then. And really, it seems like a weird thing to do."

"Maybe so, but I dare you to do it. Streak down the road Joe, c'mon. It'll be epic," Joe's friend puts out the challenge, "I'll even buy you a pack of smokes, if you strip down naked and run up to the end of the block and back. Besides, it's already dark out. Who's really going to see you? And, just like in that song, you'll be back here and dressed, before anyone might see you and call the cops."

Never one to back down from a challenge, Joe says, "You don't think I will do it, eh?"

"No way man. It seems too messed up, even for you."

"Right? Well, fine then you mutha," Joe says, as he stands up and begins to unzip his pants. His friend laughs so hard that he actually slaps his knee, "Liar, liar, pants on fire. I don't believe you'll do it."

"Believe it, you son of a bitch," Joe removes his shirt, "but you'll owe me two packs of smokes for this."

Within a minute, Joe is buck naked, except for his footwear, and true to his word, he sprints out of the shelter of his treed yard and onto the street. It's a quiet, weekday evening so there isn't much traffic. Only one vehicle slows down, driving by, and no doubt the driver is wondering if he's really seeing this. A wild man running naked. There are no pedestrians, who might be out walking their dogs, to witness. It is late enough in the evening that most people have already settled indoors for the night.

Before reaching the end of the block and returning home, Joe takes off his runners. He ties them together, throwing them up to catch and dangle on the overhead electrical wires. He figures that, what he considers his valiant act, ought to be somehow marked and remembered. He went running, naked through his neighbourhood. He figures that deserves some type of recognition, even if he's the one who created the spectacle.

So, the tied-together sneakers dangle. In this moment and in some odd way, it makes Joe proud. He accepted a challenge and carried it out.

But, that evening is topped off by mishap. Upon returning to his yard, and his friend sitting by the fire, still drinking shots and smoking, Joe trips on a log that's near the firepit. He instinctively reaches out to break his fall. In doing so, he badly sprains the wrist on his right hand. It means that he'll have to wrap it for several days while it heals. It is a seemingly minor injury, but it causes him hardship.

"Hey man, it's no big deal," his buddy comments, "just put some ice on it once in a while and keep it wrapped. You'll be back out fishing in no time."

Joe's response causes laughter, "It fuckin' hurts, man. And now what? Have you ever tried wiping your ass with your left hand?" It's at this point that Joe reaches into the cooler of beer that's been waiting for him beside the firepit. Most of the ice has already melted, causing the labels on the bottles of Bud to become unglued. "Jesus Christ, this really hurts," he baby's his sore wrist once again, "I really need to quit drinking." He lets out a loud burp and he begins to snigger as he grabs a beer and starts peeling off the soaked label. "Here!" he exclaims, "this'll do it." Joe slaps the patch over his forehead, "I'll do it using the patch, just like those smokers do."

The two continue their night of drinking around a campfire, until the early light of dawn.

That happened a while back and it's something Joe would like to forget. But, even shameful memories claim their place. Lately, and so often, he's felt like his previous life was held together by nothing more than duct tape. He shakes his head at some of the stunts he pulled.

Residents in the town do not forget either.

The shoes that Joe threw up there still hang from that overhead wire. If anyone was to ask how they got up there, and if Joe was still drinking, he would be tempted to brag about what he did, and why he did it.

Now that he is no longer a drunk, it's a moment in time that he'd rather bury. Joe can't help but cringe now, each time he is near that disgraceful and dangling reminder.

But then again, even bad decisions make for good stories.

Joe hasn't stopped his ritual of sitting on the concrete steps of the cafe, and it's here that he still overhears comments. He can't help but silently snicker. Every once in a while, someone will still express outrage, in trying to interpret the meaning of the dangling sneakers,

"I hear it's a symbol of a drug dealer or a gang member, marking their territory and letting people know that they've moved into the neighbourhood. I think the cops should investigate."

Joe knows, they have no idea that it was simply a stupid act, done by him, in a moment of drunken decision-making.

Redemption

The next morning, the first thing that Joe does is make his bed. It's in sharp contrast to his previous behaviour, as a drunk, when he'd just stumble out of bed and go directly to the kitchen. A cold beer was always waiting, and was his usual routine of how to greet the day. He now tends to arranging his blankets first, remembering something his Mother had told him, when he first moved out into the world by himself. Her words are engrained.

Making your bed is an indication of how the day will go.
If you are organized right from the start, that's how the rest
of the day will follow.

Good advice. And today, it helps Joe to somewhere find the courage to pick up the telephone, and give Hazel a ring. For months, he's hung onto a piece of paper. She gave it to him during one of those times before his transformation, when he was trying to pick her up. Holding the number in his hand now, he wonders if it's even a real phone number, or if Hazel just wrote down something to get rid of him when he asked for her phone number. He figures it would be like in that song, 867-5309. As he glances at the paper though, the number seems legit. The first 3 digits indicate it's a local number. 729. Joe dials, he hears 3 rings, and then a pleasant-sounding voice, saying "Hello."

It takes a moment for him to respond. He finds he's a little flustered, nervous, and not knowing how he'll start the conversation. He didn't write down talking points, like he considered doing but thought doing so seemed juvenile.

"Good morning, Hazel. It's Joe," his mind races on to what he's to say next, "I hope I didn't call too early. Did I wake you?" At this point, he wonders if making the call is a good idea, or just wishful thinking.

"Joe," she's sounding delightfully surprised, "what an unexpected pleasure to hear from you."

Joe's never been called that before. An unexpected pleasure. It bolts his confidence as he carries on with the reason for making the call.

Joe wants Hazel to know, that it was he who left the flowers in the planter by her doorway. He tells her, that he knew how upset she was receiving that envelope, and that he hoped that finding the flowers might cheer her mood. "Besides," he tells her, "I bought extra flowers for my own yard and I didn't have any extra planters, so I'm happy they found a good home."

"They look amazing, Joe, thanks," Hazel responds, "it's very thoughtful."

Joe clears his throat before asking, "So, did that schmuck come back to bother you at the pub again?" As if he didn't know.

Hazel goes on to describe what customers, coming into the pub after the explosion, were saying. Joe is quiet, offering no commentary, as she talks. She is the one who changes the subject,

"But, I don't want to talk about that. I'm looking out through the screen door, right now, and I have to ask. What's that grass you planted? Is it Indigenous? I've never seen it before."

It's not a plant that grows in the wild in Saskatchewan. King Tut grass has a unique appearance, that resembles what looks to be a combination of an ornamental grass with the head of the dill plant. It grows tall, up to five or even six feet, and it likes moisture. Egyptian Papyrus is its rightful name. Joe wonders if maybe that's the reason he was attracted to the tall, hardy plant. Egypt. Maybe that is the origin of Dust Man.

He finds out it's her day off. Joe is gratified when it is Hazel and not him, who suggests they spend some time together today. "There's no wind out there at all today, and the lake is calm. What do you say we meet for breakfast? Maybe even rent a paddle boat."

He'd love to say yes, but Joe knows he cannot. The morning sun scorches him. He makes up an excuse, suggesting something else instead, "There's an event at the Museum in Lumsden this afternoon. But you will have to drive. I still don't have my licence back." Hazel agrees, saying she'll come collect him around 2 pm.

Hours pass slowly when watching the clock. Joe feels like he is under house arrest, but without the electronic monitoring device that the law officials require to make sure that an accused remains confined to their home. Joe's forced to stay indoors due to the position of the sunlight.

Tick, tick, tick. The clock on the wall is a reminder that, soon enough, he'll be able to emerge and spend a day, not sitting around and feeling sorry himself, but rejoicing in knowing that the afternoon will be filled with moments of enjoying Hazel's company.

Tick, tick, tick. The big hand on the clock mocks, and Joe swears it's now traveling in slow motion. Joe finds ways to keep himself busy, like cleaning out his Mother's clothing from her closet. It's something that he's been procrastinating, in doing. Facing a final reminder that he won't see his Mom again, brings Joe back to the present. He finds it bittersweet to remember all the times that she wore a particular dress to church, or put on her big sweat pants and favourite t-shirt before going out to root around in her garden. She was his portal to humanity, and a reminder that there truly is goodness in this world. The final item that Joe places in a cardboard box is a sweater that he gave her one Christmas. It's one solid colour of pale pink, her favourite colour. She always said it reminds her of the colour of the sky, at dawn or at dusk. Joe places the sweater at the top of the cardboard box. Melancholy sets in as he closes up the flaps. He wipes a tear, then marks the box with a large black marker: "To donate."

Joe leaves his Mom's pink rabbit fur earmuffs out of the box. It's a small enough item that it cannot ever be considered clutter. Besides, the furry ear-coverings bring back feelings of delight for Joe. He smiles as he recalls teasing his Mother, when she'd wear them, which was just about every time she went outside during the winter months. He'd joke that she looked like a teddy bear, and she'd always yell back, "What? I can't hear you," pretending that the earmuffs were hampering her hearing. Then, she'd smile. It's imprinted on Joe, and something he always wants to keep. He doesn't pack her rosary either, instead, he drapes it on the doorknob that leads to his bedroom. It gives him some sort of feeling of security, as though the spirit of his Mom will always be there when he sleeps. He knows that, in some way, she'll continue to look after him, even now, and even with what he's become.

Before long, it's finally 2 o'clock. When Hazel arrives and Joe steps into the passenger side of her vehicle, he immediately notices that she has a dream catcher hanging from the rear-view mirror. He's heard the story of the dream catcher, and how evil spirits get caught in its webbing. It's what keeps you safe from harm. Hazel's dream catcher is a lovely, ornate piece. But, Joe figures this particular one must be defective. Hazel could never have guessed that she's fully invited that evil in today, and that there is a vampire sitting right beside her.

As they continue driving down Highway #54, Joe is nervous. It causes him to make small talk to take off the edge. He comments that he looks forward to the next couple of weeks, "The canola will start to bloom then."

Anyone would have to be heartless not to love that. The brilliant yellow of the blossoms, and their fragrant scent blankets the Prairies in early summer.

Hazel agrees, with an amendment, "I love it, but I find I am more attracted to flax fields. There is something about miles and miles of purple foliage, along with the bright blue sky, that really demonstrates the beauty of summer."

You are the beauty of summer, Joe thinks, sitting in the passenger-side seat, and enjoying the subtle fragrance of the perfume that Hazel is wearing. He knows nothing about women's perfume, so he can't say the name of the product, but it smells like a combination of vanilla and rain. He also detects the scent of menstrual blood again, and it makes Joe worry a bit. Hazel seems to be bleeding more often than not, lately. He hopes there is nothing medically worrisome about her condition. Joe is not a woman, and can only know what he's heard them talk about. Someone's period comes once a month, lasting a few days. This smell of blood from Hazel has been present more often than not, since he was changed and can recognize the scent.

Joe hopes that Hazel isn't sick.

It is a short drive between the Beach and Lumsden. So far, the trip has been tinged with nothing but anticipatory joy. It'll be a good afternoon.

There are no parking spots available, close to the Museum, once the two arrive at the site. That means they have to park along the roadway and walk a distance. Again, Joe is amused that Hazel stores her car key in her bra, before beginning the trek down a slight hilly area. He didn't even notice, in previous moments, that again she isn't carrying a purse.

The museum site itself is charming. It is located just south of downtown Lumsden. There is a creek that runs adjacent to the site, which is a recreation of the old township. Both Hazel and Joe have memories of visiting the place, when they were children.

The first building they visit, today, is the old chapel. It's been relocated here, like each of the other structures at the location.

As they enter the church, they are greeted by a pronounced creaking sound, as Joe pushes open the oversized wooden door, "Same sound," Hazel comments. "Same smell," Joe says. They sit together in quiet reflection for a few moments, before a family enters the building as well. Two little girls, twins by the looks of them, run towards the pulpit then sound the hand bell, which the priest used to ring during service when the church was still in use.

The moments of sitting together, on the hard wooden pew, gives both Joe and Hazel time for a time of quiet reflection.

Hazel thinks back to the last time she sat in a church. It was a couple of years ago, and she was in mourning. Kohkum had passed and a small prayer service was held in the small United Church down the hill. Kohkum had attended church services there for years. It wasn't so much that she followed the doctrine of organized religion. She liked visiting with the congregation and listening to a superb choir. All of those parishioners showed up for Kohkum's service, honouring her memory, before Kohkum being interred. Hazel is the one who dressed and prepared Kohkum, before visitors showed up for an open casket ceremony.

> She still remembers feeling the touch of Kohkum's hair, as she braided it for her final resting place. Her hair had grown thinner over time and was the colour of steel wool. Hazel had wrapped a shawl over her small shoulders. It was the same colourful piece that Kohkum would wear to a Pow Wow or a Round Dance. On her ears, Hazel placed Kohkum's favourite earrings. They are made from long, white dentalium sea shells. Hazel can still picture Kohkum's frail hands fashioning the delicate shells together on a thread, all the while telling stories about the time, she swears, she saw a UFO flying overhead. How Hazel misses hearing her voice.
> But it is after the burial that another tragedy occurs.
> No one knows, because Hazel hasn't said anything. She was eight weeks pregnant at the time of Kohkum's passing. She didn't want to tell anyone, and jinx the

growing of this sacred fetus. Hazel knows only too well that the first trimester is a test. Sometimes babies go away. Hazel knows that if her body is strong enough to carry baby past the first three months, then it will be time to sing and announce and rejoice.

She never made it.

Maybe it was the stress of the day. Hazel's hope of becoming a Mother are buried at the same time that Kohkum is put into the ground. She had a miscarriage later that afternoon. All she remembers is wicked pain and an immense loss of blood, as a lump of flesh exits her body. She's never cried so hard in her life.

Hazel holds the small fetus in her hands, and close to her heart, all the while asking God why this had to happen. Her only solace is in knowing that baby will not going to be travelling alone. Her voice will be added to those of the Angels singing, and she'll meet Kohkum on the other side. Hazel guesses that the baby would have been a girl.

She holds her own private ceremony for the unborn child, smudging it with the smoke of lit sweetgrass and sage. She says prayers before wrapping the fetus in red cloth. Hazel digs a shallow grave, right beside where Kohkum is laid to rest. She places some tobacco over the cloth, before covering it with dirt. And, she prays some more.

That thought has always provided some sense of peace and acceptance. Kohkum and baby are together.

Hazel knows that they will both continue guiding her and looking out for her safety.

All the while that she is revisiting thoughts, Joe ruminates about his own predicament. He is now a ghoul. Here, sitting in a church, only heightens his confusion about what he's become.

There is a lot of vampire lore out there. Joe grew up watching the movies and reading books about it. He has a copy of Bram Stoker's "Dracula" written in the late 1800's.

He saw the movie, made in 1922, Nosferatu. The old film was playing one night at the Regina Public Library Film Theatre. It was 2-dollar Tuesday and he was a university student, back then, and on a tight budget.

Joe realizes, there are some parallels, things that are the same, with his existence as a vampire today.

Sunlight does cause harm to him. It will kill him, but it's only a danger at certain times of day. Sitting in a church, does not bother him. Joe feels no more uncomfortable being here, than he did while attending church as a boy. The Holy Water folklore? Joe isn't keen on testing it out. He will admit, that he still does have a fear of God.

Once more people arrive to see what's inside the small chapel, Joe and Hazel decide to go outside. The nice weather has attracted throngs of visitors. It's pretty much wall-to-wall people and standing room only, as crowds stand in line to catch a glimpse of entertainment that's been hired. There are jugglers, fire dancers, and in the children's tent, storytellers. Food smells are everywhere, as local businesses offer their wares of home-made kolbassa, perogies, pies, and of course, hot dogs and popcorn.

Hazel says, "Let's line-up there," pointing towards a food stand, "I haven't had Ukranian sausage in ages. And look, they have freshly-squeezed lemonade as well." Joe agrees, knowing it's an opportunity for him to dine as well. But not on her blood.

He's happy to be dining on the sweet memories of the moment he's sharing, spending time with Hazel this afternoon.

When they get to the front of the line of the kolbassa stand, Hazel orders, asking Joe what he wants. Joe declines, saying that he ate before he came, "But, go ahead. We can walk around while you eat, and see what else is out here." As he makes the comment, Hazel slathers an excess of mustard on her home-made sausage, "Mustard is the best," she smiles, "and it's one of the crops grown right here in Saskatchewan."

In a flash of a second, Joe hears a squeal of glee, as Hazel points towards a team of horses that is approaching, "Look! They are having hay rides today, that's just fun.

C'mon, we have to go for a ride." She grabs Joe by his elbow, and starts pulling him in the direction of the wagon. He's a bit hesitant, because most of his adult life he's had an allergy to livestock. Being around them makes him sneeze, and sometimes, even causes wheezing. As a test, Joe takes a deep breathe. They are standing downwind from the horse team, so if he's going to react, it will happen quickly. It doesn't surprise him to discover that he suffers from the allergy no longer. So, he agrees and continues following Hazel, all the while she is still tugging him by the arm.

As the horses come closer, they begin to whinny and shake their manes, as though in distress. The Clydesdale at the front seems agitated, even pawing at the ground, which can be seen as aggressive behaviour. Joe can't help but feel, that his presence is the cause of this behaviour. To his relief, the teamster who is holding the reins, makes an announcement that he'll be taking a break for a few minutes. That alleviates Joe's worry that something very bad might have happened, if he had tried climbing onto the wagon, with all the horses sensing that an Unnatural passenger is on board.

"Awww. That's too bad, no hay ride right now," Hazel says, "maybe we can catch them later. But, no worries, let's see what else is being offered at this mini-festival. Good suggestion to come here, Joe. I haven't had his much fun in ages."

Several vendors are set up, and Hazel starts pulling Joe by the hand, and over towards where soap-makers, potters and jewellery-artists have their kiosks set up. But, Joe changes course.

It's because he sees an elderly woman who is struggling. She is happy to have just purchased a framed landscape painting from one of the local artists, who's set up a booth. But, it's clear to Joe, the woman finds the artwork too heavy to carry.

"That lady looks like she needs some help," Joe says to Hazel, pointing out the person he's talking about, "I'm going to go over, and see if she doesn't mind me carrying that painting for her, to her car. I'm guessing that's where she's headed."

"Good idea," Hazel responds, while wiping a glob of mustard from the side of her mouth, with a paper napkin, "I hope she's parked up near the duck pond. We can sit along the shoreline while I finish this sausage. It's really good. Sure you don't want a taste," Hazel offers, as Joe smiles, indicating that he doesn't want a bite. Not of a sausage, anyway. He can't help but glance at her neck, and he'd love to taste her. But it's Hazel, and he's vowed that no harm shall come to her while he's around. And never, never, will she ever have to worry that he'll use her as a food source for him. She is sacred. She is special to him, and Joe loves her. He just hasn't fully admitted that to himself yet. He longs to kiss her, but that perfect moment hasn't presented itself, just yet.

They approach the woman, making the offer to help carry the heavy frame. Once they see where she's parked her vehicle, they all wonder how she'll be able to back out. Her car is jammed-in with other cars hap-hazzardly parked along the grassy parking area. Joe wonders how she will be able to manoeuvre out of the spot. Joe places her newly-purchased artwork in the trunk, and stands guard, as the woman slowly attempts to back out.

That's when a golf cart shows up.

It's driven by one of the volunteers for the event today. He's giving rides to those who are mobility-challenged, and have had to park some distance away, like they had to. The volunteer driver is a jovial fellow, laughing and chatting with the passenger he's picked up. It means, he isn't paying full attention to his driving. The golf cart collides with the old woman's car, as her vehicle is partially backed out of its parking spot. No one is hurt, but the collision leaves a dent on the back fender.

Everyone assembles for pow wow, which is a discussion on how to handle this situation. Their conference centres around, who caused this to happen? There is worried, but respectful, interaction between the woman, the golf cart driver, and Hazel as an onlooker. While this is happening, Joe surveys the damage. There's not much, and it will need very little work to fix. He takes the opportunity. While everyone's attention is focused somewhere else, Joe puts his hand under the back wheel fender. It's on the driver's side, everyone else is still in discussion on the passenger-side of the car. With great, newly-acquired, strength, Joe carefully fashions the metal, and the dent, back into shape.

"I don't know what y'all are worried about," he says once everyone is paying attention, "it's likely the mid-day shadows from the trees that made it look like there was damage. But see," he points to the fender, "there's none."

Ancestral Land

On the drive back to the Beach, Hazel finds herself surprised to be thinking that spending time together this afternoon is an unexpected delight. She also finds that she doesn't want the day to end, and longs to keep the company of Joe for the remainder of the day. The man did surprise her with flowers, afterall.

She suggests they take a hike in Kinookimaw. It's the community adjacent to Regina Beach. It's a historically significant part of the valley. For centuries, Hazel's Indigenous Ancestors came to the area each summer, to harvest the land, and to hunt and fish.

Joe says yes to her suggestion of taking a hike, but to be honest, he doesn't want the day, spent together, to come to an end either. It's as though she's helping him to colour in the areas of gray in his life, that were a blacked out because he drank too much. And, he has hope that the two can build some type of meaningful relationship. Joe's prospect is like the light spectrum. No one can see ultraviolet, but everyone knows it's there. And it shines.

Travelling down Highway #54, Joe is a bit surprised when Hazel veers off the main highway and onto a side, gravel road. "We can drive a bit slower going this way," she says, "and roll down the windows. All the crops and wildflowers are in full bloom right now. May as well take in the fragrance." The gravel road runs past the local cemetery, and when Hazel approaches the sacred ground, Joe notices her struggling to breathe. He has to ask, "Why are you holding your breath?"

Her first reaction is to say that she's got something caught in her throat. But, as she glances at Joe, remembering the kindness of how he's treated her lately, she feels safe to tell him a story. And, to repeat the words of Kohkum:

The dead aren't always dead. Sometimes, mystery creeps in, allowing the dark forces that caused their death to survive, in some form. Not everyone dies in a good way. Humans cannot sense their evil presence, those of the undead, but the Jumpers can. Some call the Jumpers mythical creatures, but Kohkum says, they, too, are real. She remembers one that she'd see, even now and then, when she was a little girl. She named him, Corbitt. The Jumpers live in the tree tops and they come out at night. Some call them Watchers. They never take lives, unless it's something that needs to be done. Their job is to follow around those who do good in the world, making sure they never befall violence, or some other type of bad fate, from the dark forces. Kohkum also tells about the Little People, who are Spirit Guides and have a similar type of purpose, especially for children. The Little People are invisible, but some kids can see them. They are like Guardian Angels. Kohkum advises:
"Always hold your breath, when passing a cemetery. Those Beings have always lived here too, both light and dark Spirits. And, you can never tell if there is some type of evil just waiting to be ingested, so that it can influence human form and carry on with its plunder. Suspicion or not, best to be safe. Holding your breathe is calling on the Forces of Light for protection, and a way to ensure that a person doesn't ingest bad energy,

otherwise, some creatures might come looking for it, later."

Hazel tells Joe there are many, similar stories, within her Indigenous culture, "And, Kohkum was the best story-teller of them all."

At the same time, while delivering her story, Hazel glances at Joe and wonders why he is still wearing his sunglasses. The clouds have now rolled in, muting the bright light of the days' sunshine. She figures it's a moot point to ask, and just continues on with the drive.

Meanwhile, Joe catches an inherent glimpse into Hazel's character, kindness, as she swerves to avoid hitting one of the many gophers that run across the grid roads.

It's in sharp contrast to how he used to react, while drinking and driving.

Back then, he would specifically veer towards the rodent, with the intent of squishing them. Today, and now that he's been forced to be sober, Joe can't figure out why he took part in that destructive behaviour. The small animal was just doing what Prairie Dogs do, scavenging for food but harming no one. It's in moments like this that Joe realizes that the river of his life has been a journey of too many unseen twists and turns, most with wild water and rocky shores. He wonders if he is beyond redemption, and if maybe being turned is some type of punishment for all the wrongs that he caused, in the past.

Maybe Hazel can help him find meaningful direction, be that as it may be, given his current circumstance, of no longer being alive.

Before long, Hazel parks her car atop a grassy bluff that overlooks the lake.

She reaches for a couple of large, used paper coffee cups that litter the back floor of her car, holding them up like a prize and saying to Joe, "Here. I don't have a proper bucket, but we can use these. The Saskatoon berries are prime for picking right now. I'll show you the best spots to pick. It's where Kohkum and I used to spend hours and hours every summer."

The hill from the parking area, down towards the lake where Hazel is heading, is a steep one. It makes Joe thankful that his arthritis pain no longer affects him. He couldn't have done the trek before he was turned. While they walk, Hazel points towards the brightly-coloured Russian Thistle, that grows in abundance at the side of a road. It's more like a foot path now, and no longer used for vehicle travel. She tells Joe that her Kohkum used to pick the stems of the thistle, chewing them into a poultice, anytime the little Hazel might have been stung by a wasp or hornet. It took away both the sting and the pain.

Joe is impressed by Hazel's knowledge of Indigenous plants, especially when she says, "I remember these, too," pointing out the Breadroot plant, which some refer to as Indian Breadroot. It's easy for Hazel to identify, with its fuzzy, or what some call hairy flowers, that grow in clusters. But it's the root of the plant that Hazels knows. It's off-white and grows as a bulb, that she remembers. Kohkum would dry the root, then later boil it, to soften it for eating. Kohkum called it Tipsin, and told her the practice of harvesting was shared by the Dakota and the Lakota, on how to dig the root with a stick. It has a flavour that resembles a turnip.

While they walk, Hazel finds a heart-shaped stone, and picks it up, handing it to Joe, "The land has knowledge and gives many gifts," she says, "here. This one is for you." Joe isn't sure how to react, so he does what he's always done. Shying-away from showing emotion, Joe says, "Hey, that's cool." He tucks the heart-shaped stone in his pants pocket.

As he does so, Joe notices a discarded beer can, that someone didn't do a very good job, trying to hide it in the underbrush. By the look of it, the can has been there for a while. The paint on the lettering has become faded by the sun. Nonetheless, it is evidence of indiscretion. Joe wonders if it might be something that he threw out some time ago, when he and the boys were out partying.

While the area has been a place for Hazel and Kohkum, and celebrating the Land, it's also been a place for Joe and his drinking buddies over the years. They'd sit around a campfire at night, looking for love at the bottom of a beer.

There's been a heat wave these past days, and today is no exception. As Hazel, once again, reaches for her water bottle, she can't help but wonder why Joe isn't doing the same. He carries a backpack, but he hasn't opened it once. And, like she, he hasn't made any effort to remain hydrated. He's not even sweating.

A story Joe figures that Kohkum never shared is that animals respond when a vampire is near. At least, that's Joe's hypothesis.

In this case, it's because there are cows grazing along the hills. When he and Hazel arrived, the cows were grazing all over the valley area. As Joe approaches, their behaviour changes. They form a single, straight line, like wanting to line up at for a bank teller, and they walk slowly towards where Joe is standing. He doesn't want to call attention, and he doesn't have to, with Hazel's next response,

"It's getting late. I suppose we should get going before the sun starts setting." As they walk back towards her vehicle, Hazel sees something else that is familiar to her. Hey," she says, "we might even find some wild potatoes here. I remember Kohkum teaching me how to dig those, as well. She'd put them in a fish chowder, along with the day's fresh catch from the lake. Which reminds me. Would you like to come over for dinner tonight, Joe? I'll make a great chicken, bacon and garlic recipe for pasta. I'll add a lot of cheese."

Joe wants to say yes, but he cannot. He's got his own hunger to feed, and it doesn't include noodles. He tells a lie, "I'd love to, but I'm allergic to garlic," Joe tells Hazel, "but, I'll take a rain check. Not only that, I did tell the Old Woman who lives down the street from me that I'd come over tonight and move some heavy things from her shed and to the curb. She's got someone coming to take the stuff to the dump tomorrow."

Joe isn't lying. He did volunteer to help out his elderly neighbour, saying that he'd be there for her with downsizing, getting rid of what's become old waste and clutter in her shed and basement.

Walking back up towards where Hazel's car is parked on the bluff causes Joe to wonder about another vampire myth. Hazel is wanting to cook with garlic. He knows it wards off nothing for vampires, not for him anyway.

Garlic. Joe has always loved the flavour that it adds to food. It does have so many useful purposes, though, other than using it for cooking. He's heard it has medicinal purposes. Joe smiles, remembering a funny story, which has to do with a toothache and a clove of garlic.

> He is a boy, and Joe's Mom is trying to get her son to stop squirming, while she tries to put a clove between his cheek and his gum. He's got a cavity that needs to be looked at, and it's causing pain. It'll be a couple of days yet before he gets to see a dentist.
> "What is that, Mom? It smells funny."
> "It's a clove, Joe. Here, put it in your mouth and it'll help numb the area. Trust me."
> It works. The essential oil from the clove brings relief. But, the little Joe had only heard the word - clove.
> So when he gets another tooth ache, as a young adult, Joe does what he thinks is his Mom's remedy, putting a clove of garlic beside his gum.
> This time, it hurts.
> There is a terrible burning sensation. So, Joe calls his Mom to ask what he did wrong.
> "I put a clove between my gum and cheek, just like you did back when I was a kid. But now, it just stings and my breath smells like garlic."
> He can hear his Mom laughing at the other end of the telephone receiver. She's giggling so hard that it takes a minute before she is able to catch her breath and respond, "Not a clove of garlic, you silly. You need to use a dried clove, like something you use for baking or cooking. Oh dear."

Joe doesn't have any negative reaction to garlic today. Plant life is sacred and feeds the body.

He needs to feed as well.

After saying good night to Hazel, he goes into his home to pull on a warmer sweater before heading off to see the neighbour. Joe will help her out with moving boxes and keeping her company.

He'll wait and see what else the night hours might bring.

A Kindness

Joe goes to his neighbour's home, just minutes after bidding adieu to Hazel. But, not before taking care of Xavier.

The cat is waiting for him, when Joe gets home. Xavier is prancing on the veranda, giving a loud purr, and he wants to be fed. Joe unlocks his door and heads to his pantry where the cat kibble is stored, pouring a scoop into a metal pet bowl. Yes, he's bought a pet bowl because it's official, Xavier is now a regular part of his life. Joe leaves the bowl outside, near the front door, before walking over to see Mrs. Carter.

Her caragana bushes are in full bloom, reminding Joe of the lush bush on the bluff, the one growing right beside where Hazel parked her vehicle. Seeing it is a reminder. Joe wishes that he hadn't made the promise to move Mrs. Carter's yard waste and other items to the curb tonight. He's just enjoyed a great day with Hazel. One that he hopes is the beginning of something else that might become routine.

Joe needn't knock on the Old Woman's door. She opens it before he arrives, "There you are, my sweet, Dark Prince. I was wondering when you'd show."

Joe has no idea why she makes such a reference. Does she know something about his change? And, if so, how does she know? What she says next makes it clear to Joe, he doesn't need to worry.

"Oh hello, Dear. Who are you?"

Joe holds her wrinkled hand, "Mrs. Carter, it's me Joe. Your neighbour. You asked me to help you move a few things that need to go to the dump, remember?"

"You're taking me to the dump, you say? Whatever for?"

"No, dear, I'm here to help you." Joe notices that her kitchen tap is running, draining into a sink filled with dirty dishes. The water stopper, used to plug the sink, sits on the window sill, right beside a house plant. It's clear the plant hasn't been watered in some time. It's sad-looking and wilted. Joe goes to turn off the tap, but not before catching some water in one of the used tea cups in the sink. He waters the plant as well. Joe doesn't know how long the tap has been running. He hopes it hasn't filled Mrs. Carters septic tank, to the point of overflowing.

"Are you here to make me dinner?" she asks. Joe figures, why not, and opens her refrigerator door. The shelves are pretty much empty. Joe decides that moving boxes can wait a few more minutes, telling Mrs. Carter that he'll head up the road and grab her a sandwich at the gas station. He glances at the clock on her wall, realizing he'll have to hurry. The store extends its hours, during summer months, but he only has a few minutes now before it closes for the night. He arrives to find that there are no pre-made sandwiches left in the cooler. Joe purchases a block of cheddar, a package of ham and a loaf of bread. He'll make her a sandwich instead.

Upon his return to her home, she answers the door in the same way as before, "There you are my sweet, Dark Prince. I was wondering when you'd show."

Joe can feel that the veil between life and death is thin for Mrs. Carter.

She goes to the bathroom to put in her dentures, then returns to the veranda. Joe thinks that she looks frail and unsteady, and he wonders, when was it that she last ate?

Her hands are shaking, as she takes her place in the wicker rocker, out on the deck. Mrs. Carter eats her ham sandwich, while Joe starts moving black garbage bags filled with dandelions that have been dug out of the ground. There are boxes, marked with black ink that say "dump", over by her shed. Joe moves those out to the edge of her driveway as well.

When he's done, Joe pulls a lawn chair up beside Mrs. Carter's rocker. As he does, Mrs. Carter grabs a hardened piece of old clay, that she's had displayed in one of her outdoor flower pots. It's in the shape of a trilobite, one of the ancient bugs, only known today because they are so often dug up by geologists. As she hands it to Joe, she says, "I want you to have this. My grandson made it for me at school. You take it now, because it seems to me that you have a lot in common with this insect. The history of the trilobite is as old as you, and the stories of your own people and history, now," she stops to clear her throat, "You are no a killer, my dear boy. You are a saviour, cleaning up what needs to be gotten rid of."

Joe is puzzled, and ever worried, by her comments. How does she know? His concern lessens by what she says the very next moment.

She starts talking to him as though he's someone else, "You know, Royal," Joe knows that's the name of her deceased husband. He died more than 20 years ago. "I want to dance tonight. Can we go to the club?"

Joe knows what she's referring to. There used to be a dance hall, out here at the Beach. It was called The Ark. It would have been the ultimate romantic place, dancing on the floating barge, while travelling up and down Last Mountain Lake. But that was a long time ago. It was at The Ark where his own parents met.

There is a romantic history of dance halls on the Prairies. It started in the 1920's, known as the Jazz Age, when the dance craze grew. Waltzes and fox trots were popular, alongside the Charleston and the shimmy. Swing music was all the rage by the 1930's, and the jitter-bug became the dance that everyone moved to. The social celebration carried on for the next few decades, until the 1960's, when rock and roll music changed the scene forever.

Joe is touched that the widow remembers those happy times. Her husband, Royal, adored her and took care of her. Joe decides that he will take care of her tonight, as well, but in a different way that will allow Mrs. Carter to be with her husband again.

Realizing that she is no longer fully present, Joe touches Mrs. Carter's hand, saying, "Come Dear, Fats Waller awaits." He leads her from the deck and back into her home, to the living room where an old record player cabinet has been gathering dust in the corner. It would be considered an antique today. Joe sifts through the old vinyl discs beside the big, wooden cabinet, selecting Fats Waller, a jazz pianist who was popular in the 1920's.

Joe places the vinyl disc on the turntable. There are sounds of scratching on the old disc, before the music even begins to play. When the piano sounds, Mrs. Carter blossoms.

Joe takes her hand, and slow dances her to the beat of the couples' favourite song, "Ain't Misbehavin," Mrs. Carter tells Joe, it was the song that was playing, when Royal proposed, all those years ago.

I know for certain, the one I love, I'm through with flirtin'
it's you that I 'm thinkin' of. Savin' my love for you.

As Joe holds her, he can feel her ribcage protruding, like she's more skeletal than a mass. She's lost so much weight, since he remembers seeing her when he was a kid. Her flowered house dress now hangs, in a sad way, from her bony body. She's been reduced to weighing no more than 90 pounds. He smells her hair, and it's clear that she hasn't washed herself in some time. Her scent is not unpleasant, just old and in need of care.

"Oh, Royal," she says, "you always knew how to spin me, just like when I was a girl. Oh, how I have missed you, my love." Mrs. Carter gently places her head on Joe's chest, and closes her eyes.

When the drums sound on the recording, Joe knows it's time. He sinks his fangs into her neck, until she is drained. When her heart stops beating, Joe carries her back outdoors, and seats her on the wicker rocker. She's still wearing her kitchen apron. Joe goes back into her house, and fetches a framed photograph from the living room mantel. He noticed it while they were waltzing. Joe places it in Mrs. Carter's hand. It's a picture of she and her husband, taken on their wedding day. She looks so young, beautiful and happy.

Joe gives Mrs. Carter a tender kiss on the cheek, whispering, "Be well, my friend. You and your Royal will be dancing together again, soon." Joe removes her wedding ring to add to his collection. It is a symbol of love, and something that Joe wants to attract into his own life.

He knows that whoever it is, who's coming to pick up her boxes and yard waste, will find her in the morning. Because of her age, no one will suspect anything but natural causes.

The death Joe delivered is much more merciful than the other one she would ultimately have had to suffer, dying slowly and painfully due to her disease. He feels no guilt in taking her, almost like giving her a gift. She's always been kind to Joe, for decades, starting when he was just a boy.

Mrs. Carter met the end of her life, sealed with a kiss.

The Watchers

Joe considers what he's just done, as an act of mercy.

Although, that isn't the consensus of everyone, or everything. Joe's deed isn't gone unnoticed. The Jumpers know what he did.

They've been watching her, from the treetops, for the past five years, arriving shortly after Mrs. Carter was diagnosed with Alzheimer's disease. The Jumpers have the ability to change with their surroundings, so if they are watching from the many aspen trees, which flourish on the Prairies, it's unlikely they will ever be detected. They are like chameleons, blending in, thereby remaining invisible.

It is they who have been turning off her water sprinkler at night, when the Old Woman has forgotten that she'd turned it on. The Jumpers are the ones who close and lock Mrs. Carter's front door at night, when she forgets that its wide open. It's the Jumpers who wail and squeal from the bush, if any ne'er-do-well intruder decides that an old woman, living alone, is an easy target. They throw rocks, if they have to. That scares them off, and it's the reason why some neighbourhood kids say that her house is haunted.

For the most part, the Jumpers purpose is to protect.

It's the Unnatural, named Corbitt, who has the eyes of a raven, who's been specifically assigned to look out for Mrs. Carter.

There's a mean dog who lives down the block. The night that dog was running loose and had the intention of pouncing on the Old Woman, was stopped. Corbitt made sure of it. He watches for the safety of children in the neighbourhood as well, but it's the well-being of Mrs. Carter that is of his most concern.

Corbitt doesn't like what he's witnessed tonight. Joe killed her.

He follows as Joe walks home, Corbitt silently catapults through the tree tops. Things that go bump in the night. It's not just a saying.

While Corbitt may resemble a monster, he isn't. His is not the purpose to battle. And he moves like the wind, invisible and silent. His translucent, skin and oversized muscular legs allow him graceful movement amongst the tree tops. He's naturally white, in colour, but his chameleon-like ability allows Corbitt to blend into any surroundings.

Joe arrives home, unaware that he's been followed.

He's already fed, on Mrs. Carter, so that hunger is subsided. And, he's lost his interest in spending time watching action movies. As always, Xavier is there, sitting right next to Joe's longboard.

Joe decides he'll go for a spin on his longboard, and have a gander at what's happening around town tonight. But, before he's able to reach the hedges at the edge of his drive, Joe is confronted by some tall, opaque figure, that seemingly fell from the sky.

Joe is startled.

"Hey, what's up Daddy Long Legs?" Joe doesn't know what to make of this creature, that resembles Gollum from the movie Lord of the Rings, but without the mean face.

Corbitt doesn't speak with words. He communicates as a telepath, casting his thoughts as they come, without using words.

He tells Joe that what he's done to Mrs. Carter is no act of sympathy. It's nothing short of murder. Although, Corbitt does say that how Joe treated the body, placing her on her outdoor rocker, was a decent thing to do. Taking her wedding ring, was not, and he appeals to Joe to return to Mrs. Carter's body and put the jewellery back on her finger.

Joe voices his defence, "She was slowly dying, and a painful death at that. Seeing how she lived, like forgetting to turn off the kitchen tap, it was just a matter of time before she, maybe, set the place on fire. Now that, my friend, is a cruel way to go. I always liked Mrs. Carter. She's been kind to me my entire life. No matter what you think, what I did was done out of kindness."

For the first time since becoming a vampire, Joe transforms. His physical characteristics change. He's never felt threatened enough to allow it before, until now. He can't be sure that Corbitt won't try slashing out at him, with his sharp and sloth-like claws, which allow him to move amongst the trees. Joe's forehead protrudes, giving him the appearance of a Neanderthal, bulges appear under his eyes, looking like he's got severe sinus trouble. And, it isn't a myth, Joe grows pointy ears. He's ready for battle. Even snarling at Corbitt, who isn't at all frightened.

Corbitt tells him that he didn't show himself tonight to pick a fight. He's a Watcher, who some refer to as a Jumper. Joe remembers that Hazel had mentioned the Jumpers, while retelling a story from Kohkum.

Corbitt sends another message, doing so, without uttering a word.

> I was there the night that you were turned. I saw it all. I've been following the Dust Man around for years, too. He comes to this part of the valley only during summer months. But now that he created you, I haven't seen him. He left after knowing you might be okay and able to fend for yourself, finally. That's right, even Dust Man didn't sense that I was near, watching, and you have never sensed my presence. In your human

form, you were always too drunk to notice or care, now that you are one of those blood suckers, you've been too aloof or arrogant, thinking that you're the only one who hunts at night. There are others, many of them. All supernatural, some with the intention of a demon. You be careful of how you dispose of the dead. Rigor mortis sets in faster than you know, and the Unnatural ones can smell it. You are putting everyone in this town at risk. Be more careful. There is a reason why people bury their dead. Being laid to rest isn't just a saying. It is necessary, otherwise the evil undead take notice. Like it or not, you are one of those now. The evil, even though you think yourself not.

As quickly as he appeared, Corbitt disappears. In a fraction of a second, like a lightning strike, he jumps up towards the tall aspens in Joe's yard. And then he's gone. Joe is impressed with his ability of flight, and snickers, knowing that popular vampire myth suggests that he should be able to fly, too. He can't.

Just as well that Corbitt left when he did.

A little army of ferals has taken notice of the Jumper's presence, and are approaching with a stance that spells fight. The fur on their backs stands straight up, and their claws and fangs are showing. He's seen cats fighting each other before. It's brutal. Joe finds that he's thankful there isn't some sort of confrontation with Corbitt, with him or with the ferals.

With Corbitt's disappearance, the stray cats disperse, heading back into the bush to do whatever it is that ferals do. It's possible that they sided with Joe, because the ferals remember that it was Joe, who had earlier left the door ajar, on the home of the mean man who used to leave out poisoned food. They were able to dine on the fat man's corpse, for days, before the stench of decomposing body finally attracted attention and someone called the ambulance.

For a split second, seeing the cats gather, sparks a memory for Joe.

It was last Halloween, before he became a vampire. That night, Joe stumbles home from the bar, carrying an 18-pack of beer. He was short a couple of dollars when he got to the off sale, but he swiped a toonie from the waitress tip jar, before she noticed him waiting at the cash register, so she didn't notice his pilfering. There is a fresh layer of early snow on the ground, which causes Joe to slip and fall because he's wearing his old runners which have seen better days. There is no more tread and the bottoms of those sneakers are like a banana peel. Joe's only thought is that he's glad to have had the foresight to buy cans of beer, instead of glass bottles. Surely, they'd have been broken with his fall. It isn't a late hour. In fact, twilight is just setting in. But, it's getting dark enough to turn on his front porch light. There aren't many kids in his neighbour- hood anymore. Everyone has grown so quickly, and the little kids he used to see out riding their bikes out on the street are now driving cars. But Joe has just done something that invites them in. Everyone knows that turning on an outside light at Halloween has its own unwritten code. It's an invitation to trick-and- treaters, that says, this is a house that is giving out candy.

Joe shouldn't be surprised when a group of three teen- agers knock on his door. It's two boys and a girl, each of them dressed as some Star Wars character.

Joe forgot about Halloween, so he hasn't purchased any candy. But, there might be something he can give. He remembers buying a box of granola bars not too long ago, so he goes to check his pantry. The box is still sitting in the cupboard, but the carton is empty. He feels bad about letting the youth leave without offering something. That's when an idea occurs to him. In his drunken state, Joe grabs 3 cans of beer, and puts them in their treat bags. The boys give a puzzled look, but don't complain. As they walk away, Joe spies a jack-o-lantern that he carved earlier in the week. Someone had dared him to enter the local pumpkin carving contest.

The bet was that, if Joe carved a penis image, then took the pumpkin to the contest, he'd win a 6-pack from the joker who issued the dare. Joe did his part. He got the pumpkin, took it home and precisely carved the shape of an erect penis. But it would never be allowed to be seen at the competition judging. His entry was immediately disqualified, and the judges insisted that Joe take the porno pumpkin away. It's been on his veranda ince.

Joe turns off his outdoor veranda light after that.

It causes him to ponder about the purpose of Corbitt's appearance, tonight. It startled Joe, which is the reason why he transformed. But, when he sensed Corbitt's energy, Joe felt that it's almost like a friend coming to visit to give a cryptic warning. A piece of advice that might even keep him somehow safe.

But about what? Joe didn't get the chance to ask him about other Unnaturals. Corbitt said some of them are evil. Who are they and why would they be interested in him? Joe has never noticed any odd beings hanging around, prior to being turned. Why are they showing up now? Joe figures that he'll have to accept that he isn't the only Unnatural. Why would he be the only one? It's clear to him that he just wasn't open to meeting, or seeing, any of them, before his senses became heightened. He hopes the others are like Corbitt. That they are Watchers but not intent on causing harm, although, he has a sinking feeling that there is no guarantee of that.

Even though it's been a pleasant evening, weather-wise, Joe is surprised when storm clouds move in as quickly as Corbitt had appeared, and then disappeared. The sounds of thunder roll in the distance. "I guess I won't be heading out for a longboard ride tonight," Joe tells Xavier, now that the cat has calmed down since Corbitt's departure.

Joe thinks about what Kohkum had said. That an unexpected storm is a sign that someone has died. The rain comes to wash them clean. He knows who died tonight, and that it was a passing not due to natural causes.

Maybe this storm was sent for the benefit of Mrs. Carter, who Joe hopes is dancing again, with her Royal now.

Heavy drops begin to fall from the darkened sky.

Rejuvenate

The next morning, Joe is awakened by a phone call. He checks the time on the digital clock radio across the room. It's after 10 am.

"Hey, sleepy head. If you're not already up, it's time to get your ass out of bed," it's Hazel, "there's a farmer's market today down along the main street. I'd like you to come with me."

Joe wants to say yes, but he knows he cannot.

"I can't make it out for the next little while, errands that need to get done, and I can't put it off any longer. How do you feel about a rain check, until later this afternoon?"

"A girl can't say no to that. How about I pick you up around 3:30. You're not afraid of heights, are you?" Hazel asks.

"No, why?"

"Just wondering. I have the perfect afternoon planned for us. You need to say yes, when I tell you what it is. Otherwise," she giggles, "I won't cook you dinner. I was planning on getting fresh steak from the butcher, who's at the market. And, I know you like barbecue because I remember you mentioning once. But, that's for later. I'll see you at 3:30."

Hanging up the receiver, Joe feels giddy in knowing that Hazel has been thinking about him, too. She's planning meals that he used to enjoy. Who doesn't love barbecued steak and baked potato, along with a frosty, cold Kokanee beer? He loves it, or, the memory of it. Joe can't have any of it, anymore. He wonders how, someday, he'll be able to tell Hazel the reason why.

That's something to deal with at some other time. For now, Joe just feels genuinely happy. Something he hasn't felt in, too long to remember. He'll be spending time with Hazel again today. She has an interest in him. His long-uttered prayer for inclusion into her life seems to have been answered.

It is now mid-afternoon, and Hazel arrives to pick up Joe.

"So, what's the mystery?" he asks, "And, it's a hot day. Why did you insist that I wear long pants and a wind breaker?"

Hazel tells him, it's because she's planned an afternoon of sky diving.

"It's something that's been on the books for me, for a while now. I pre-paid last month. A friend of mine and I were planning to take the jump. But, she had to cancel, just last night. Sorry to spring it on you so suddenly, but I really didn't want to postpone. So, that's where we are headed. There's a drop zone just outside of Moose Jaw. We are going to be jumping out of a plane."

Once at the hangar, Joe feels an excitement that, he can't remember the last time, while he's being suited up with straps and other safety gear. The instructor gives a tutorial on what to expect, saying that because both Hazel and Joe are novices, they will take the tandem dive, which means being attached to an experienced jumper.

A Jumper?

The word has a different point of reference for Joe, after encountering Corbitt last night.

Hazel suggests that someone at the hangar take her cell phone, to snap a photo of the two of them before they get loaded into the aircraft. Joe has to decline, not that he doesn't like the idea of a photo with Hazel. He's worried that, because he can no longer see his image in a mirror, what if there is also no image in a photograph? It's too much to risk, so he changes the topic, saying it's probably a good idea for him to visit the washroom, right now. "I have to admit, I'm scared to go up there. I just don't want any surprises after jumping out of the plane, and plummeting down. Best to be safe." He excuses himself, and is gone long enough that Hazel forgets about the suggestion to want to take a photo. There is too much excitement in the air, with all visitors to the hangar anticipating what's about to happen. A staff member approaches Hazel for the second time, now that Joe is no longer by her side. He says it's to check her harness one more time, although he is taking his time and engaging in personal small talk. It makes Hazel wonder if he's attempting to flirt with her.

He disappears when Joe returns, and it doesn't take long before the two are up in the air, and the small Cessna 182 plane reaches a safe height above the drop zone. Joe is mentally preparing himself to be dropped from the sky, 3000 feet above ground. It seems daunting but it's too late to change his mind now. He'll do it.

Joe finds himself being a bit spooked when his diving partner opens the door. "Time to step out," he says. Opening the door of a moving vehicle, to Joe, it's unheard of. The rush of air coming into the aircraft takes his breath away, and a terrifying thought enters. He worries that the rush might cause him to transform again, and that he won't have any control on whether that happens. It is a possibility. Joe reconsiders his decision to jump.

Instead, his tandem partner takes control and within seconds Joe finds himself standing at the open doorway, with only an open expanse of Prairie below.

They make the jump, and in those first few moments out of the plane, Joe can't help but feel that this is what it's like to be sucked up in a vacuum. That initial rush lasts a matter of seconds, before a peaceful free-flight down. A bird's eye-view isn't just a saying. The view is spectacular.

It's so windy up here. It's little wonder why birds can soar at these heights without having to flap their wings. As he mentioned before, Joe has always loved the vibrancy of canola fields in full bloom, but at this height, he thinks it looks more like a painting.

It is a peaceful soar back down to the ground, and it's the one time that Joe wishes, that some vampire lore was true, and that he did have the ability to fly. What an amazing experience!

The free flight down ends almost as quickly as it began. And, apparently the jump has given Hazel an appetite. She suggests that, instead of driving directly back home, that they make a little side trip, and drive in to the heart of the City of Moose Jaw. She tells Joe about a fudge shop on the Main Street, that she wants to visit, "And, don't laugh when you hear what I have to say next," Hazel gives Joe a wink, "but, I'd really like to hit a KFC drive-thru before heading back out on the highway."

"Anything you want," Joe responds. He knows that the take-out chicken is a family tradition that Hazel and Kohkum shared, whenever they were in a community that had a KFC. Now, it's like Hazel is inviting, that Joe be included in continuing to build memories of love and togetherness, in sharing this KFC tradition. Joe looks forward to hearing the stories about this one.

After the side trip in to the city, it takes no time at all to make the drive from Moose Jaw and back to the Beach. During the trip home, all discussion centres on exhilaration, and how abandoning fear has allowed for unforgettable moments in time. Jumping out of a plane is fun. Joe thanks Hazel for taking him, "Skydiving. It isn't something that I would have normally planned for myself. But, I would do it again, anytime," he smiles, "count me in. Maybe we could make it an annual activity."

It's the first time that Joe has indicated an interest in spending time with Hazel, for the long-term. She responds by grasping his hand, and saying, "It's a deal."

Now, back at the Beach and at her front door, Hazel finds that she looks forward to spending even more time with her new friend. She's purchased some steak to barbeque, and she hopes Joe is up for sharing a meal together, even though they just stopped at KFC, on the way back from sky-diving.

It's then that Joe softly touches her hand, this time, as she shifts her car into park. It's the first time that Hazel has invited him into her home.

As Joe steps over the threshold of the blue door, he is immediately drawn to Hazel's sense of style. Her home is decorated with original artwork, like paintings and drawings from local artists, and sculptures from metal artists, who she met in the city when she worked as an arts reporter, full-time.

One of those sculptures is located right near Hazel's front door. It's a tall structure, about 4 feet or more, and it vaguely resembles a rib cage and a spine. It's eclectic. But, Joe's only comment is, "Hey, cool coat rack." He unzips his wind breaker and hangs it at the top of the sculpture.

This makes Hazel laugh out loud, even though she tries hard not to. She simply holds out her hand, and motions Joe inside.

Upon further entering, he sniffs the calming scent of Dragon's Blood incense, which Hazel had burned earlier that day. She's mentioned to him that she meditates each morning, first thing, even before morning coffee.

A beautiful piece of beadwork, framed and proudly displayed, hangs near the entryway. It's a saying:

> *A house is made with sticks and stones,*
> *but a home is made by love alone.*

Hazel notices that Joe is looking at the artwork, and she comments, "I made that for Kohkum, one Mother's Day, a long time ago. It's one of the first pieces of beadwork that I ever worked on. Kohkum loved it, and hung it up. It's been hanging in that same spot, for years."

"It's the perfect greeting," Joe says, "I'm glad you left it hanging."

It's a lovely moment that Joe doesn't want to spoil. He tries not to fidget, but he is doing his best to hide his hands. He's been keeping them covered, ever since jumping out of the plane. He sees that his fingers have become longer and more boney. It's subtle, but a change nonetheless. Maybe it's because he allowed himself to physically transform the other night, when coming into contact with Corbitt. He experienced fright then and again today, plummeting out of a moving aircraft. It makes him snicker out loud, remembering that Hoyt Axton song from his youth, and the chorus lyrics:

> *Work your fingers to the bone*
> *What do you get?*
> *Boney fingers. Boney fingers.*

That's when that frightening thought creeps in again, with Joe realizing he may have unintentionally started to transform, while falling from the plane. Even with all the safety precautions, it was still scary for him, but a breath-taking experience. With his still elongated fingers, Joe worries that maybe he's starting to lose control, and hopes that unintentional transformation doesn't happen again, in some circumstance where Hazel might see, or take notice.

But he needn't worry about safety now.

Standing in Hazel's kitchen though, Joe finds that he is bothered by her florescent lighting. He worries that odd shadows cast by the lights might cause his eyes to become luminescent, like a cat's eyes in the darkness. Joe clicks the light switch to turn off the overhead lighting, and flicks on the table lamp, that Joe spots on the kitchen table. He tells Hazel that the softer lighting of lamplight better matches his mood, and that he hopes she doesn't mind.

She doesn't. She's happy to say that she's already made some comfort food, for Joe. They can get to the barbeque later.

Hazel has baked him a pie with the Saskatoon berries, that the two of them picked together, during their Kinookimaw hike.

"Here, you will love this," she says, cutting into the sweetened berries. She places a couple of slices on a paper plate and wraps it with plastic, making an apology.

"I picked up some nice steak at the farmer's market, as you know, but there's no time to barbeque it right now. I just got some news. I wasn't shifted to go in to the pub tonight, but I just got a text. Someone called in sick, so the pub is short-staffed. I really wanted to just hang out here, though, and spend some more time with you," she glances directly and deeply into Joe's eyes, "rain check?"

Joe gives her a nod and thanks her for a surprisingly different way to spend the afternoon. Hazel sends him home with a doggy bag, filled with berry pie, and a promise to barbeque steak at some later point in time.

He isn't disappointed, because it is within Hazel's character to help out when it's needed. Joe tells her that he may pop down to the pub later, just to say hello, and maybe even order a plate of nachos.

As he walks home, Joe is feeling uplifted and hopeful. He's carrying sweet berry pie made by the sweetest girl he's ever known.

Joe leaves a slice out on the veranda, once he gets home. It's an offering for Corbitt. Hazel had told Joe that some Unnaturals like sweet things, and because Hazel made this pie, he knows, it's ingredients are sweeter than anything that could be found in a bakery.

He places the remaining slice in his freezer. A reminder of another perfect afternoon.

Out in Public

By the next evening, it's another date night. Hazel has sug-
gested that they head up to the golf club restaurant. "I
hear they have this most amazing artichoke appetizer," Hazel
says, "I want to try it out, and see if I can figure out how to
make it myself, at home."

Joe brings his backpack to the restaurant, because he
knows he'll need to sneak his food off the plate and put it
somewhere. It's odd behaviour, but Hazel doesn't question
Joe on why he's wearing a backpack again. To a restaurant?

When the server arrives, Hazel asks about the artichoke dish. She wants to know what goes into the mixture of
ingredients. There is some banter, as the server comments that
it's one of the most popular orders. She tries to guess at what
goes into creating the recipe, when Hazel suggests that they
go right to the source. Ask the Chef.

Hazel orders the artichoke appetizer and a main meal
of chicken parmesan, and the waitress disappears back into
the kitchen area. She returns minutes later, with two glasses
filled with water and a hand-written note, with instructions. It
is signed by Chef Moya, himself. Hazel squeals with delight,
glances at the recipe, then folds the paper, tucking it into her bra.

Her action prompts a huge smile from Joe, who wonders what else is in there?

While Hazel enjoys the first few bites of her artichoke dish, she talks a bit about how peaceful it always is to take a bicycle ride along the trail by the lake. It's her cue to suggest that the two will need to make that trek soon. Joe agrees.

He finds himself being enchanted by Hazel's description of the bicycle that she rides, "It's old," she says, "although, these days, I suppose that calling it vintage gives it more panache." She goes on to explain that the wheels used to belong to Kohkum, who also made a birch bark basket. She figured out a way to attach it to the handle bars,

"We'd go berry-picking, with her riding that bike, if the distance was too far for her old legs to walk. Her comment, not mine. The birch bark basket is still attached, and these days, I still ride her old bike, mostly to gather interesting stones, or plants that I pick along the way."

Hazel pauses, taking time to clear her throat and gather her thoughts, "I love how Kohkum stayed active, almost right up to the end of her life. I miss her."

Her voice becomes quieter. She stops talking, and breathes a heavy sigh. Not surprising to Joe at this point, she reaches into her undergarments to retrieve a tissue.

In the case that Hazel would appreciate finding a way to lighten the moment, Joe waits for a few seconds and then changes the subject. He talks about how he's always been amazed by the turtle ponds, which are located alongside the trail, in a wilderness area just east of Town.

"We most certainly need to head up that way, when we do get on the trail with our bikes," he suggests, "and, make sure to bring your camera." He knows that Hazel has a keen interest in photography.

Before long, the dinner order is served. Joe uses his power of hypnosis one more time, to allow Hazel to think that he's eating, when really, he's putting the food in some plastic sandwich bags that he brought from home. He ordered liver and onions with mashed potatoes and gravy. He figures it'll be a nice treat for Xavier. Being a stray, Xavier is not a picky eater. Joe makes sure to remove the onions before placing the food in a baggie.

When Hazel excuses herself to go to the washroom, Joe observes others who are also dining out tonight, and what he's seeing is sad.

There's a couple.

The woman looks at the menu and figures she'd like to order some pasta. Fettucine with blackened chicken. The man, who she is with, tells her that she should order a salad instead because he's noticed that she's put on a few pounds lately. When the waitress comes, he orders her a glass of water and a Greek salad. He orders himself a surf and turf, which includes mounds of shrimp served atop a New York steak. And he orders himself, a double scotch and water.

It's a surprise to Joe that he's able to read this woman's thoughts. That hasn't happened before. He knows what she's thinking, as easily as if she were having a regular conversation with him. Joe thinks it may be happening because she's having her period. Joe can smell it. Or, it could be that he's able to know her thoughts because, it's clear, she is experiencing extreme emotion.

After ordering, the man takes out his cell phone, and starts looking at email messages, Joe supposes. The husband totally ignores the woman he brought to dinner. Joe can sense that she wonders if maybe, the messages might be from one his mistresses. She has reason to wonder, as Joe listens in on her thoughts,

"You've cheated on me, so many times over the years, you fat swine. That's how I ended up getting syphilis. You lied to me, again, saying it couldn't be, and that if you got that STD, it must have been because of using a public toilet. As if. But, thankfully got yourself checked out. Damn cheater, and you wonder why I cringe anytime you try to touch me, always after one of those poker games with the boys. If you are even playing poker. It's likely more a case of poke her. Arse, you couldn't even manage to get me a Mother's Day card this year, treating me like I am nothing more than some type of hood ornament. Oh yeah, you'll get yours someday, soon I hope. And, I won't feel sad. Not at all. I'll rejoice, maybe even throw a party."

Meanwhile, she sits quietly, only thinking these thoughts but never saying anything out loud. It's like she begins to wilt, a flower in dire need of being watered.

Moreso than Joe wanting to sink his fangs into the man's neck, it is she who wants to kill. Her husband.

It's further exacerbated when his cell phone rings. The husband takes the call even though, it's clear his wife wants to talk, about something, anything. He pays no attention to her again, but he is animated, laughing and joking with whoever it is on the other end of the telephone line. He's more interested in his outward appearance, totally making an effort to gain hand, in whatever meaningless game he plays.

When the food arrives, he digs in, offering no commentary on whether he's enjoying his entre. He doesn't ask if his wife is liking her Greek salad. She isn't. She wanted an actual meal instead of just a salad. He shows disinterest, until she reaches out to grab the garlic toast that she asked for, with her order. He stops her from tasting, "Carbs". He starts eating the toast instead.

Joe hears her thoughts again, "Fine. You pig. Scarf it down. Maybe it'll give you a heart attack, you eat so many damn fatty foods."

The guy orders his third double scotch and gives the wife the keys to drive home. As a point of coincidence, Joe arrives at the till to pay his bill, at the same time the man is fumbling to bring his credit card out of his wallet.

Joe can sense that the wife is seething, and internally weeping, at the same time.

It's already dark out when they all leave the restaurant. Once in the parking lot, Joe overhears the man admonishing his wife, who didn't drive to the city today to pick up his dry cleaning. He's criticizing her, saying, "What are you good for? All I wanted, was for you to pick up my dry cleaning, and you can't even remember to do that! I've worked so hard in my life to give you everything you want, and you can't do me one small favour." He throws his hands up, as if in disgust.

The woman stops to think, again Joe reads her thoughts, and he's saddened to know what this woman has had to endure,

"No, that's not true, you don't give me everything I want, asshole. I wanted pasta tonight. And, I wanted a husband who pays attention to me. I still can't believe you locked me out of the house, last weekend, when there was a tornado causing all sorts of property damage, to everyone around us. It's by the Grace of God that I wasn't killed. The neighbour's roof was ripped off, and it was terrifying for me to see her living room curtains, floating through the air, like some kind of kite. What pisses me off, is that you acted like nothing happened, after that twister threatened, even denying that you locked the door on purpose. You said, you thought I was downstairs at the time. What horseshit kind of lie is that? And now, here you are, forcing me to be your designated driver again. Drunken sod. I'd leave you, if I could, but honestly, I'm afraid to do so. You've been violent with me before. I know you would beat me again, if I mention it, and I get tired of having to wear sunglasses, indoors, when I do something as simple as going to get the mail."

This guy needs to go, Joe's thoughts, as he drives Hazel home.

It's now been a full year since getting his DUI, and he's finally got his driver's licence back. He's even more happy to be behind the wheel of his dream car again. It's a fully-refurbished 1969 red Dodge Charger, the same type of vehicle featured on the 1970's television show, The Dukes Of Hazzard. Joe's Mom had left him a substantial inheritance when she passed. This is his gift, to himself. But, Joe does make a note to himself. He needs to get a new licence plate. The old one reads 24JOE, referencing his drinking days, and constantly picking up a case of 24 beer.

He's going to have to breathe into a device now for the next 12 months, each time he wants to start the vehicle. The installation of the breathalyzer is a court-ordered provision, just to ensure that Joe isn't too intoxicated to drive anymore. Joe blows. He isn't embarrassed doing so. Hazel knows his story.

It's during Joe's contemplation that Hazel has an observation.

It's why she secretly smiles as Joe continues the drive towards home. Old vehicles have ashtrays. Joe doesn't smoke, but Hazel notices that his ashtray is where he stores his quarters and dimes. But, prominently displayed on top of the change is a round object. Hazel recognizes it as a chip from AA. It celebrates one full year of sobriety. She knows this because a friend of hers has the same. Hazel even attended her one-year birthday. It makes Hazel proud for Joe. She thinks she's just found some sort of answer, as to Joe's behaviour, from horrible to heavenly. It's because he's sober, she tells herself, mistakenly believing that the recovery chip is something that he earned.

It's as though, Hazel has altered the reality of things that are real, but unpleasant to know. It's because she's falling for Joe. It is like she's blocked out the memory of what Joe was really like not that long ago, just as the summer season was starting to get busy. And, Hazel should know. She's the one who served him, vodka after vodka, the night of Joe's encounter with Dust Man. She knows that Joe didn't walk home that evening. He staggered out of the pub because that was all he was capable of doing.

She also couldn't have known that the real reason that Joe carries this AA chip, now, arranged visibly in the ashtray of his car, is because he sees it as a defence. Displaying it is his response to the old habit of drinking and driving. Joe figures, should he ever get stopped by police again, the chip will be the first thing the cops will see. He guesses that it's likely he'd be let go, when police see the one-year chip. And, that he'd be granted freedom without discussion or interrogation, because of the presence of a sobriety chip.

Hazel can never know that it wasn't earned.

The coin comes from a place of someone home alone.

When Joe first started driving again, he was worried about blowing into that breathalyser device. He had thoughts that his breath might not even register anymore. For some reason, that wasn't a factor the first time he turned on the ignition. He once again knows the freedom of being able to drive a vehicle.

Never again. It's a promise Joe's made to himself hundreds of times before. This time, he knows he'll be able to keep that promise. The thought causes him to wonder.

Who is the real vampire? Is it him, or was it the alcohol? It's taken more lives, ruined more lives, than Joe can imagine himself ever touching with his fangs.

Once he drops Hazel at her home, Joe decides to take a drive.

He knows where the couple, who he just saw at the restaurant, lives. He's seen the man before, sitting out on his front deck, drinking a short scotch and swilling down a bowl of tortilla chips, with a side of guacamole dip. The oaf never once waved to say hello, and acknowledge Joe as he walked by his home.

That was before Joe got this licence back, and was forced to walk everywhere.

The man has a violent undertone to him, at the best of times. He has a sour telltale expression.

As Joe drives past the home tonight, he's hoping that he will not witness the shadows of a man punching his wife. There are no curtains on the large, living room window.

Joe is relieved, for the wife, that there's no violent behaviour going on. This time.

He remembers seeing the woman, sitting alone on that same deck. As Joe passed by, once before, he wondered if he should stop to offer help. She was crying. But, she carried a body language that said - leave me alone - so he did. He could almost feel her pain back then, even without being given the dark gift that he now carries. And yes, she was wearing sunglasses, even though the day was cloudy.

The guy is so thoroughly insensitive, it's clear he doesn't care about bothering his neighbours either. Tonight, he's out mowing the lawn, the cutter is loud and roaring. It's still early enough that he's not violating any noise bylaws, but really? Who cuts their lawn after it's already dark outside? Anyone with young children will surely be bothered by the sound. It's their bedtime.

It causes Joe to cringe when he thinks back to a time when he did something similar. He can't claim innocence to never having taken part in a similar type of ruckus. Again, alcohol was involved.

It happened one Fall, when Joe had been day-drinking all afternoon. He'd been procrastinating in cleaning up the fallen leaves that littered his yard, even though it was on his to-do list. So, just as darkness was setting in, Joe took out his leaf blower. But, he doesn't like the task of bagging all the leaves, so he did something woefully insensitive. His next-door neighbour had gone away for a few days, so there was no one to witness as Joe blew all of those leaves right into the neighbours' already-raked yard. He didn't feel bad about doing so, figuring he'd tell his neighbour about how a big wind storm came up, while he was away.

That was back then. Joe makes a mental note that he'll have to go over to his neighbour's, once the snow begins to fall. He'll shovel his walk and driveway, as a gesture of peace and to try eliminate the memory of previous bad behaviour.

For now though, Joe stops and unbuckles his seat belt. He never used to wear it, but it's best not to tempt fate any further than what he's already come to know. It's the weekend, a time when everyone knows, there is likely to be a RCMP presence in town. These days, they are patrolling around in unmarked vehicles. Getting a seat belt violation, so soon after regaining his driver's licence, isn't something that Joe wants to face. It would mean even more points being taken from his driving record. He's already lost so many. It's not worth the risk.

Joe confronts the man, yanking him by the hair, which turns out to be a comedic moment. The man wears a toupee.

Before the guy has time to react, Joe grabs him by the shoulder, sinking his fangs into his neck, which smells of too much aftershave. What little hair he has, on his balding head, is greasy and smells of sweat. Joe tucks the fake toupee into his pocket.

The lawnmower sound stops, as the man's hands release the safety control cable.

Joe's granted the woman her wish. Her husband is dead. Given the man's lifestyle, that he eats fatty food and he drinks too much, everyone will point to heart attack as the cause of death.

He checks the trees to see if Corbitt might be watching. And if the Being is monitoring Joe's actions again, he doubts the Jumper will make an appearance tonight.

It's a case of good riddance to bad rubbish.

The First Kiss

By the following evening, Joe finds himself feeling giddy, again wishing that he could see his reflection in the mirror, to check out his appearance. Hazel has invited him into her home again, suggesting that she cook dinner. He wants to arrive looking dapper, so wearing a t-shirt is out of the question. As he sorts through the clothes hanging in his closet, Joe wonders about all those Hollywood movies about vampires. The women, who are vampires, always look so nice, wearing fresh make-up and their hair has been perfectly teased and coiffed. How is it that anyone can apply eye liner, that precisely, without the use of a mirror?

Joe chooses a basic, buttoned-down dress shirt. It's light pink in colour. He got it from his Mom. It's a birthday gift from a few years ago. It warms his heart when he recalls her comment, while Joe's unwrapping the gift, his Mom says, "Who do you think you are, Johnny Cash? Stop wearing black all the time. You really have to get more adventurous and start wearing different colours. And pink is a good colour, it shows that you are sensitive. Girls like that."

It causes Joe to smile, as he remembers the comment. His Mom always wished for him, that he'd find love.

Maybe now he has.

Joe tucks his shirt into the waistline of his stone-washed jeans. The pants have purposeful rips, showing his knees. That's the look, these days. It makes Joe snicker, when he thinks back to his childhood, and how his Mom would have been embarrassed to send her kid out in public with tears in his pants. She always had those iron-on patches handy, which she'd attach, if his jeans got torn. They were stiff and uncomfortable, and Joe usually ended up ripping them off, after not too long.

It was around this time, when Joe was maybe nine years old, that he had first taste of alcohol.

It's after a game of scrub baseball, and one of his friends' pulls a bottle of home-made dandelion wine from his backpack. His parents had produced a batch, and left it to age, on a shelf down in their basement. His friend isn't a bad kid, just curious about the wine. So is Joe.
They both sit by the shoreline and empty the bottle of home-made brew, before the sun sets.
It's Joe's first night of staggering home, and one that's been repeating way too many times over the years. He falls into his bed, immediately that night, and doesn't get up until his Mom calls him for breakfast the next morning. She doesn't even know that he'd been drunk the night before. How could she know?
Even way back then, Joe finds that he is good at hiding. That afternoon, he heads up to the corner store to buy some eye drops. He remembers hearing that advice from an older classmate at school. Visine gets rid of the red caused by alcohol dehydration.

Joe's made sure to have a bottle of the eye drops, in his bathroom medicine cabinet, ever since. But, he hasn't needed to use them, anytime lately. There is no way to remove the stain that he's now afflicted with.

Joe moves his hands across his chest, making the sign of the cross, before heading out the door. He's going to meet

Hazel, and he hopes their evening together will be tinged with promise.

It is.

Hazel wears an apron as she opens the door. She's been cooking. A 3-bean spicy chili recipe and a nice-looking loaf of bannock. It's not what anyone would consider a romantic meal, but since serving Joe at the pub all these months, it's what he often orders. He's commented that there is nothing as good as a big bowl of chili, along with his usual vodka. So, Hazel knows that the spicy meal is something that he likes.

The chili is still in the slow-cooker, so that the flavours can properly mix. Joe is right on time, and carrying a bouquet of flowers that Hazel recognizes were purchased up at the local grocery store. It's a mixture of daisies, some of which have been ornamentally-coloured into bright purple shades, greens, and pink.

"I am not going to become a victim of my past just because I remember it." Joe wonders why that thought popped into his head.

He keeps trying to shake the feeling of being sorry for himself. He can't help but guess that it's likely, that if he had sobered up long ago, this is how he would have been spending his nights. With Hazel, and not alone with a bottle.

He never had any real reason to feel sorry for himself. If his Mom was strong enough to let go of bad memory, and rebuild, surely he could too. But, he never did, instead drowning it, with beer and vodka. At first, it was called fun and socializing. The drinking quickly turned into a place to retreat and hide, alone, often sitting in the darkness on his deck while the rest of the neighbourhood turned in for the night.

Shameful.

He hopes that feeling can be shaken off and discarded, soon. He still ingests alcohol, through the blood of those on which he feeds. Maybe he carries their sins, and bad memory, too, because he drains them of tainted blood.

Bad habits die hard. Or, in the case of Joe, they don't die at all. They just change.

He knows that he has so much work to do, to better himself, starting with his alcoholic behaviour. He needs to quell the tendency to spout out crude words, that he once thought were clever. Especially with Hazel. She's moved into a place in his heart now, and it's a feeling that he wants to grow, with care. She is as lovely and delicate as an imported and rare orchid, and she deserves the same tenderness. Joe already loves her. He just hasn't told her yet.

Maybe it's the dress that Hazel wears, a long, yellow, off-the-shoulder sundress that clings to her slender body. Even though Hazel's still wearing the apron, Joe can't help himself but stare at her breasts, remembering that she's worn the dress before, when he used to drink alcohol. He made a stupid comment back then, while at the pub. Something like, "You like look a banana. Let me peel you out of that."

He'll not utter something so disrespectful tonight.

"These are just lovely," Hazel smiles, taking the bouquet to the kitchen counter, then reaching into the cupboard, above the stove, to grab a clear, glass vase. While she fills it with water, Joe comments on how the kitchen smells amazing, "Lots of spices, I can tell," he says, inhaling the scent of what's stewing in the slow cooker, "and, you have outdone yourself," he points to the loaf of bannock, that's cooling on the stove top, "I haven't had a good piece of bannock in ages. I can hardly wait until we eat. Thanks."

"The chili will be ready, soon," she says, "but first, I'm putting you to work." Hazels open a kitchen drawer and grabs a couple of sharp paring knives. She tells him they need to cut some rhubarb. The leafy, perennial vegetable grows in abundance at the edge of her garden. "Here," she says, "this one is yours." She hands Joe a Tupperware bowl, and gestures, pointing with her lips towards the door. It's a gesture indicating that they are to go outside.

Once in her garden, and cutting the rhubarb, Joe notices that Hazel's crop is a healthy one. She's planted numerous tomato plants, side-by-side, that are already starting to bear fruit. He makes a point of commenting on the new growth, to which Hazel responds, "Yes, it's something Kohkum taught me. She always said to plant them together, so the plants can pollinate each other. They grow best when planted together, encouraging growth." Her comment leads Joe to a thought towards realization. He has never planted his heart beside anyone, in the past. Maybe the time to begin anew is now.

After a moment, he makes a suggestion, "Hey, it's karoake night at the bar tonight. We can head down there, after dinner, if you like."

Hazel rebukes the suggestion, saying she doesn't want to mix with the bar crowd, tonight, "It's so much nicer to just spend quiet time, at home, with you." She blushes. "Besides, what would you sing if we went down there?"

He doesn't forget the lyrics, now that he's lucid. Joe serenades her, singing Folsom Prison Blues. Not the most romantic of songs, for sure, but Hazel is impressed with the sound of his singing voice. He's a baritone, just like Mr. Johnny Cash.

I hear the train a-comin, it's rollin round the bend
And I ain't seen the sunshine since I don't know when
I'm stuck in Folsom Prison, and time keeps draggin on.

When they get back into Hazel's kitchen, she tells him that she'll bake a pie, "Kohkum taught me how to make the best crust. While I fix that, you cut up the rhubarb."

While Hazel crumbles the softened lard into the flour mixture, that she's put in a bowl, Joe gets busy slicing the rhubarb into small pieces. How did she know that rhubarb pie is his favourite? Saskatoon berry pie is awesome but Joe prefers the tartness of rhubarb. He's never mentioned it, but then again, maybe it's a given. Everybody loves rhubarb pie.

Silently rejoicing in spending these moments, Joe isn't paying attention for a fraction of a second. He slices the tip of his left index finger with the sharp paring knife. He feels no pain, and doesn't call attention to himself, but he begins to bleed. Out of the corner of her eye, Hazel notices, saying,

"Just call me Florence Nightingale."

Florence is the considered the founder of modern nursing, and that is what Hazel intends to do. Take care of

Joe's wound. Hazel immediately heads to her bathroom to grab some medical gauze, Polysporin and band-aids from her cabinet.

When she returns to the kitchen, it's like she never had to make the effort. She sees Joe continuing to cut the rhubarb, as though nothing has happened.

Hazel shakes her head. She could have sworn on a Bible that she saw blood, but now, there's no reason to fret, and there is no injury. She has to ask. But before then, Hazel takes a good look at Joe's hands. They aren't rugged, the way a farmer's hands might be. Instead, they look like they might be soft, and she wonders if he uses hand lotion. Then she figures, it's probably because he works in a kitchen. There'd be a lot of humidity in a place like that.

Hazel wonders if she'll be able to hold those hands, any time soon? She does wonder, though, about a strange and crudely-fashioned tattoo across Joe's right hand knuckles. They are the letters L B T. Her first thought is that maybe it's some type of statement on sexuality or identity. If that's the case, it puzzles her. She wants to ask what the letters mean, and why Joe had them permanently printed on his body, but she won't have to. He notices Hazel looking at the tattoo, so he offers an explanation,

"Oh, this," he says, "it was just one of those questionable decisions that I made, back when I was still partying quite a bit. One night, someone had a tattoo gun, so I asked him to print the letters of my favourite sandwich. Bacon, lettuce & tomato. He either wasn't paying attention or maybe he is dyslexic," Joe shakes his head, continuing, "Or more probably he was a bit drunk, and that's how the lettering came out, as lettuce, bacon & tomato." he giggles, "the guy apologized for the mistake, but it's been there for so many years now, that I just don't even notice it anymore. I thought, once, about getting it removed. But that would probably hurt. Besides, now you know my favourite sandwich."

Hazel also notices that Joe's fingernails look dirty, like he's been gardening. Well, in reality, he was, being just outdoors and picking her rhubarb. She has no way of knowing that it's dried blood from the night before. Even though Joe had washed his hands, before cutting the rhubarb, that stain cannot be removed. It's an ever-present reminder.

Joe tells her that he didn't cut his finger. He didn't even nick it. He only poked himself with the sharp end of the knife, like being poked with a stick. "Thanks, though," he says, "this rhubarb is pretty much ready now to be sugared-up." How could he ever explain to Hazel that, now that he's a vampire, he's got the power to rejuvenate, almost immediately. It's far too early in the relationship that he longs to build with her. But he vows that someday, he'll find a way to tell her. He makes that promise to himself, and it's one that he will keep. Just when? When the time is right, but when can that time be? "I'm a vampire now, hope you don't mind," is that how he'll start the dialogue? It, too, needs to be given thought and care.

While the pie is baking, Hazel goes to her spare bedroom. But, before doing so, she instructs Joe to fill a couple of glasses with water and meet her on the veranda. She joins him outdoors, and she's carrying a container filled with paint brushes. The pocket of the apron she still wears bulges with small bottles of acrylic artist paint, of all sorts of colours.

Joe wondered why there were two blank canvasses, waiting on the heavy, metal patio bistro furniture, when he came out to set down the glasses of water. Now, he knows.

"I didn't know you are an artist," Joe says.

"Yes, it's something I've been playing around with for years. Kohkum is the one who got me interested. I can't remember how old I was when she bought me, my first paint set. It would have been around the same time that she first started teaching me how to bake. After a banana loaf or a batch of cookies went in the oven, we'd sit down and paint, waiting for the baking to finish. So, here we are," Hazel smiles, "carrying on a with another cherished tradition, I guess."

Hazel reminds Joe of a maestro, the way she swishes the wet paint onto the canvas, or makes a dab here and there. "I like painting images of flowers, the most," she says, "usually

I give them away as gifts, otherwise my house would be filled up by now. Actually, I think I will gift this one for you tonight. For some reason you remind me of a sunflower, so that's what I'll paint for you."

It's a sweet moment for Joe. No one has ever told him before, that he reminds them of a flower. It's ironic too. She's painting a sunflower. The sun is not necessarily a friend to him anymore.

He snickers a bit, with a retort, "Well, it's good you didn't say that I remind you of an onion, because I have lots of layers."

Joe has no idea what he'll paint, but a moment later, he grabs two shades of gray acrylic paint and squeezes a glob onto the top of a yogurt container. Hazel saves the lids for this purpose, rather than spending money on a proper artist pallet.

"Okay, I've got it," Joe remarks, "I'll paint Xavier. He's that feral cat who's been hanging around my place, regularly. He comes up on the veranda, everyday, now that I started feeding him."

"Oh him!" Hazel exclaims, "I still can't believe you managed to teach him how to travel with you, when you longboard."

There isn't a great deal of conversation, as they embark on their paint night. But, there are plenty of furtive glances. Joe wonders what Hazel might be thinking, and he doesn't want to spoil the moment by saying something stupid.

When the timer on the oven sounds, that it's time to take out the pie, Hazel suggests they take their spicy meal out on the deck.

At the first mouthful, or what Hazel is mesmerized into thinking that Joe is eating, Joe can't help himself but say, "Hey! This is awesome. Why don't you enter that chili challenge event that is held up at the school gym every summer?"

"You think so?"

"Absolutely, this meal is perfectly spiced, not too hot but definitely piquant. If you don't mind, I'll take some home with me tonight."

Joe is surprised to find that he's started to salivate. The chili does smell great. He hopes his reaction isn't an indication of anything else, like wanting to feed, now. He forces himself to change his thought process, so that he isn't fixated on thoughts of blood.

He's already mentioned the chili challenge, so may as well start there. Hazel is still considered to be relatively new to the community, and she's never attended the event, so Joe explains:

The contest is held each summer, at the Beach. It's organized, mostly to bring the community together and share a meal. But it's also a fundraiser. Money goes towards supporting kids' sport and art programs. Similar to a Fall Supper, Joe supposes. There's music, decorations, lots of visiting and good, friendly competition, as those who attend cast their vote for who's got the best recipe. Joe looks forward to this year's gathering. Now that Joe has brought it up, he hopes that Hazel will attend with him, as the better part of a couple.

The distraction works, and Joe is able to come back into the present moment, enjoying his time with Hazel. After serving the chili with a large chunk of bannock, on the side, she brings out the warm rhubarb pie. Joe longs for a taste of it, because the smell is glorious. Instead, his joy in experiencing the flavours comes while watching Hazel's reaction. He loves how she helps herself to a second slice, topped off with gobs of home-made whipped cream.

The moments are lovely, but fleeting.

10 o'clock arrives so quickly.

It's already dark out, but the summer air is still mild. Joe says it's time for him to head home, "I've got a few things planned for tomorrow, so best to get an early start." He doesn't feel the need to tell Hazel that he isn't able to face the morning sun. He figures it's something best kept secret right now.

"Oh, okay," she says, "but wait. Before you head out, I'll run in and put some leftover chili in a Tupperware container for you. You can get the sunflower painting at some other time. I want to make sure it's completely dry, before you carry it home."

When she returns, their hands touch, as Hazel passes over the plastic bowl, filled with chili. It isn't an awkward moment, and seems the perfect time for Joe to give Hazel a kiss goodnight, but not on her cheek.

Joe can smell the aroma of rhubarb and whipped cream on her lips, as he reaches out to softly hold her chin. He puts his lips on hers, but delicately so. No need for an open mouth, just a heart- felt gesture, to let Hazel know how he feels.

"I had the best night ever, tonight, Hazel. Thank you for - everything. See you tomorrow?"

"I'd love that," Hazel replies, "I'll bake us some bread pudding and make some tea. We can just hang out on the deck again."

Joe gives Hazel one more soft kiss, before he leaves. He's feeling like Jesus on a good day, and he prays there's never a need to roll the stone away. He's happy and he hopes she'll never betray him, because it would kill him to lose her affection.

It is time for him to go. Even though the two just had dinner, so to speak, Joe needs to feed his hunger for blood. So he does, heading out along the pathway again, to see who has had too much to drink and has passed out tonight. He reverts to his initial practice of taking only what he needs, and stopping before he senses that the heart might stop.

Joe usually feels like he needs to rest, after taking someone down. But, this night is different. He finds himself being inspired by his evening spent with Hazel, and her ability to paint. Joe has no art supplies in his home. Why would he? He does take out pencil and paper, though, and begins to draw the soft features of Hazel's face, beginning with her full lips. After some time, he's finished the pencil drawing, and he's quite proud at the resemblance. Joe is amazed that he has a little-known talent, that he never knew he possessed, before.

It also surprises him to realize that, since the change, he has also become ambidextrous. He now has the ability to write or draw with both his right and left hands, with the same precision.

But, to Joe's main delight, he kissed Hazel tonight.

And he can draw.

Only Women Bleed

The next evening, Joe brings a gift of Rhubarb Rose. It is a mead, brewed at the Prairie Bee Meadery in Moose Jaw. It's one of their best sellers with a zest of rhubarb, and sweetened with honey. Joe knows that it's important to Hazel to shop local, as much as possible. She told him, it's the reason why she shops at the local farmer's market. She had also mentioned liking the mead, on the drive back from Moose Jaw and the afternoon of skydiving. Hazel isn't much of a drinker but she does enjoy a glass of wine or mead every now and then.

Joe made the effort to find the rhubarb mead, having never taken the time to actually browse for products at the local liquor store. In the past, he usually went straight to the beer cooler, or grabbed a bottle of vodka, which is placed right near the door.

"Oh, how lovely, it's rhubarb, just like the pie we made the other night," Hazel remarks, as Joe hands over the bottle, "and it's chilled too. Here. I'll pour us a glass." It momentarily slips her mind that Joe no longer drinks alcohol.

Joe has a quick response, "I can't, Hazel. You know that I am a vodka man. But enjoy."

His keen sense of smell tells him that Hazel is bleeding again. So does her appearance. She looks, both, tired and drained of energy. Her next comment informs him that his observation is correct.

"I hope you don't mind if we stay in tonight," Hazel asks, "I had a really bad sleep last night. Correction. I didn't sleep at all." As if on cue, she makes a grimace, and puts pressure her abdominal area, clutching it with her hand.

"Hazel! Are you okay? Here, sit down," Joe helps her towards a kitchen chair, "I'll pour you some mead."

It's while he's uncapping the bottle that Hazel tells him that she suffers from some feminine problems. It's a condition called fibroids, which are common amongst women who are perimenopausal.

"But, I can't be ashamed of a natural process of how a woman's body ages. This is just one of those realities. I just didn't think it would happen so soon." Hazel whispers. She changes the subject.

Thinking that it might be uncomfortable to talk about heavy flow, and having irregular periods, which includes delivering heavy clots of blood, Hazel lightens the conversation by trying to make a joke.

"Whoever said that women can age gracefully was a bald-faced liar, Joe," she takes a sip of the mead, "I went to the doctor the other day to have this condition checked out. He tells me that there's no reason to worry. Lots of women suffer from this, so it isn't a serious condition. But, he did say that I should make the effort to eat foods that are rich in iron," then, Hazel giggles, "Ironically enough, rhubarb contains iron."

"Did he give you some medication to help with your pain?" Joe asks.

"No. Because heavy flow, and sometimes developing fibroids, is a natural process for women my age. He says I just need to tough it out. Eventually, it'll stop. But then he told me that it could take years for my reproductive system to move into its next phase. That's when I'll stop producing eggs, and this excessive bleeding will stop then, too. It's an inconvenience, but mostly, it makes me tired. And the cramps are so severe, sometimes, that I feel like I can barely cope."

Hazel describes to Joe that the doctor also gave her the option of having this condition, medically treated, through surgery. It would mean having her uterus removed.

"The removal will stop the pain," the doc says, "but you also have to realize that you will never be able to have children, once this crucial part of your reproductive system is taken out. So, give it some thought." The doctor calls fibroids, and what Hazel is going through, a common condition. He asks her if she wants a referral to a specialist. She says yes.

"So, that's it Joe. I am going to have surgery soon. I can't say that I am happy about it, but I also know that I don't want to live with this pain for another 10 years or more." A soft tear drop makes its way down Hazel's cheek, "Also, it makes me sad that I'll never be able to raise a family, once the surgery is done. It's always been a dream of mine to have a daughter or a son. So, I'm just feeling fragile tonight, that's why I hope you don't mind staying in. Maybe we can watch a movie."

Joe agrees, and Hazel puts on a DVD. It's an old movie called, *When Harry Met Sally*. As they watch, Joe can't help but think it may be some type of commentary that Hazel is trying to make.

When friends become lovers.

It's a tender moment for Joe, when Hazel asks if it's okay that she places a pillow on Joe's lap, so she can lay down while they watch the movie.

"It feels better when there is no pressure on my body. I hope I don't fall asleep," she says, "I am such a heavy sleeper, you'd have to carry me to bed."

Hazel tells Joe a story, of something that happened in her youth.

> She's an adolescent, and thrilled at the opportunity to show off her new pow wow dance regalia. Kohkum has been working on designing and creating it, throughout all these past winter months. It's a jingle dress, that's yellow in colour with accents of red and blue beadwork. For this, Kohkum's designed flowers.

Dozens of shiny silver cones accent the outfit. The cones create their own joyful song, swaying and touching each other, as Hazel moves. The jingle dress dance is significant to Hazel. It's a dance that represents a prayer for healing.

There's a pow wow over at the Piapot First Nation. The community is located less than an hour north of the City of Regina. The dance arbour is packed, as thousands have made their way, to visit, eat, dance and listen to the beat of the drum.

Hazel always finds it amusing when non-Indigenous people ask her, "What time does the pow wow end?"

There is no answer for this question. The drumming, dancing and visiting comes to an end, when people start getting tired and want to go to bed. That could be at midnight, or it might be at 3 in the morning.

This factor is at the crux of Hazel's story.

She's been dancing up a storm since early afternoon, and she's tired now that the sun has set. The food trucks are even packing up for the night. But, the drummers keep going, which means people like Kohkum plan to stay until the very end.

Hazel tries to stay awake, but exhaustion takes her, and she falls asleep, sitting up straight and right in her lawn chair, "My cousin says that I slept so soundly that they couldn't wake me up, so he carried me to his truck. When everyone else piled into the cab, I spent the trip laying on some blankets on the cargo bed at the back of the truck. I can't believe that I slept through the whole thing, only waking up an hour later when we finally arrived back at home," she giggles, "so, yes, if I do fall asleep tonight, don't be upset. It's not your company. And, I am a heavy sleeper."

Joe covers Hazel with a blanket, and strokes her hair, while the movie plays. Hazel whispers another story about how she has always been able to sleep through, just about anything,

"I also remember Kohkum saying to me, 'You sleep like the dead, my girl," at this point, Joe perks up his ear, in the normal way, wanting to know what Hazel will say next, "Kohkum says that she always had to carry me to bed, when I'd visit. She did that right up until I was about nine years old, and I had gotten too heavy for her to pick up. So, she'd just leave me there, on the couch, covering me up with one of the blankets that she knitted for me. Actually, Joe, it's this blanket right here, that you used to cover me up. How did you know?"

He didn't know that the knitted comforter he'd chosen, had been made by Hazel's beloved Grandmother. It makes him feel special and needed, that Hazel is so comfortable, that she does fall asleep on his lap, long before the movie comes to an end.

Joe finds that, what Hazel just said, about how she sleeps so deeply that she is unaware of her surroundings, bothers him. He wonders if he's the same, after feeding. He always falls into heavy slumber.

But, do I sleep so hard that I, too, am unaware of my surroundings? He thinks to himself that the way he nods off, after a feed, is no different than in the days when he'd pass out after blacking out. And, if that's the case, isn't that a danger to me? It's a fleeting thought, as Joe once again finds delight in stroking Hazel's long hair.

When the final credits play, Joe tenderly picks up Hazel to carry her to her bed. She doesn't weigh much, Joe thinks, or, maybe it's just because he has increased physical strength now that he, too, is one of the Unnaturals. As he gently places Hazel's head on the pillow, the ending song for the movie plays on.

It had to be you. It had to be you.
I wandered around, and finally found
the somebody who could make me be true.

It's at this moment, Joe knows that he has the ability to alleviate Hazel's suffering. She is excessively bleeding again. He has a thirst for blood. Joe uses his power of hypnosis, allowing Hazel to believe that she's having an erotic dream about him.

As he removes her panties, guiding his lips towards her vagina, Joe thinks of a flower. The Bird of Paradise. He wants to remove the rest of her clothing, so he can see her naked body, which he's been fantasizing about, since first meeting her back when he was still drinking heavily. But, he thinks that taking off her clothes is too much of an invasion of her privacy, and it violates his level of respect for her.

As he glances at Hazel's vagina now, Joe feels guilty, knowing that he is embarking on sexual assault. But, he also believes that what he is about to do is not guided by a sexual impulse or desire. He wants to help ease Hazel's pain. In some twisted way, it is an act of love.

And then, he drinks. He puts his lips on Hazel's second set of lips, between her legs, which Joe has longed to kiss since long before he was turned.

There will be no need for additional feeding tonight. Joe can feel the fibroids from her abdomen loosen, and enter his own body. Most of them are the size of a loonie, although a few that go down are as big as a hen's egg.

Unlike the doctor, Joe can remove them without the need for surgical procedure, which means that Hazel won't have to have a body part removed, thereby giving up on her dream of becoming a Mom, and raising a family.

It's like Joe's giving her two gifts, taking away the abdominal pain, and ensuring that Hazel won't be forced to abandon her deep-felt desire of someday having a child.

For the moment, it's Joe's purpose.

As he swallows, the fibroids go down as easily as Angel Food cake.

Second Time Around

Hazel awakes the next morning, and acts as she always does, yawning then there's a big stretch. She gets out of bed to turn on her coffee maker. As part of her usual routine, she's already set the coffee grounds and poured the water, the night before. It saves time during sleepy moments, making it easier just to flick on the brew button.

For the first time in a long time, Hazel decides to forego her usual morning meditation. There is something different about this day.

She's filled with a feeling of optimism, as she opens the refrigerator door to get her coffee cream. It makes Hazel smile to see the half-emptied bottle of rhubarb mead, brought as a gift from Joe the night before. She is flattered that he remembered her mentioning it, paying attention to the details of their conversations. Not many men do that, pay attention. Hazel's heart is given a tug. Could Joe be the one? He's always been such a derelict in the past, an ass-pinching, crude talking jerk. He is no more. Hazel feels her emotions move towards beauty. She realizes that she loves Joe. But how can she tell him that? And, where will it lead?

It occurs to her that she's known Joe for a long time, but she really doesn't know anything about him.

Still, she feels lighter somehow, both physically and emotionally.

The abdominal pain that she's felt for months, is gone this morning. Hazel realizes, it's the first time in too long of a time that she's enjoyed a full night's rest. She remembers nodding off, while laying her head on Joe's lap and watching the movie. Then, she woke up, comfortable in her own bed. She supposes that Joe might have carried her, but she can't be sure. There's always been a history of sleep walking for her.

Hazel thinks back to a time, when she was a little girl and spending the night with Kohkum.

Getting up and walking in the middle of the night, without even knowing. It's something that happens to young Hazel, only when she's visiting Kohkum. She wanders out of the house and onto the front lawn. One night, she's is startled by seeing some strange creature, who's eating ripe raspberries from Kohkum's berry bush. The thing has long legs and pale skin. He looks like a big frog, or a grasshopper. Little Hazel isn't afraid, and she walks towards the Being, wondering if it'll talk to her. It doesn't, instead it quickly disappears, jumping straight up towards the tree limbs, and then it's gone. The girl stands there for a moment, hoping he'll come back. He doesn't. Instead, it's Kohkum, who comes to the front veranda, taking little Hazel's hand and leading her back inside, and back to bed. Without knowing, the little girl has just encountered Corbitt.

In the morning, the girl asks Kohkum whether she knows anything about it. She does, telling Hazel the Jumper has been around for a long time, for as long as she can remember. She's seen him too, even when she was a little girl.

"He's harmless," Kohkum says, "and he generally only comes out at night, which is why you haven't

seen him before," she ruffles her granddaughter's hair, "but, you shouldn't be out at night anyway, my dear. There are others, not as nice as Corbitt, that also wander around."
Over the years, Hazel is convinced she's seen Corbitt again. He shows up as a flash, seen from the corner of her eye. But she can't be sure. It's just a feeling that she has.

The memory quickly vanishes, because it's thoughts of Joe that are at the forefront today.

She had an erotic dream about him, last night, and making sweet, tender love with him. He's like the Prince in fairytales that Kohkum read to her when she was a child. He's like the characters in the movie, that she fell asleep watching with Joe. She's just so comfortable with him, that being vulnerable feels safe.

Joe. Hazel wonders if it wasn't too personal of information that she told him about her medical condition, and that she needs to have surgery. It's not the usual date type of conversation, especially with a new love prospect in her life.

She also wonders why she woke up wearing no panties, but, she quickly puts it out of her mind. Hazel sleeps in the nude on a regular basis, and figures she probably removed them herself, before REM sleep because she doesn't like the feel of elastic around her waist while she rests. She is also delighted to realize that she's no longer bleeding, which is a welcome change. So often, her erratic periods last up to two weeks, sometimes longer. This morning, she counts her blessings that it's gone away.

Then, her thoughts turn back to Joe.

Hazel holds only hope that it won't be like before, where she's fallen for someone who acts like a Prince at the beginning, then turns out to be some piece of shit later.

She admits, to herself, that she's fallen in love with Joe. She thinks it safe to give him a chance, or give herself another chance at offering her feelings and her heart. Joe is no longer the ass-pinching, vodka-swilling, insensitive asshole who she'd served at the pub, not that long ago. He's flirted with her so many times before, but in his drunken state back then, who would want to accept the offer?

Something has happened to change him.

Hazel wonders, what?

Pondering

The next day, Joe wanders out of his home when the sunlight is no longer at its peak. He feels some guilt, wondering if the non-consensual sex he performed last night might be feasibly considered a date rape.

Joe always dreamed about how ethereal his first intimate touch with Hazel might be. He imagined that the two of them would be engrossed in warm embrace, whispering of mutual wants and needs, and caressing each other in moments of passion that only lovers can express.

He'll have to hold those thoughts, and promise to himself that he'll never admit to Hazel, what he's done. She is totally unaware that she's been violated, although, if she did understand the reason why Joe acted as he did, he wonders if she might actually thank him. What he did, he did as an act of love.

He knows that it is a faint hope only, that he'll be forgiven by the Universe, because the truth is out there. What he's done is immoral, Joe is aware of that as well. For the first time, in a very long time, Joe feels utterly ashamed, in a way that feels sinister, as never before.

Then, he rationalizes that it's true that he used his powers to mesmerize Hazel into believing that she was only dreaming. But, in his own defence, he did it to help her. She's been living with pain for far too long. He took that away, ingesting the fibroids that were causing her anguish.

He wants to give her a call, and suggest that they meet up after her shift at the pub tonight. It's when he remembers a stupid piece of advice, given to him by another drinking buddy, back in the day. It's the 3-day rule. Never phone a girl for at least 3 days after having sex, otherwise they'll think it's some kind of commitment. Joe used to follow the so-called male rule, but he won't today. He decides that he'll call Hazel after he showers.

Joe hasn't taken a shower or a bath in quite some time. There's no need to, now that he no longer sweats and doesn't cast any body smell. Today, the water isn't needed to cleanse his skin. He's hoping it will cleanse his soul, if he even has one anymore. He wants to wash himself clean, remembering the story Hazel told him about how Kohkum said, that water is sacred. He figures that maybe any water will do, even if it comes from a faucet.

While the rush of spray cascades over his face and hair, Joe can't help but continue to wonder if his actions, in performing oral sex with Hazel, without her knowing, might constitute nothing short of him being a rapist. He cringes at the thought. Joe would never hurt her. If anything, his instinct now is to protect her.

After towelling down and getting dressed, Joe decides he'll go for a walk, instead of calling Hazel right away.

He heads down to the main beach area, where he can dip his feet in the sandy point, which is between the pier and an area where people often bring their dogs to cool off in the water when the days are hot. Today, it is scorching, with temperatures above 30-degrees. It means that the beach is swarming with visitors.

Joe decides to walk back towards his home, along the shoreline. It quickly becomes quiet, as he exits the main visitor area of town.

He's been strolling along for about a half-kilometre, when Joe spots an old woman, who is also along the shoreline.

She's out throwing a ball into the water. Her dog, who's big with mostly black fur, happily swims out to retrieve. The scene plays itself out again and again and again. It's great exercise for the dog.

When the pleasant stranger notices Joe, and moves towards him to outstretch her hand in greeting, it's clear to him that she has trouble walking. That'd be the reason the dog exercises in the lake, instead of taking walks along the pathway.

"Oh, you startled me, dear boy," the woman smiles, "it's usually so quiet and isolated in this little spot that I found. It's why we come here. Hi. My name is Holly and this is my little dolly. Her name is Saffy."

"Hi Holly," Joe smiles and shakes the woman's hand, "my name is Joe. So, Saffy? That's an unusual name."

"I call her Saffy, which is short for Saffron," the woman finds a moment of joy, an anecdote that she shares with Joe, "my granddaughter laughs when I tell her that saffron is a spice. 'Oh, you live with one of the Spice Girls, she said. I had no idea what she meant, so, my granddaughter played me some of the Spice Girl music, after finding it on her cell phone. Some lively song called *Wannabe*, that my granddaughter says everyone is dancing to, these days. Kids and technology."

Holly doesn't seem very old, maybe she's in her early 70's. It's clear that she enjoys gardening. She's still wearing her gloves. Joe isn't sure if it's to keep her fingernails from getting dirty, or from coming into contact with poison ivy. So much of the noxious weed grows out here, and it's a damn itchy and uncomfortable ordeal, coming into contact with that plant.

Joe knows.

Poison ivy has sent him to the walk-in clinic more than once. Just one touch of the plant develops into having a bad rash, that's so invasive and itchy, it can drive a person insane.

Good for Holly, Joe thinks, gloves are essential when rooting around out here. He also takes note of the sun hat that she wears. It will protect her from the sun's rays, but it won't protect her from Joe, if he feels it's necessary to feed. It's getting to be that time of the day.

"It's just too hot to walk her today, and she loves the lake. I'm just happy that my dog is also one of those to retrieve a ball, as well," the woman gives Joe a smile, "did you want to join in? Saffy loves it when we get company."

Joe takes the ball, and starts the game of fetch. While doing so, the two make small talk about gardening and how both of them are wishing for rain.

"Do you live here at the Beach? I don't remember seeing you around town before," Joe asks.

The woman tells him that she's a seasonal resident, who inherited a cottage along the shoreline.

"It's been in our family for decades," she says, "I remember visiting out here when I was just a girl, it's been that long. Oh my," she stops chatting for a moment, "it's just so hard to believe that the years have travelled by so quickly. My, it seems like just yesterday that I would have been in the lake with my Saffy, instead of standing here on the shore."

Joe can sense that Holly is kind. The wrinkles on her face indicate that as well. She has more laugh lines than frown lines. She smiles even through her pain.

Holly hasn't mentioned to Joe that she is sick, and that it's sometimes excruciating for her to just walk around in her home. But he knows.

There is a smell of medication, coming through her pores. He figures the medicine no longer helps, to alleviate the pain. Her movements are laboured, as she reaches to pick up the ball for Saffy. She gives a little wince. The actual throwing of the ball into the lake is likely even more difficult. It is as though each time she uses a joint, it screams in pain. Still, Holly tries to carry on, as though everything is alright. She is wanting to enjoy her time spent outdoors. It may very well be her last summer.

Joe knows that Holly rejoices in taking in the moments now, because she accepts that soon enough, she'll be bed-ridden and relying on others just to provide basic needs. No one wants that.

Joe knows this.

He is familiar with the smell of stage 3 bone cancer, which hits hard and fast, and is not treatable. He knows about this disease all too well. He watched his favourite uncle, slowly and painfully die from the same. And, he remembers the smell of the medication. The sour reek could be detected, even back then, when he just had the ability of detecting scent in the same way that anyone would.

Joe talks about him to Holly, "You know, right where we are standing now, I remember being here with my uncle. It's the exact spot where we'd go fishing. Uncle Gabriel was like a father to me."

What happens then is so intimate that it surprises Joe. He's never fully admitted to anyone, how devastated he's always felt, witnessing family violence, when he was such a young boy. He tells Holly that it was difficult for him to grow up without a father, although it is preferable to the alternative which would have been growing up with an abusive dad. He tells her that his father was an alcoholic and Joe admits to being an alcoholic today, although he doesn't tell her that he's now a vampire.

Essentially, just being in Holly's presence is like being able to put on some type emotional salve, that soothes and heals. She is one of those rare people who brings out the best in everyone. And, it's also what she offers the world, her best. It's like they are kindred spirits. And, even though they just met, Joe feels like he's known her for a lifetime.

It's why he can't figure out why God causes someone like Holly to endure so much suffering. But, she doesn't complain. She just accepts.

When Joe is finished speaking, he feels exhausted at having unloaded so many hard truths. Holly gives him a big hug. Medication aside, Joe decides that she also smells like Home, which to him is a combination of freshly-baked bread with a tinge of cinnamon. She thanks Joe for trusting her,

"You remind me of my favourite grandson," she says, "he's the one who I can always count on to come over, anytime I need some heavy yard work done, or something repaired around the house." As if Saffy is following the conversation, it's at this very moment that the dog licks Joe's hand. He laughs.

"Saffy! You little stinker," prompting Holly to make a suggestion, "but yes, saffron. I have some in my pantry, Joe. I think I'll cook it up with some rice tonight, after picking some fresh corn. It's grown very well this year, in my back yard. Amazingly, I haven't seen too many deer out lately. Last year, they pretty much ate all of what I planted," she pauses, "you know, young man, you are welcome to come over for dinner, if you wish. I get so tired of eating alone all the time, and, it's always good to host company. Consider yourself a new friend. I've already defrosted some chicken, that we can barbeque and I'll even bake us a rhubarb crumble."

"How lovely," Joe then says, "and how can anyone say no to that offer? Dinner. I'd be delighted. Is there anything that I can bring?" He asks, knowing full well, there will be no dining at this woman's home tonight.

He can smell death, and he can cause death.

Should he perform, what to him, is another act of kindness? No one wants to die in pain. This woman surely will suffer badly, as this disease is allowed to progress. Assisted death? There will be no need for paperwork here.

Joe says a prayer for Holly,

"God speed that she travels well, and without pain, towards all those who have been a part of her life and have loved her. There must have been many. She's shining a light so bright, it looks like the morning sun. If there is such a thing as an Earth Angel, Holly surely is one of them."

Joe will let her endure suffering no more. There's no point. His dark curse can release her pain. He'll do it.

He wonders if Corbitt is watching, as Joe sinks his fangs into the woman's neck, draining her of her life force.

Saffy watches Joe, as he continues to suck, but the dog doesn't react. It's like Saffy somehow knows that there is no threat here. No intent to cause harm, just an act to ease Holly's pain and suffering.

Once she is dead, Joe leaves Holly's body next to the pathway, where he knows someone will find her corpse and call the proper authorities.

He removes Holly's gardening gloves, before putting Saffy on the leash that the woman was holding in her hand, and he says to the dog,

"I guess I will be introducing you to Xavier tonight. I hope the two of you figure out a way to get along."

But, before leaving, Joe picks some brilliantly-coloured wild flowers that grow along the shoreline. He gently places them in Holly's hands. She deserves to leave this earth, clutching beauty. She's at peace now. Joe only wishes that he would have had the opportunity to meet Holly, years earlier. He would have adopted her as his favourite Auntie. And, he wishes that Holly could have met Hazel. They absolutely would have adored each other.

"Dear woman, rest in peace. I hope you soon find yourself dancing to Spice Girl music, up in Heaven which is surely where you are heading. May you be proud of all those beautiful moments that you brought into this world. You will be ravaged by pain no more."

Joe kisses Holly on the forehead, and brushes her soft cheek, before heading back towards his own home.

He also makes a promise that, someday, he'll have a hot dog roast in Holly's memory. No big gesture, just a way to say, 'Thanks for blessing this Earth with your love. And for helping me wade through horrendous memories that have been holding me back and weighing me down."

Somehow, Joe knows that Holly will be there to join him, sitting around that fire.

Slow Dancing

Later that same day, Joe sniffs the pronounced smell of bacon, cooking on the stove, as he gives a slight knock on Hazel's screen door. Bacon was always one of his favourite foods. He's surprised the aroma still sparks a craving, knowing that he can no longer ingest it. But, holy cow, there is never such a thing as a bad piece of bacon. Joe wishes he was still able to eat it, feeling the crunch of goodness, and salty satisfaction, before swallowing.

He sees Saffy's nose twitching for a sniff as well.

Joe's brought the dog with him, figuring it's the least he can do, considering he's the one responsible for taking away the dog's owner, earlier today. Leaving Saffy alone in his house, which she's not familiar with, just didn't feel like the right thing to do. And, he didn't want to take the chance that Saffy might get slashed up by the ferals, if they were brave enough to make their way through the pet door that he's now installed, so Xavier can come and go as he pleases.

Hazel looks rested, and it's clear that she's taken some time in applying fresh make-up, as she answers the door. Joe thinks to himself that Hazel needs no make-up. To him, she's a natural beauty. She tells him that she's taken the night off, from working at the pub, in lieu of the night that she was recently called in, unexpectedly, and disrupting her date with Joe.

"Oh! You brought a dog," she giggles, "is that another gift for me?"

As Joe makes up a lie, saying that he found Saffy wandering by herself along the pathway, he once again feels a twinge of guilt. He's already forced a sexual experience, without Hazel's knowledge, and now he finds himself having to make excuses to cover up the reality of what he's just done. She is spending time with a killer, and doesn't even know it. He can't even imagine how Hazel might react when he fesses-up to what he's become. It will break his heart, if she rejects him, if he even has a heart anymore, . She has become the centre of his life, or what life he now finds himself wading in. But, she's the only light that he knows, the only light he's ever known, in terms of a romantic interest.

Hazel knows his past, and seems willing to give Joe a second chance. He longs to take it.

Is it time to confess? Again, Joe wonders. It's something he asks himself on a daily basis. He just can't seem to let go of that deep-ceded fear that she'll abandon him. The words that he longs to say and finally tell the truth, remain glued to the tip of his tongue. He's afraid to say, I love you, because he can't be sure how she'll respond.

"What a pretty girl," Hazel says, patting Saffy on the head, "both of you, come on in. I'm cooking us some breakfast."

"Breakfast?" Joe asks.

"Why not?" Hazel says, "It occurs to me that you and I have never enjoyed pancakes and bacon before. You always say that you are too busy in the morning to meet me. I'll fry up some eggs, too."

Joe finds himself inflicting another charade upon Hazel's perception, as he uses his power of persuasion into having her think that she's watching him eat the meal that she's prepared. Bacon, eggs and pancakes with maple syrup and whipped cream. While, in reality, he's placed the plate of food on the floor for the dog to eat.

When will the lying stop? This is no way to begin a new relationship.

While Hazel enjoys her pancakes, the conversation turns to talking about Saffy. She's a big girl, covered in thick fur. Hazel jokes that Saffy looks like a bear, but guesses she might be part Border Collie because there are white markings on the dog's tummy and paws. "She reminds me of an Oreo cookie," Hazel giggles.

"I'll grab my Nikon, after we eat," she says, "I'll take a photo of Saffy. And I have a printer. We can make up some posters to put around town. If anyone's missing her, maybe they'll see it and she'll find her way back home. Meantime, if you're not up to keeping her, Joe, she can stay with me. I've always loved dogs. In fact, I've thought about getting one, myself. She'd be good protection, and right now with so many dead bodies randomly showing up around town, I'd feel more safe."

Again, Joe feels the prick of guilt, knowing that he's the one responsible for recent, unexplained deaths in the community. He shakes the feeling away, by agreeing with Hazel's idea. Saffy will stay with her.

Once the meal is finished and the dishes are done, Hazel, Joe and Saffy make the trek around town. Joe marvels at Hazel's sense of caring, as he watches her pin up the posters that say:

If you have lost your dog, we have her.

The notification has a photo of Saffy, and gives other contact information. Once at the grocery store, Hazel pins the poster up right next to other announcements about upcoming garage sales, and fundraising bake sales. There are a few more community announcement billboards around town, so they will visit all of them.

Hazel cares, always helping out wherever and whenever she is able. That's obvious again, in these moments. It's one of the many reasons that Joe loves her, although he hasn't found the courage to tell her yet.

Joe is heartened that, before heading out with the "Lost Dog" posters, Hazel filled up a wicker basket. Her garden is bountiful this summer, and she's already started sharing the harvest. Her garden produced more than enough Swiss chard for her own needs. She's giving away the rest, to any neighbour who happens to be out in their yard, as the couple walks by with the dog. She's sharing the gift of food, because she can.

While walking back home, Hazel makes a comment about how beautiful the sunset is tonight. The sky is pink.

"What is that saying?" she asks, "Red sky at night, a sailor's delight. Red sky in the morning, sailor's take warning?"

Her comment gives Joe pause, making him wonder if Hazel is suggesting intimacy this evening. A delight. If he's reading her correctly, Joe is happy to oblige in romantic touch, this time, with her consent.

When they return to Hazel's home, the dog takes a spot on her couch. It's been a good, long walk. Saffy is tired and still full of pancakes and bacon.

Hazel puts on a CD of Gordon Lightfoot's greatest hits. When the song, *Beautiful*, begins to play, Joe takes Hazel by the hand. He holds her tight to chest, as they sway to the music.

> *At times, I just don't know, how you could be*
> *anything but beautiful*
> *I think that I was made for you*
> *and you were made for me.*

It's a feeling of warmth and belonging for Joe. How he wishes that he'd not wasted so many years, being drunk, before getting to know Hazel like this. Although, Joe figures the Lightfoot song that best describes his own life is more likely to be the song, *Race Among The Ruins*.

> *If you plan to face tomorrow, do it soon.*

Then, another reality makes its way into Joe's memory. The last time he slow-danced was with Mrs. Carter, only moments before he drained her.

But, Joe still holds no remorse for doing so. In his mind, that too, was an act of love.

Into the Night

By the next evening, Hazel has outdone herself. When Joe comes to call, he's greeted at the door by Saffy, who wags her tail and licks his hand. The dog probably knows, but doesn't seem to mind that he's a vampire. Again, the fragrance wafting out through the screen door, makes Joe's mouth water. When he goes in, it's little wonder why.

Hazel has roasted lamb this evening. She bought it at the farmer's market just yesterday, so it is as fresh as fresh can be. There is a big bowl of garlic mashed potatoes on the counter, with a pot filled with gravy on the stove top. Rounding it off is a a magnificent-looking salad, topped with strawberries and toasted almonds, and of course, cobs of fresh corn that Hazel has already slathered in butter. She's grown the corn in her garden.

Hazel has often remarked to Joe that each meal is a celebration.

She tells him that food is a joy for her to prepare, knowing that the effort will make someone happy. Special meals, like Thanksgiving and Christmas dinners, are great, but for Hazel, it's the everyday meals that say a lot. It's why she doesn't eat fast foods very often, unless it's made on the barbeque or over a fire. It's also the reason that she slow-cooks most of what she prepares. The main ingredient in all her dishes, is love, and that's what she's serving up for Joe tonight.

It is a feast indeed, and a feast for the eyes. Joe wishes he could indulge, but knows he'll have to resort to his usual trick of making Hazel believe that he's dining, when all he really does is push his food around on the plate with his fork.

She's gone to so much effort, in preparing this lovely, romantic meal. She's also taken the time to get herself ready. She's wearing a sheer, full-length sundress. It's light blue with some floral pattern along the hemline. And, she put on her favourite beaded earrings, that were made by Kohkum. Joe has mentioned, in the past, that she looks very pretty when she wears her hair up, so that's how it's coiffed this evening, showing off her delicate neck and shoulders. Joe counts his lucky stars that he's managed to gain the attention of such a beauty, wishing he could hold on to this very moment for the rest of his life.

He considers that maybe tonight is the night to come clean and finally admit to her that she isn't dating just some regular guy-next-door.

But something seems off.

Hazel is restless tonight, fidgeting with her hair and breathing heavy sighs. Joe knows that it can no longer be that she suffers from menstrual cramps. He took care of that the other night. He sucked out all of the fibroids that were hurting her, and he was amazed at how many came out. It was like dining at a smorgasbord, with way too much food. Joe has to ask.

"This meal is the best I've ever had. Thank you," Joe begins, "but you seem upset. Have I done anything wrong?"

"There's nothing wrong," Hazel says, then admits, "it's just that, well, I love you Joe, and I don't know if you feel the same way about me. I was hesitant to say anything, but I just can't keep these feelings to myself anymore."

He puts down his fork, and advances to her side of the kitchen table.

"Hazel, you are the most beautiful thing on God's green earth. I've loved you for months, but just didn't know how to say it, so I tried to show it instead. I put that heart-shaped rock that you gave me, right on my bedside table, so that I think of you the first thing when waking up each day. You are always the last thought on my mind too, before falling asleep. I love you too, Hazel. Loving you is the only thing that makes sense in this world."

He takes her by the hand, and it is Hazel who leads Joe to her bedroom. She's been waiting long enough. She unzips the pretty sundress that she's wearing. Joe watches as the light chiffon material floats down towards her wooden floor. This is the moment that Joe has been dreaming about, seeing Hazel's slender body, naked. He kisses her, clutching her soft breasts. In her excitement, her nipples have grown hard. Joe lovingly caresses them with his hands, then puts his tongue on her nipples, so he can begin to suck. Hazel moans, and begins to undo the zipper on his jeans. He wants to do it himself, knowing it would be faster to get the pants off, but he'll be patient, allowing Hazel to explore as she wishes. If his skin is cool to touch, Hazel doesn't notice. Her own body temperature is already rising, and she's starting to sweat,

"Make love to me," she whispers.

Joe gently picks her up, and once again, places her head on the pillow. His penis throbs and he'd like nothing more than to enter her. But, he'll wait, wanting this night of passion to be forever implanted as part of Hazel's memory. Joe moves his tongue towards the middle of her breasts, and runs it slowly down her ribcage. He suckles the fleshy domain of her inner thighs, and for the second time, his tongue enjoys licking her Bird of Paradise. Joe clutches her buttocks, so that Hazel won't be able to wiggle, as he begins to suck on her clitoris.

It's ecstasy for her. Joe can taste her milky fluid, as she comes to orgasm. But he's not finished.

It is Hazel who guides Joe into her body, pulling with force. When he's on top of her, she wraps her legs about him, and grabs his ass so that he might be able to thrust harder. He wants to come, but uses whatever self-control he can muster to make this moment last.

Joe can tell by the sound of her breathing that Hazel is ready to orgasm again. One more hard movement, and the two reach satisfied frenzy together.

Hazel begins to cry, "I love you, Joe. Hold me."

He lays down beside her, and strokes her hair, then he embraces her in a way that ensures, these moments were not just about a sexual experience. He's tender, wanting Hazel to feel safe.

She falls asleep in his arms.

Reap What You Sow

Joe has no feelings of guilt, as he leaves Hazel's bed, and he goes tip-toeing towards the front door so that he can leave. She's told him that she's a heavy sleeper, and judging by the soft snoring sounds coming from the bedroom, Joe isn't worried that he'll wake her.

Joe needs to feed.

He decides to take Saffy with him, grabbing her leash to go for a late-night walk.

Rather than taking the time, to wander the streets or walk down the pathway, and wait, Joe figures he'll go right to the source. It's closing time down at the bar. There will surely be people leaving, who shouldn't be driving home. Joe plans to make sure, that tonight, they won't be in any shape to drive after he's done feeding on them.

As he walks, Joe replays in his mind, the beauty of what he's just shared with Hazel. But, that tender moment of memory comes to a violent end, as he spots two men, kicking someone in the parking lot at the bar. A man is on the pavement, and it's clear that he's badly hurt.

"That's what you get for coming around here, you faggot," one of the assailant's yells.

"Yea," says the other, delivering a boot to the victim's groin area, "go back to where you came from, you ugly Indian."

Joe can see that the man on the ground is in critical condition. He isn't moving, yet the two thugs continue with their assault. When one of the abusers takes a jackknife from the upper pocket of the jacket he's wearing, Joe knows, it's time to step in.

Joe doesn't know if these two plan on stabbing the victim, or if they were planning on cutting the man's hair. Joe can tell that, whoever was on the ground, is likely to be First Nations. He's wearing a braid. Maybe these assholes are planning to cut his braid, and keep it, like some sort of trophy. Something they can brag about later on. Fucking, racist bastards.

"We kicked the shit out of him!"

What sort of victory is that? High-jacking someone, two on one, and for no good reason other than this man's skin is brown.

Racist punks. Joe decides that he will take them down, hard.

He moves quickly, and is standing directly behind one of the assholes', when the other notices.

"Who the fuck are you?" the punk yells, while spittle flies from his mouth, "you just fuck off, eh. This is none of your business, otherwise, you're gonna get it next."

"Who's going to get it?" Joe calmly asks, a moment before he grabs the man by the neck, breaking it, as though it's nothing more than a twig. The other clutches the knife hard, and begins to run. Joe is right behind him, grabbing his shoulders and yanking him to the pavement. His plan is to pierce his jugular immediately, but he thinks differently, just before doing so. Instead, Joe plants a harsh kick to the man's groin, delivering another to his ribcage. Just like this deadbeat did to the man on the ground. As the goon begins writhing in pain, Joe bites. He lets the abuser suffer for a bit, just so he knows how it feels to be assaulted so violently. Minutes later, it's over, and both men lay dead.

The dog has been the only witness, and she didn't react one way or the other, to what's been going on.

Joe collects the car keys from one of the man's pocket. He'll keep them as a reminder. He then moves their bodies towards a nearby boat launch, where he dumps them on the rocks, beside the lake. A stretch of shoreline where the water kisses the land. If anything, someone might believe that the two killed each other in a drunken rage. The man who was earlier holding the knife, still has it in his hand. It's like having his neck, violently yanked and broken, caused the nerves and reflexes in his hand to buckle.

Joe checks the victim who has been beaten. He still lays on the ground and is obviously in need of medical attention, by a professional. His breathing is laboured and the man is bleeding from the head. Joe doesn't feel right, just leaving him, where he was senselessly assaulted by the hooligans. He wanders back towards the bar, where the head waitress is just about to turn the dead bolt, locking up for the night,

"Hey, I'm sorry. We're closed," she says.

That's when Joe explains that, he was just out walking his dog, when he found someone injured, "You need to call an ambulance," Joe says, "he looks to be badly hurt." Joe waits for the paramedics to arrive, before walking back towards home. There's no need for Joe to make any kind of statement to police. He tells them that he saw nothing, and that he found the victim laying on the pavement, while he out, walking the dog and minding his own business. By chance, he came across someone in need of help. Joe feels satisfied that the man will now receive the proper medical attention that he requires. He hopes he'll be alright.

Joe isn't too worried about leaving the other bodies by the boat launch. The corpses are visible enough, he knows someone will find them in the morning.

But, he wonders about the warning that Corbitt gave, the Jumper that showed up after Joe took mercy on Mrs. Carter.

Be careful about how you dispose of the dead. The Unnatural ones can smell it.

Joe figures that it is only a matter of time before he knows what that warning means. That time is now.

As he walks through the darkened streets, Joe sees

something approaching. It is not a someone. The figure is too large, with a thick, muscular body. It's Bushman, the Being that others might refer to as Sasquatch.

Joe's instinct races towards flight or fight. He's only fully transformed his appearance once before. That happened when he met Corbitt.

It happens again now. Joe's hands change, looking more like claws with extended fingers and long fingernails. He's ready to take on the challenge of battle, but there's no need.

Bushman hardly glances at Joe, when he passes him, while Joe is also walking along the road. Saffy doesn't react at all. It's like she just enjoys being along for the ride, and meeting Unnaturals is part of that. It is no big deal for her, and because she is a dog, without any sin, she never has to worry about harm and bad intention. God did a good job in creating animals. They are pure.

Joe senses that the creature has no intention of causing a ruckus, with him. Bushman is heading towards the area where Joe's left the dead bodies, in the parking lot near the lake front. He wonders if Bushman plans to eat them right where the bodies were dumped, or if he'll drag them off somewhere, for a snack at some later date. Bushman's footsteps are not silent, like Joe's. Instead, the brute sort of shuffles, as part of his elongated gait. As he passes, Joe catches his scent. It's like a combination of stinky, wet dog, and rotting old leaves, raked into a pile in autumn. Bushman's breath is laboured, the same way someone would wheeze if they suffered from a bad cold. He briefly meets Joe's eye, and lets out a grunt.

There's been no confrontation between the two Unnaturals. Joe assumes that Corbitt is watching somewhere, but puts it out of his mind and continues walking towards home.

Hazel should still be sleeping.

A light rain begins, as Joe walks. Again, he wonders if it's enough to wash him clean. He killed two tonight, and even through their hateful act, he wonders if he did the right thing. This time, it was outright murder that he committed, and there will be no rationalizing away that fact.

Joe is a cold-blooded killer.

Afterglow

Joe decides to let the feelings of guilt slide. He feels confident that all turmoil is now behind him, and it's a future with Hazel that he will build.

He'll start tomorrow, by introducing her to places along the shoreline.

A while back, he discovered a private area, right at the water's edge, that is perfect for swimming. It's where he wants to take her, later in the afternoon, and once the sun has risen to a point in the day where it's safe for him to go out.

Hazel is still lightly snoring when Joe arrives back at her home. He pats the dog on the head, before turning in himself. It takes only a minute, after he locks her door and climbs into bed, that he falls into a deep sleep. He's holding Hazel, the same as he did before he went out to feed.

Just before sunrise, Joe he wakes early and feels bad about having to lie to her again.

As he is gently placing a kiss on her forehead, Hazel wakes up. She is surprised to find that Joe is already fully dressed and planning to leave. She asks him, why. They'd just spent hours, exploring each other as lovers. Leaving so early in the morning doesn't make sense to her.

"Oh, no need to worry, I'll be back later," Joe says, "I should have mentioned to you earlier that the boys and I are planning to head out on the lake this morning. Dawn is the best time to catch whitefish. They like to bite early, so we're meeting down at the dock in the next half hour," he touches Hazel's hair, "If I catch something, I'll clean it up and bring it over for dinner tonight. I'll even barbecue it myself. Go back to sleep, my beauty."

Hazel closes her eyes, with Joe's reassurance that he isn't leaving because he feels uncomfortable. He's made plans to go fishing with the boys. Her light breathing indicates that she's already fallen back into slumber. Joe pulls the blanket up over her shoulders, before he leaves.

The truth is, Joe didn't want to be at Hazel's home during the morning hours. He figures that she is likely to suggest again, that the two of them go out for breakfast, or that they take an early morning walk. He could never risk that. Telling a fib is easier, which delivers a sad reminder for Joe. This behaviour is no different than when he would constantly tell lies, living as an alcoholic. Anytime he wanted to get out of a difficult situation, or, if he needed to borrow money to buy more booze, he'd just make up a lie.

Joe keeps his word about bringing a fish for dinner, though. He does so by calling up a buddy who he knows was out fishing yesterday. He offers to make a trade: a six-pack of beer for a whitefish. Joe will have to head down to the liquor store again, but he figures that's probably a good thing, in terms of keeping up appearances. For years, he's been one of their best customers too. No one needs to know that the brewskis aren't for him today.

It's 4 o'clock when Joe meets up with Hazel again, for their afternoon rendezvous of frolicking in the lake. Hazel looks breath-taking. She's pulled her long hair back, into a ponytail and she's wearing a hot pink bikini. The slender curvature of her body reminds Joe of some statuesque bronze sculpture. Her smile indicates glee. Joe thinks she's like a little kid, as she spends a few minutes blowing up a triangular-shaped floatie device, that's decorated like a piece of pizza.

She hands Joe a few small rocks that she's painted. They are oval-shaped, and Hazel's coloured them red, with black spots, to make them look like Lady Bugs.

"I've been leaving painted rocks along the pathway for years," she says, "it's something I used to do with Kohkum. This is so great to think that another tradition will continue, this time with you. I love our time together, Joe."

There is no dawdling to be had. Joe puts the whitefish that he's brought into Hazel's refrigerator. He grabs Saffy's leash, and a bottle of Gatorade that Hazel's left on the table by her front door. The time for another adventure begins.

While they are walking, down at the pathway by the lake, they come across the very spot where Joe remembers waking up, that first morning after being turned by Dust Man. It's the one of the many times that he's felt regret, knowing what he's become. He watches, as Hazel stoops to pick some of the brilliant yellow flowers from the goldenrod plant, that grows in abundance at the side of the path. He loves her zest for life, when she tells him,

"Kohkum and I used to pick this," Hazel says her grandmother would dry the plant, and use it anytime the little Hazel would come down with a cold or a flu, "she'd boil it into a tea, and it didn't take very long before I was feeling better. Oh, I miss her. She told me that it was her gift to pass down plant knowledge." Hazel gathers up an armful of the plants as she and Joe continue to walk. She wraps the goldenrod, that she's picked, in her beach towel.

Passing down knowledge, Hazel's story gives his heart a tug, and Joe finds himself again wishing that he'd become sober years earlier. Maybe he and Hazel could have had a family together by now. A life filled with love, instead of the sorrow that Joe has chosen over these many years of being alone, with a bottle in one hand and faint dreams in the other.

Hazel has made his dreams come true now. His prayers for finding love have been answered. She is his shelter from the storm. But, how can they make it work? Joe can't even face the sunlight. He wonders if her light for him might dim, once she knows what he's become.

She interrupts Joe's train of thought, remarking about the beauty of a flock of pelicans that soars overhead. Joe knows, because Hazel has told him, that seeing pelicans signals a need for focus and persistence. It carries a message that abundance and a bounty of joy are about to arrive. It is Joe's wish for he and Hazel.

There is no wind today, and the lake is calm, looking like a mirror. A reflection on which Joe finds the need to ruminate.

Joe is determined that he'll find the courage to tell Hazel soon. The pelicans arrived with a signal that it's time to come clean. He needs to tell her, that he has a dark secret that he can only pray that she will accept.

A Little Misstep

By the following day, Joe has convinced himself that he's finally worked up the courage to confide, unearthing the unknown, to the most important person in his life. He is determined that enough time has passed. He'll tell her that he is no longer human. Hazel has a right to know, and today is the day.

He'll suggest that they take a long walk, to some public place outdoors, where it is less likely that Hazel might feel trapped or unsafe, once Joe breaks the news that she's dating a vampire. He can't even take a guess at how she might react.

A strange thought occurs to him. What happens if she asks to see his fangs? It would mean transformation, and he'd be forced to show her the entire package, of pointy ears and long fingers, a puffy face and protruded forehead. Joe hopes it doesn't come to that. He doesn't want her to see him like that, ever.

He knows that Hazel is working the day shift today, so he's got about another hour to figure out how to arrange his wording, somehow gently, so that she isn't frightened or startled. In his mind, he keeps going over what opening words he might use.

Have you ever seen one of those movies?
I have something difficult to tell you that's hard to explain.

Here, you might want to sit down before hearing this.
How would you react if you found out that I am not
the person that you think I am?

As he ponders on those opening lines, Joe trashes all
of the above, figuring most of them sound like he's going to
confess that he's married.

The hour passes quickly, and Joe picks up the phone,

"Hey Beautiful, if you aren't too tired, what do you
say we go for a walk tonight? Maybe even visit the ice cream
place, before it closes for the season?"

Hazel is happy to oblige and suggests that the two
meet up at the treat shop on the main street,

"I'll get Saffy's collar on and meet you there in about
20 minutes. Sound good?"

Soon, the dog is wagging her tail, so vigorously that
her entire back end sways like a flag on a pole, when Saffy
spots Joe in the distance. It may be that she's happy to see him,
but more likely it's because the dog knows that Joe always
buys her a puppy sundae. At least that has been the routine,
each time he's walked her and they happen to pass by the ice
cream shop. The treat for dogs consists of a bit of ice cream
surrounded by 3 or more dog biscuits. She loves it.

Hazel gives Joe a quick kiss, and says, "Did you want
to order? My treat." Joe decides it's easier to order something
rather than try to trick her, as he so often does, "How about
a rootbeer float," he suggests. Hazel smiles and squeezes him
by the hand, while they wait in the line up.

It's a busy evening and it takes about 15 minutes before Hazel is at the front of the line. As she puts in an order,
Joe does his best to not fidget, instead he keeps his eye on the
menu board, making comments about how amazed he is that
there are so many flavours of ice cream available.

He still doesn't know what wording he will use to
break the news to Hazel. He glances her way and it causes
him to smile. Joe notices that Hazel has just pulled her bank
card from her cleavage. Again, he wonders why she doesn't
just carry a purse, seems like it would make things easier. But
she is also physically carrying something today.

It's a cloth bag, which is slung over her shoulder. Joe asks why. She tells him that it's filled with books that she's already read,

"I was planning to walk up to that little library at the top of the hill. You know the one, it looks like a small cupboard, with a glass window, so that the books are protected from the weather. There's a sign that says, leave a book, take a book. I wander up there all the time," she takes a book from her bag, and shows Joe, "I have finished reading all of these, so I wanted to go up and leave these ones, then take a look at what else might be available."

"Sounds good to me," Joe replies, "but here, let me take the bag. It looks to be bulky, and maybe even heavy."

"My handsome gentleman," Hazel responds. She gives the bag to Joe, then turns her attention to the tiger-tiger flavoured ice cream that she ordered. While they walk, Joe pretends to sip his rootbeer float, all the while making comments about how good it tastes. As they walk by a garbage can, he throws the large cup in the trash. He asks her about her work day, then he lets Hazel do all the talking.

She tells him about customers who came into the pub earlier in the day, and one couple who brought their six-year-old daughter in for lunch. They are out-of-towners, and just visiting the lake for a few days. It's the kids' birthday, and because she's not at home with her friends, they let her order anything she wanted on the menu,

"Oh my Lord, you should have seen her, Joe," Hazel glows with happiness, as she continues to describe, "the kid loves pizza and she ordered every combination that we have on the menu. Needless to say, they all went home with a ton of leftovers. It was a good day."

Before long, the couple arrives at the little library structure. Hazel stretches out her right arm, and motions with her lips, towards Joe's arm. She asks him for the cloth bag so that she can donate the books that she wants to leave for someone else. Once she finishes arranging them, and leaving them on the shelves, she says,

"Now, let's see what else is in here. Oh look! I was hoping I'd find a cookbook."

Joe glances at the title of the book, and he can't figure out why Hazel seems so excited. He knows how she cooks, and she loves her meat, especially wild meat. It's as though she can read his thoughts, and she bursts out laughing,

"Yes, I know it's for vegetarian dishes," Hazel giggles, "I've heard that joke too, you know. What do you call an Indigenous vegetarian? Answer, a bad hunter. I have an uncle who just loves that joke. But practically, this is a good book for me. I'll be taking my garden off, for the season, soon enough. I can't remember the last time I had such an abundant harvest, and I mean for all the varieties of vegetables that I planted this year. I may as well get ideas for some new recipes."

Hazel is excited. So much so that she's turning the pages hurriedly. She's not paying attention to the dog, who is still on the leash that attaches to her wrist. Saffy sees a squirrel, running towards a nearby tree, and the dog lunges forward ever so slightly for a closer look. This causes a shift, with the book that Hazel balances in one hand. It falls. She tries catching it before it hits the ground, but in that fraction of a second of trying to grab, she gets a paper cut instead.

It's a deep but clean gash, that leaves her right index finger bleeding,

"Ouch!" she says, then instinctively puts the tip of her finger in her mouth, "wow, this is bleeding fast. Joe, do you have anything, like a tissue?"

He doesn't, instead suggesting to Hazel that he will run across the road, to the gas station, and pick up some napkins. That takes a matter of minutes, and when he returns, the bleeding has slowed somewhat. While he was gone, Hazel covered the small wound with a leaf. She told him that the sap on the leaf will help to cauterize the wound.

"Does it still hurt?" he asks her.

"Just a bit," she says, and takes one of the napkins that Joe's retrieved, "it's nothing serious. In fact, what will make it better is a kiss, like Kohkum used to do when I was a kid. She'd give my boo-boo a kiss to make it better. Here," Hazel holds her bloody finger up towards Joe's face, but his reaction startles her.

In the flash of a second, Joe turns away and places his hands, to cover his face. At the sight of her blood, Joe feels the sensation of unpleasant tingling. He thinks of the pain as being the same type of unexpected shock that anyone would feel, after stubbing their toe: hard, unexpectedly and without warning. When Hazel asks, what's wrong, he lies, telling her that an aphid just flew into his eye.

"Oh, those damn, little bugs this time of year," she says, "but don't worry. It happens all the time. Just keep your eyes closed for a minute or so, and it'll work its way out."

As Joe stands there, still covering his face, he begins to panic. The smell of her bloody finger has caused him to start transforming. He can feel his eye-teeth begin to elongate into sharp and deadly fangs.

It doesn't help that Hazel keeps insisting that Joe kiss her boo-boo. Once again, she holds her bloody finger up, close towards his face.

He can't chance it. Instead, Joe quickly turns away from Hazel, and he starts to run in the opposite direction. All the while, he's yelling to her, "I'm sorry, this really stings my eye. I can feel it squirming! I've got to get home and grab some Visine."

He leaves Hazel and Saffy just standing there, abandoned in bewilderment, at the top of the street. It leaves her feeling foolish. She reaches down to grab the fallen cookbook from the sidewalk, puts it into her cloth bag, and stomps down towards her home, which is just off to the side of main street.

While walking, a few tears are shed, with Hazel thinking that she doesn't want to spend time with Joe anymore. Her thoughts cascade, like we've been intimate so many times, he's seen me naked, I've welcomed him into my life, what the hell was that all about? He ditched me!

By the time she reaches her home, the telephone is ringing. Hazel guesses that it is probably Joe.

She doesn't answer.

On Weathering the Storm

By the next morning, Hazel finds that she still feels miffed. True, it was her decision to not take his call last night, but it worries her that she hasn't heard from Joe since. Has he rejected her? It begins a series of thoughts, with Hazel wondering if she should have followed Joe home, to make sure he was alright, instead of storming straight to her own house instead. Maybe she should have answered his phone call? What if he thinks of her as being too dramatic now, over something that happened that, really, was just so minor? A paper cut.

Second-guessing. It rarely leads to anything good, and more often, it always jumps to a wrong conclusion. She checks her clock, only to realize that she's slept in today. That shouldn't surprise her. She tossed and turned most of the night, before finally falling into a fitful slumber. That aside, it is time to get up. She has responsibilities, and the first one is staring her straight in the eye. Saffy has become accustomed to being walked, even before Hazel has her morning coffee, or mediation.

A beautiful day greets her as she opens the door. The sun is bright, there is no wind, but most importantly, she finds a gift on her doorstep, along with a note from Joe.

I'm so sorry that I left you in such a rush last night. That bug really was hurting my eye, but that isn't the real reason I hurried away. This sounds like an excuse, but it isn't. I have this terrible aversion to the sight of blood.

When I saw your finger bleeding, I could feel my stomach start to well. It's happened before at the sight of blood, to the point that I actually threw up. I know that sounds gross, but I didn't want to do that in front of you. So I fled.

Please forgive me. I love you and hope we can work this all out, later today.

All my love,
Joe.

Joe is lying again, about his reaction to seeing blood, but at this point, Hazel doesn't know this and she finds it in her heart to accept his explanation. Some people do suffer from unusual phobias.

Joe experiences a feeling of guilt again, at not being honest with Hazel. It's as though, all his adult life, he's been picking at his own scabs, so that they don't heal. The scar serves as a constant reminder of all the wrongs that he's done in the past.

Again, he promises himself that he will tell Hazel about his predicament, today. But as with past behaviour, it may very well be a promise that he won't find a way to keep.

Alongside the note is another lovely bouquet of flowers. Finding it lifts Hazel's spirit, and she exhales, as though a way to get rid of bad feelings. Can she forgive him?

The answer is yes.

First fights are a natural course for any new couple, and this one was so childish because the whole thing was based on nothing of real importance. There was no real conflict. At least, this is how Hazel sees it. She blames herself for not being more sensible. She remembers Kohkum's advice, to carry herself with kindness, and to not be quick to condemn or be judgemental of others. You can't always know their story.

She admits, to herself, that her reaction may have been extreme and juvenile, and that the punishment of silence doesn't fit the crime. Joe didn't abandon her. He just can't handle the sight of blood, she tells herself.

Although, she has no way of knowing the real reason that Joe made such a marked escape. He started transforming at the sight of her blood. Fangs started to protrude at the smell of her blood, as Hazel kept sticking her bleeding finger right under his nose. It's something she'll never know.

When Hazel returns from walking the dog, it is she who makes the first phone call of the day. Joe answers on the first ring. It's because he's been waiting by the phone, all night and now, into the morning. He didn't even take the time to go out and feed. He's relieved to hear the sound of her voice.

"Are you okay?" Hazels asks.

"I'm good now that you've called," Joe responds, "and I am so sorry that I just up and ran away like I did. But, puking right there on the sidewalk, and right in front of you, is something that I just never want you to see." He pauses, "Are we okay?"

The remainder of their conversation is conciliatory. Hazel invites him to come over. Joe agrees, saying he'll be there in a couple of hours.

Before that time, he gets in his car and makes a trip to nearby Lumsden. There is a florist located there.

During one of their recent conversations, Joe remembers Hazel telling him about her high school prom night. She'd been the valedictorian, and graduated with honours, but she didn't have a date for the dance. He'd developed a case of the stomach flu, which took him out of the mix. But, that wasn't Hazel's regret for the night.

It was the flowers.

She's always loved the idea of a wrist corsage, talking about how special it would be to wear pretty flowers on her wrist. It's something that she has always wanted to do, but has never done.

Today is the day that will happen.

Joe waits while the floral designer fashions together a wrist corsage of vibrant red roses, mixed in with the delicate, white baby's breath flowers and limonium, which is also known as sea lavenders. All of it is presented with just a touch of greenery and tied together with a soft pink ribbon. While hanging out there, Joe notices some rose-scented bubble bath, deciding to pick that up as well. It's a beautiful thought that he'll share in taking a bath with Hazel later today. He figures, may as well put out the suggestion by bringing her the bubble bath.

Floral artistry takes some time, so instead of continuing to wait, Joe suggests that he'll step out for a minute and grab a cappuccino at the coffee house next door.

Once out in that little corner of a marketplace, he sees that a new business has opened. It is a deli. He decides to pop his head in, figuring that maybe it'll have the items needed to put together a romantic charcuterie platter. Hazel adores cheese, any kind of cheese. He knows that she also enjoys gherkins, black olives and sour dough breads. The shop has it all, and while Joe is making a few selections, he also comes across a locally-produced bottle of ice wine. Hazel has mentioned that she likes the taste of the sweet dessert wine. It is his pleasure to charge it all to his Visa card, before he begins the journey back to the Beach.

There is promise is in the air. Joe can smell it. Or, maybe it is the salami that he just bought at the deli. Whatever the case, he's feeling hopeful and happy.

His Mother's Ring

There is no gentle way to break the news that you no longer walk as one of the living. By the next morning, Joe gives Hazel a soft kiss, as he gets ready to leave her home, again before dawn. He doesn't know what type of excuse he'll come up with this time, for leaving her after another night of passion. She doesn't wake up, as he quietly gets dressed, so he leaves another note.

> I love you, my sweet beauty, and
> I'm sorry I had to leave early again this morning.
> Chad's got me doing inventory, down at the cafe,
> and he wants it done before we open for breakfast.
> 'll call later, my Love xoxox

Joe reaches his home just before sunrise. Xavier is waiting. The cat allows Joe to pat him on the head, knowing that he'll be fed now. Joe takes a plastic baggie out of his backpack. He's filled it with the barbecued whitefish.

Joe didn't feed last night, instead he ended up spending the night, holding Hazel. He wants his thoughts of love to provide enough nourishment, but it doesn't. He still needs blood.

He decides there is a bit of time, before sunrise. It's enough time for him to find someone passed out along the trail, after they've had a long night of too much imbibing. It happens everyday. He should know. He's found himself at that very place in the past.

The first person, who Joe notices along the pathway, looks to be one of those power-walkers. He can't help but think, it's still so early, the sun hasn't even risen yet. Why is she out, by herself, at this hour? There are no witnesses, should anything happen. It's not safe.

He could have easily taken her down that very moment. Even though, she's obviously looking after her health, it's clear she isn't looking after her safety. The woman is walking-and-texting, which in these moments, are just as dangerous as driving-and-texting. She is totally unaware of her surroundings. But, Joe decides not to stop her. He lets her pass, without the knowledge that she's just circumvented disaster. And, only by his good grace, which has never been much to count on, in the past.

He decides that he'll wait, instead, for his usual prey, of someone who has passed out along the pathway, after a night of too much partying.

As history repeats itself, Joe comes across a man, who obviously tried riding home on his bicycle last night. The pathway is not lit, and it is pitch-black after dark, so it's not easy to manoeuvre. This bloke, drunk as a skunk, slid right off the trail and drove his bike down the bluff. Joe finds him, uninjured and now sleeping it off, at the bottom of a rocky slope. Joe sinks his fangs, but not before removing the red bandana that his man wears around his neck. He tucks the cloth into his pocket. He won't kill on this day. The man has done no harm, other than to himself and he'll find that he's waking up with bruising in the morning, from hitting the rocky surface, when he comes to. Joe drinks, then stops when he knows it's time to do so. He can still hear the man's heart beating. He'll leave him to rest, and to nurse, what's sure to be, a giant hangover.

Before leaving, Joe glances up towards the trees. He wonders if Corbitt is watching.

Joe needs to rest after he feeds, kind of like falling asleep after eating a big, Thanksgiving, turkey meal. He heads back home, and falls into his bed, but not before pulling the heavy window shades that blocks out the sun. And, for the first time in a long time, Joe has a dream.

> They are at a playground, and Joe watches as Hazel pushes a little girl who's playing on the swing.
> The child has Hazel's features, of long, brown hair and a delicate, oval-shaped face. There are squeals of playful joy and the girl keeps yelling, "Higher! Higher!"
> Then, she looks towards Joe, saying, "Daddy, can you help?
> Mommy doesn't know how to push me, as good as you do."

Joe wakes up, wondering if his dream was a scene of something that might have been, or if it's just something that he wishes that could have been, at some long-ago-forgotten point in time. It hurts him, in this moment, to admit to himself that he allowed his life to amount to nothing more than waiting for the off-sale to open, so that he could buy more booze.

He rubs his face, again, feeling a sense of regret. If he'd only made the effort to embrace sobriety instead of constantly nursing a bottle, how different everything would be today. Living the dream, instead of just having them surface, during heavy sleep.

It's at this precious moment that Joe makes a decision.

He gets up, and starts rooting through a dresser drawer. It's the place where Joe has stored memory: old photographs, a copy of his university degree, an old rosary that he used to pray with, long ago, in the days when he was a boy at church. But, what he's searching for holds even more significance. He finds it, pulling a weathered jewellery box from the hiding place, amongst other items in the drawer. Joe opens the box, and in it is his Mother's old wedding ring. It is a white gold band, and instead of one large diamond, the ring catches the eye because of it's being unique. It is a large emerald, surrounded by three small diamonds on each side.

Even though the marriage relationship, for his Mother, was a disaster, she kept the ring. She wore it every day. Joe remembers how sad he felt, taking it off her finger, after her death, and while he was helping to prepare his Mother's body for cremation.

He wonders if the ring, itself, might be cursed.

Joe has no memories of happy times spent with his father. He only remembers the night that his Mom woke him up in the middle of the night, telling him to be quiet. His Dad was drunk the night before and passed out on the couch. Joe's Mom had bruising on her face, and she told the little boy that they were leaving to go visit his Grandma. They never returned home after that night, but his Mom worked to rebuild. She put herself through university, started a lucrative career and bought the house, where Joe still lives today. How he loved her, and her strength.

For some reason, she continued to wear the ring for the remainder of her life. Even if there was some type of curse, both real or imagined, placed on the band, Joe figures it's been long removed, because of a Mother's love. His parents' would have shared some moments of joy. He was born after all. Joe wonders if maybe his Mom continued to wear the ring, as a celebration of marking Joe's birth, and all the good years that she and her son spent together.

That was real. That kind of love holds magic.

Joe chokes back tears, as he holds the ring in his hand, realizing that he has known great love before. It came from a Mother's heart. It's the kind of steady love that needs to be realized again. This time, with the beauty named Hazel. Joe hopes she'll agree to be his wife.

He'll propose to her tonight. He can figure out how to explain the rest, later.

Tortured Beginnings

Joe has no idea how he's going to propose to Hazel. He's never been this far before, emotionally, and the thought is both exhilarating, and it scares the shit out of him. He knows, they can never be a regular couple, if Hazel even agrees to have him as a husband.

She's been patient with his erratic behaviour, like leaving her during early morning hours, and then not resurfacing again until late in the afternoon. He, so often, carries a backpack, even when there's no need to carry one. It's where Joe has been storing the food that Hazel has gone to the trouble of making for him. But that isn't really a correct description. Preparing meals is a labour of love for her, celebrating gifts offered by the Land and sharing them with someone special. Hazel has never asked any questions. And, for that, Joe is grateful. He wants to, but still can't find a way to explain.

He waits until late afternoon. When he's able to go out later that day, Joe makes a trip up to the grocery store.

He's already made arrangements to borrow a pontoon boat from a friend of his, and he's planning a romantic picnic on the lake. That's what he's told Hazel. Joe makes a mental check list of what he needs to buy. He remembers Hazel saying that she adores freshly-squeezed lemonade.

One of the kitchen items that Joe never got rid of, after the passing of his Mother, happens to be a clear glass jug. It'll be perfect for lemonade. Hazel's also told him that her favourite sandwich is egg salad, so he needs one of those too. And, to ensure that the grocery store deli has egg salad, Joe's already made a call to put in the order. Hazel told him that she likes her sandwiches with the crust cut off, so he makes sure to put in that request as well. He figures that it doesn't matter what type of snack, he buys for himself. It should be something that has meat in it, though. He's going to allow Hazel to believe that he's eating, again, then he'll hide it in his backpack to feed to Xavier and Saffy once he gets back later. Oh, yes, he almost forgot. Hazel also likes Eatmore chocolate bars, so he'll grab one of those as well.

On the drive back from the store, Joe makes a mental note to set his oven on low, so that he can dry some of the kale that he planted earlier in the growing season. Joe's always appreciated the healthy snack, which was introduced to him at a party, years ago. He can't enjoy it anymore, but he hopes that Hazel will develop a taste for them as well. The crunch of kale chips celebrates a season. And the vegetable has four times the vitamin C content, as spinach. But to be honest, Joe remembers it tasting really good.

By the time Joe returns home, he finds that he's literally shaking with anticipation. He has no way of guessing what Hazel's response will be. Naturally, he hopes she says yes.

Joe makes a point of paying attention, as he slices the ends off the lemons. He wants the squeezed delight to be as enticing to look at, as it is to taste.

He's still jittery, and his hands are shaking. It reminds Joe of those many, many days when he'd wake up feeling so woefully hungover. His hands were shaking then too, but it was a symptom of alcohol withdrawal, so much so, that he couldn't even spoon his coffee grounds into the filter, without scattering the coffee all over his kitchen counter.

The case couldn't be more different right now. He feels elation, paying attention to detail, before squeezing the lemon juice into the glass container. He doesn't want to cut himself again, not that it would matter. He'd heal up within moments. There's some wild mint, and strawberries, growing in his backyard. Joe decides to go out and pick some, so that he's able to infuse the flavours with a mixture of club soda and water.

He's been watching the cooking channel, on those nights when he's not with Hazel, and he comes home after feeding. While Joe no longer ingests food, he knows how much joy cooking and food preparation brings to Hazel. He's making the effort to learn more, so that he can please her.

He knows there is a small camping cooler out in his shed, so he'll dust it off and put in the ice packs that are in the freezer. He's feeling kind of proud that he no longer uses this gear, just to carry around beer anymore. Today is a special occasion. In his mind's eye, he paints the scenario for a perfect afternoon.

Joe toys with the idea of also bringing a CD player, maybe the two of them can do some slow-dancing again. But, he scraps that thought, knowing that hearing the sounds of soft waves, and the songs of birds will provide the ambience he wishes to create, for the moment that Hazel says yes, and his life will be changed forever. Again.

His deliberates on to what to wear. He doesn't want to appear too casual, but they will be floating on a boat, so he doesn't want to be too dressy either. He chooses a light-coloured golf shirt that has an upper pocket. It's where Joe will hide the ring. He'll wear a pair of baggy shorts, of course, and flip flops. Joe doesn't need to worry about whether he needs to shave anymore. His facial hair stopped growing the night of the encounter with Dust Man.

Like a first kiss, Joe knows that moments, like what he's about to do, are burned into memory, forever. They become the stories, that will be told about this type of gesture, to be told, and retold again, may times over.

He wonders if Hazel might consider taking his last name. Kiedrowski. It's the surname of his grandparents, who immigrated to Saskatchewan. Joe's Mom never did change her name when she got married, which, for the times was unusual.

The surname hails from a place called, Kiedrowice, near Gdan-sk, Poland. That part of Eastern Europe is one of the places where vampire lore begins. Again, Joe considers that, what has happened to him may have been pre-ordained, and that per-haps Dust Man might be some type of kin, long-forgotten and never spoken about. A dark family secret. His secret now.

Joe has always had an interest in vampire lore. He just never would have guessed, that he'd become one of them.

Even though the popular myth carried is that vam-pires originated in Transylvania, there is folklore that is even older, originating as far back at the 4th Century AD. Vampires in that part of Eastern Europe, are still, to this day, referred to as upierzs or upiors. The stories that Joe remembers, being uttered by others when he was a kid and listening in, was that a vampire is born evil. A Being with two souls, one of them for use during the living years, the other soul that comes alive after death.

With the introduction of Christianity, the rituals of baptism and conformation, eliminated the second, bad soul, which meant vampire numbers dwindled.

But, Christian faith and practice has been waning in recent decades. Perhaps that's the reason that Joe finds him-self in this predicament today. But, he was baptized. There are even photos, as evidence.

At this point, Joe imagines what it must be like when powers collide in the Universe. How is it anyone could de-clare to be a winner, if that's the plan? When good and evil meet, and clash.

Joe can hear himself repeating the words to The Lord's Prayer.

> *Thy Kingdom come, thy will be done*
> *on Earth as it is in Heaven.*
> *Give us his day, our daily bread,*
> *and forgive us our trespasses.*
> *Lead us not into temptation,*
> *but deliver us from evil.*

He's said the prayer hundreds of times, throughout his lifetime. First, as a boy in church, and in recent years, as a way of finding a source of power that would help him to quit drinking, before Dust Man caused that by turning him. For Joe, the prayer has obviously not worked. It happens again that Joe reflects on whether his being turned was something that happened by chance, or was it something that would have happened, no matter the circumstances. He can't be sure.

But, he is sure of his feelings for Hazel. Again, he makes the sign of the cross, as he begins packing up the cooler. Although, he can't be sure that God even hears his prayers anymore. He's already wandered too far into the darkness, and he did it long before being turned. He was a shit-ass drunk who never cared about anything, except where to find the next drink.

Joe checks his watch. It's almost time to pick up Hazel and head down to the boat. The radio is playing, as he finishes packing up. It causes Joe to also check the calendar. He didn't realize that he's planning to propose to her on Friday the 13th.

More folklore. Fears are based upon this day. As he listens to the radio interview, he prays that he is not walking through fire, and provoking the unmentionable, of things that are inevitable. Things that will keep he and Hazel apart. The radio guest states:

> Fear of Friday the 13th originates from the last supper and the 12 apostles. That meant that 13 people sat around the table, and one of them betrayed Jesus and the crucifixion happened as a result. So it started as a fear of 13 people at a table. Friday had already been a bad day because in Europe hangings were done on Friday, so it was known as hang man's day. The two combined make Friday the 13th a day filled with superstition.

Joe hopes to find a day of wonderment and love instead, on this Friday the 13th. Again, he prays.

For Better or For Worse

Well, they slow-danced anyway, even without a CD player. Joe and Hazel, holding each other, tightly as if one, together on the boat. There is no need for actual music, when you both have a natural rhythm together.

Hazel asks Joe why he's shaking, considering the temperature is up near 30 degrees, even still, this late in the afternoon.

"You're not sick, are you?" she asks, "If you feel like there might be something coming on, I can brew you up some goldenrod or sage tea, once we get home. Maybe you caught some type of bug, while out fishing with the boys the other morning."

Joe reacts with tenderness, holding her soft chin gently in his hand, and saying, "I did catch a bug, Hazel. It's called the love bug, and it all has to do with you," Joe looks deeply into Hazel's wide eyes, "In my over four decades, I swear, nothing has ever felt so right, as much as spending time together with you. I have never felt this sure, about anything, before. Hazel, I love you," he removes the ring from his pocket, "My beautiful friend, will you marry me?"

For a split-second, Hazel is dumb-founded, and at a loss for words. And, there is an eerie silence in the air that Joe can't quite put his finger on. It's like there is some sort of witness to this proposal. A Watcher who doesn't agree with what Joe is proposing.

It worries him, momentarily, until Hazel's expression changes to delight, "Yes, Joe, yes. I will marry you." They kiss and embrace, holding tight, like some beautifully sculpted piece of art.

The two of them toast, with a glass of frosty lemonade. Hazel immediately begins making plans,

"There is that little, historic chapel up at the Museum on the hill," she says, "I always imagined, that if I were to ever get married, that would be the place. It's one of the first structures that anyone sees, when driving into the community. And, it's perfect for us."

The building does hold a lot of stories, although hosting a vampire is likely not amongst that history. The church was built in 1910. It's seen many weddings, funerals and congregations amass. It's been moved three times since the turn of the last century, first being located at a busy intersection right in the middle of a residential area, where people may have been more likely to just drive by, and make comment, rather than stopping in for reflection and prayer. The chapel was then relocated, right in the middle of the business area. It's a little-known fact that, these days, that location is now where a busy ice-cream stand operates. The building was eventually moved to the Museum location, at the top of the hill, where the little blue church sits today.

Now that Joe knows, that he suffers no adverse reaction to being in a place of worship, he agrees. A church wedding is what they'll do. It's what Hazel wants, "Whatever you wish, my love."

Joe is aware that the chapel is named after St. Bartholomew, who was one of Christ's Apostles. He can't say that he'll live up to that name and the stories written about Bartholomew, who was considered to be incapable of deceit. Joe read the information in a pamphlet that's available at the front entryway of the church, when the couple visited that Museum, as well, earlier this summer. Joe knows that he can never claim that badge, of being eternally honest. He certainly hasn't been with Hazel, in too many ways to count.

Following the crucifixion, each Apostle scattered throughout the world, to spread the teachings of Jesus Christ. Bartholomew fled to Armenia, where he was eventually captured and beheaded.

With all the recent warnings from the Unnaturals, Joe can't help but think that history might repeat itself, and that he, too, might be walking into facing a similar fate. Being beheaded, or killed in some other way for his belief that he is deserving of great love.

In this case, Joe believes in his love for Hazel.

She breaks his train of thought, by next bringing up something to consider.

Practical decisions need to be made, like where will the two of them live? Joe has his own home, a place that holds so many memories for him, about his childhood, about his Mother. But, it also holds other, not so fond memories.

His house is where, these past years, Joe has found himself passed out, after way too many nights of hard drinking. It's where he has found himself so drunk, too many times, that he wakes up to find that he's shit himself, again. His bowels had loosened to the point that he couldn't even control his own bodily functions anymore. He'd pissed himself too. The alcohol abuse had taken over to that extent. That, is a memory he has no trouble in wanting to leave behind. It's not something that he ever wishes to share, even with Hazel, who he swears he'd tell her anything. Except, for one dark secret that he can't figure out how to bring up. He's a vampire. The secret eats away at him, Joe wants her to know, but it's been easier that she doesn't these past months.

Hazel, on the other hand, is connected to recollections of Kohkum, in the house where she lives. That's what brought her out to the Beach. It's those strong feelings, of love and family, that keeps her here in this community. Now, she's about to begin another chapter in her life, her family will now include a husband. Joe has been so good to her, kind and respectful in recent times, that she can't imagine, now, living without him.

She wants them to begin sharing a life together, immediately.

"Oh, and, we need to pick a date, Joe. I'd say sooner, rather than later," Hazel says, "a summer wedding, or early Fall. The little chapel on the hill closes after the September long weekend. But, I'm sure if we make special arrangements, the wedding date could even be after Labour Day. So, we need to make a decision soon."

She marvels at her ring and the emerald, that dances in the sunlight, as she holds up her hand to admire. Joe feels perfect contentment, in the moment. He gives thanks that Hazel said, yes. His love. His new bride. He can't wait for the moment to say - I do.

But, will that even happen?

Just as he's reaching to open the cooler, to grab another handful of ice to top up Hazel's lemonade, he sees movement out of the corner of his eye. Joe's peripheral vision has increased as well, likely a defence of sorts, in case anything tries to sneak up on him, catching him off-guard. Like the way that Corbitt did, the first night Joe was confronted by an Unnatural.

Joe swears that he just saw Mermaid. Her large, powerful tail fin splashing back down, creating large ripples, as she descends towards the depths of the lake.

He has no idea why she might have been wanting to keep an eye on him. Was she?

Joe can sense Mermaid's telepathic warning, as the ripples on the water subside, "Stay away, it's forbidden. You will only cause harm. You will bring disaster upon this union."

She's a fish that will never be caught. Maybe Hazel is supposed to be the same, Joe begins to wonder. Is Hazel a beauty that I have come to enjoy but can never really have? Why?

He also realizes that the Unnaturals have been surfacing a lot lately. They all come with the same message, ever since Joe started building a relationship with Hazel.

Stay away, our kind does not mix with humans. No good can come of it. It is forbidden.

Unnaturals. They bring messages and seem to keep appearing, now that Joe's senses are heightened. Or maybe, they've always been there. He just never noticed before, or maybe he has and just ignored it.

He remembers another point in time.

It was last summer, and through alcoholic delirium, Joe vaguely recalls that he has heard the swish of Mermaid's strong tail fin before. She was there, one early morning, after he'd passed out along the shoreline. He remembers that she touched his hair, pulling it away from his eyes, before turning Joe on to his side. It's a safe position for someone so drunk, just to make sure that they don't choke on their own vomit. That can happen, if left lying on their back.
Mermaid was there once before as well, but not that Joe would ever recall.
It happened one hot August night, last year when Joe was still heavily drinking. After the bar had already closed, Joe was already in a blacked-out drunken state. He decides to skinny dip under the Full Moon. He's never been a strong swimmer, and he goes out too far from the shoreline when it becomes clear, he isn't going to be able to make it back, safely. Joe flails and calls for help, but at that late hour there is no one around to see or hear. He starts sinking, until Mermaid intervenes, pulling Joe back to the safety of a sandy shore. Joe lay there, naked, all night long, waking up in a haze as seagulls begin their morning mew.
Joe might not remember that specific incident, but Mermaid does. And she doesn't like what she's seeing today. Joe is playing with fire.

Mermaid has been there to help Joe out before. Then she always quickly disappears.

Joe prays the same won't play out with Hazel. That she will quickly leave him, once she knows his secret.

Silence in the night. It's now unnerving for Joe, wondering what will happen next.

Start Spreading the News

As they come off the lake, Joe notices an unusual cloud formation that seems to be following him. It's shaped like an Angel, with a wide wingspan and arms outstretched. It reminds him of a story once told that seeing such an image represents that the seer needs to pay attention to intuition and guidance. An angel in the clouds. Joe knows he's certainly had a lot of visitations lately, but they come more like cryptic warnings from the Unnaturals. He wonders if everyone can see the Angel in the clouds, at this moment, or if it's an entity meant only for his eyes.

While Joe refuels his friend's boat at the floating dock of the Yacht Club, he glances down towards the gas tank. What he sees causes his hand to shake while self-serve refueling. He swears that he's just caught another glimpse of Mermaid. It's like she was following under the surface of the boat, and now flees towards deeper water and fewer onlookers, away from the shoreline. This time, there is no splashing of a tail fin.

Once docked, it isn't surprising that the first thing that Hazel does is to start making a series of telephone calls. There is a lot of planning to be done. She's getting married, and figures that she needs to call in the troupes, of her girlfriends. That's the best place to start. As she announces the news over the telephone, Hazel continues to gaze at her ring, which still glints in the sunlight, even as the suns' rays weaken. The day is approaching twilight.

It's also when Hazel brings up the topic of where to have a honeymoon. "I have always wanted to go to New Orleans," she tells Joe, "there is something romantic about the history of the French Quarter and its famous jazz scene, plus, we'd get to eat fresh seafood."

It all sounds good to Joe, who finds himself being relieved that he already has a current passport. Again, he worries about whether his reflection would even register, if being photographed for a new one. Which leads him to another concern. Wedding photos. Joe figures the best way to find out if his image can be captured on film is to take cell phone selfies. That'll be the test, for some later point in time.

But, New Orleans? Joe doesn't know if the lore about the city is true. That it is a vampire haven, according to modern media, folklore and storytelling. If that is true, Joe doesn't embrace the thought of coming face-to-face with another one of his own kind. A killer. Mythology does have its roots in reality. If this one is true, Joe figures he might just suggest a honeymoon somewhere closer to home.

His thoughts about catastrophe, and meeting up with other vampires, quickly change, realizing that he's about to marry the love of his life. Hazel.

We can take a road trip, he thinks, and never leave the Province. It can still be magical. Joe describes to Hazel, how the two of them can travel across Europe together, with a quirky twist. They never have to leave the Province, he explains,

"We have so many small towns in Saskatchewan, with names like Strasbourg, Aberdeen, Montmartre, Odessa, Amsterdam, Orkney, Penzance and Hague that we could totally make- believe. We can visit these places right here at home, and make the best of it. Besides, that is a large area to cover, we can pretend, and imagine, just as though we are driving across Europe. We'll dine at local cafes, visit small town marketplaces, bakeries and art galleries, and fall asleep in a new location every night. What do you think?"

Hazel loves the idea, and the two begin talking about how spending their nights in small town hotels, and eating at small town restaurants has its own cultural flair. The Prairie settlers come from all parts of the world, so there are sure to be unique findings, in both food and other flair.

"And, in those places where there is no cafe, we can forage through small town corner stores, and see what they have," Joe shares a cherished memory, "After that, we can have a tailgate picnic, like Mom and I used to do, when I was a kid."

Joe describes how that particular adventure always began as a drive in the country, with no real destination. They would just get in the car and drive. But, before leaving home, Joe's Mom would pack up sandwiches, fruit, cookies and something to drink. When they got hungry, they'd stop, wherever they happened to end up. They'd just spread out a blanket on the grass, in some ditch at the side of the road, and enjoy scenery that was new to them. It was always a good day, taking a trip but never really leaving home.

Hazel loves this story, and they both agree that, on their road trip honeymoon. Hazel insists that one of the destinations has to be at Love, Saskatchewan. It's a small village located near the City of Prince Albert, which is often referred to as the gateway to the north.

Love was a booming railroad community settlement in the early 1900's. Since then, its population has dwindled to 50 residents. But, it still has its charm, with a special postmark, should anything be mailed from Love. The postmark is that of a teddy bear holding a heart. Hazel says, "We totally have to write each other a love letter and mail it from there, with a Love postmark. Let's do it!"

This makes Joe happy, and he encourages Hazel to bring her Nikon, for their road trip. She's adept at photography, and it's a skill he thinks she should give some more thought to developing. There are so many abandoned grain elevators, and ghostly old and deserted homesteads, dotting the Prairies, as well as other unique landscape features. Joe suggests that Hazel might even give some thought to working towards publishing a book.

"A Saskatchewan History in Photos," Joe proposes, "you could do some historical research, or write short stories or poems, along with each photo. And the pictures would be a chronicle of our honeymoon trip. I like the idea."

"That name for a book sounds too boring," Hazel responds, "but I do like the idea too. Capturing moments in time. Our special time."

Whatever that outcome might bring, in putting together a book, Joe finds himself overwhelmed with joy, and the thought of building a future together.

It will begin by just getting in a car together, and driving.

Undercurrents

Once back on shore, and having delivered the pontoon boat back to his friend's house, Joe makes a suggestion, on what the couple might want to do this evening.

Hazel has never visited his home before. He suggests they spend the night there. Her first overnight with Joe, in his home. To him, it makes sense for Hazel to see how he lives, because eventually he'll have to be down-sizing. He can head up to the grocery store, and get some boxes to pack up things, that aren't to Hazel's taste.

She agrees to spend the night at Joe's, but not before suggesting that she goes to her own home first. Hazel wants to throw together an overnight bag, and retrieve Saffy. She doesn't want the dog to spend the night alone.

When they arrive at Joe's, Hazel snickers at seeing a dead mouse on his doorstep. She knows that it's his cat who left it there as a gift. Cats instinctively do those sorts of things, as a way of saying, thanks for feeding and taking care of me. A gift. "Thanks Xavier," she says, before opening the screen door, as she does so, she snickers to herself at thinking a corny thought, "If I were a cat, I'd spend all of my nine lives with you, Joe." Hazel sighs and once again checks out the ring on her finger.

When she enters the place, the first things she notices is that Joe has hung the sunflower painting that she made, when the two of them had a paint night during one of their first dates. The artwork is in his entry way, and it's the first image that greets a visitor upon arrival. On another wall, is a water colour of a hummingbird, exacting nectar from some bright red bouquet of flowers. Joe tells Hazel that he painted that one himself, an experiment in his ability to draw. He says he used her paints to colour it in, one night while she was asleep and he was still awake. He doesn't mention that the painting was created, during the wee, quiet night hours, after he'd gone out to feed.

Ironic, that Joe dances towards the same movements now. Needing to feed, like a hummingbird.

The small bird, on red nectar. Him, feeding on red blood.

Is Joe a monster? Hazel's love doesn't leave him feeling like one.

It is at this moment that Joe realizes that Dust Man didn't suck the life out of him. Alcohol had been doing that for years. It's as if God created the Devil, and in this context, Joe isn't referring to himself. He only wishes that, all those years ago, he'd been standing by the door, guarding, and making sure to never let that Devil in and, that Devil is alcohol.

He is more grateful that, after waiting years of wishing and waiting, he's finally found a place to belong. With Hazel. He'll do whatever he can to make it work, make it last. Also knowing that it means, starting with telling the truth about what he's become. That'll happen, but not right now.

There isn't much more artwork to view on the walls. There are some lovely antique pieces, left by Joe's Mom, including a wooden sitting bench. It is hand-carved and in the shape of an elephant. Hazel thinks it's a piece that will look good in her home, a place they will start to furnish together. Although, it isn't furniture that makes a house, a home. It's love. She knows that they will share plenty of love no matter where they live, and no matter how they decorate.

While Joe's place can't be described as a bachelor pad, Hazel thinks it's likely best that he moves in with her. It's been her place of strength and wonderment, ever since childhood. Sharing their lives in that same space will allow for that to carry on, and grow. Maybe even raise a family. That's her wish.

Once in the kitchen, and before putting down her purse, Hazel has a little giggle upon realizing that Joe doesn't have a table. Instead, it's an upright ironing board that he appears to be using, as his place to dine, or at least it's where he places items, like a sugar bowl and salt and pepper shakers. She finds it curious that he has a child lock on his pantry door. Joe doesn't have children. She has to ask why he's got a lock.

He tells her it's because of Xavier.

The cat still has his feral tendencies of wanting to keep some distance, except when he's hungry. He regularly comes up on the veranda, asking for kibble. But when the weather turns, and there is a deluge of rain, Xavier actually comes indoors. He can smell the bag of cat kibble stored in the pantry, and he's a clever, little bugger. The feral has figured out how to clutch his paw under the door, forcing it to open. The first time Joe let Xavier in the house, the cat ripped the bag open, helping himself to food. Joe was left to clean up the mess, which included strewn pet food, and Xavier's puke. The little dude had gorged himself, to the point that his stomach couldn't handle an excess amount of kibble.

"So, now that we're here, would you like me to fix dinner for us? I don't mind," Hazel offers.

Joe tells her that he's already got that covered,

"It's been such a great day. I love you, and don't want you to be fussing around in the kitchen tonight."

He says that while he was out earlier in the day, and getting things ready for their picnic on the boat, he also picked up some hot dogs and fixings, "We can have a wiener roast and just enjoy sitting by the fire tonight. Sound good?"

Hazel nods in agreement.

Contrary to popular belief, Joe is not afraid of fire. Indeed, one of his favourite childhood memories is sitting around the pit, and roasting wieners or marshmallows. He looks forward to continuing that, as a tradition with Hazel now. He finds himself also wanting to become a student, of sorts.

Hazel's mentioned that she wants to teach Joe how to make bannock on a stick, over the open coals of a firepit. It's something she learned as a girl, taught by Kohkum, when the two went out camping on the Land. It sounds like an interesting, and necessary skill, to know. Joe toys with the idea of suggesting that she begin teaching him tonight, until he realizes that he has none of the necessary ingredients in his pantry. He's given all of that away to those in need, to the Community Fridge in the city.

Also, for the first time in his life, human or otherwise, Joe finds himself wishing for an early autumn. It's because of another story that Hazel's told him, the evening they went for a walk to the little library, and before the transformation mishap occurred.

Again, he finds himself planning for their future. Joe experiences a hope and joy that he hasn't felt in a very long time.

Hazel had told him that, throughout the month of September is when chokecherries are perfect for smashing. It's another of her family traditions that Joe wants to learn. The way Hazel describes it, ripe berries are placed on a flat rock and smashed with another large stone, so that the meat of the fruit can blend with the chokecherry pit. Kohkum says eating the pit is good for digestion. The berry mixture is then placed in a cast iron pan, over the coals of the firepit. Lard, a bit of salt and a sensible amount of sugar, depending on desired sweetness wanted, are both added, to blend it all into a type of paste. Hazel swears that it is the tastiest thing that anyone could ever eat on their bannock. And, it needs to be eaten fresh. Her words and instruction on how to smash chokecherries, replays in his mind again and again. He gets choked up as he imagines the family closeness of Hazel's memory. He's especially touched by how the story ends. In addition to the bannock on a stick, Kohkum brings a cookie cutter with her, while out in the bush. It's in the shape of a gingerbread man. She cuts pieces of bologna into the shape, and lets them slowly fry until crunchy and browned. It too, was one of Hazel's favourites, when she was a young girl.

Joe longs to carry on with these traditions. Her memories and her stories are another way for him to imagine his life, together with Hazel.

Even though he'll never be able to actually taste the mixture of smashed berries, he longs to try making it, knowing that his sense of smell will capture the flavour, and become a part of his own memory. That, along with knowing the happiness that being out on the Land always brings to Hazel.

For him, new adventures, experienced together, can't happen soon enough.

Joe kisses Hazel on the forehead, as she stands beside his make-shift ironing board/table. He heads out the door, towards his chopping block, where he'll cut some wood for tonight's bonfire. Saffy follows, maybe to see what Joe is doing, or maybe to get away from Xavier, who's been growling at the dog. The cat has taken his place, sitting at the edge of the deck. The two animals might become friends, maybe not. Xavier has his own way of doing things. And, cats rule, as if anyone didn't already know.

While Hazel is now alone in the house, she can't help herself but do some snooping. They are going to share a life together, after all.

She opens Joe's backpack, which he's left near the front door. Inside, Hazel finds some empty Tupperware containers, but nothing else.

She opens his refrigerator door, to find, only a package of hot dogs, some mustard and ketchup. It makes her wonder, has he not gone shopping recently? Joe always talks about how much he loves the food that she's prepared for them, since they began to date. She's always had the impression that he enjoyed cooking as well. But there are no ingredients in the fridge to suggest that.

In his freezer, there is a curious find. Hazel notices some frozen bacon, but it isn't in its original packaging. Instead, Joe has separated each piece, then wrapped them piece-by-piece individually and placed them in to freeze. It seems odd, Hazel thinks. But then again, he does live alone, so maybe it makes sense in some way. He freezes individual portions.

Of course it makes sense. She remembers Joe telling her that he sometimes cooks for Xavier. The cat has developed a taste for crispy bacon, bite-sized pieces of beef jerky and pan-fried fish from the lake. Still, Hazel has to shake her head, wondering why there is so little food in Joe's home.

While continuing to root around in his freezer, she also finds some food items that she's sent home with him in the past, like it's some kind of trophy. A piece of frozen Saskatoon berry pie, and a container filled with chili. For her, this is starting to border on being creepy, too much mystery at the start of what should be their lives together. She checks his pantry and cupboards, there is nothing there as well, except for a bag of cat kibble and a package of hot dog buns.

She wonders if she should mention something, but decides against, for the moment. The day has been filled with his love and attention. Hazel doesn't want to spoil the mood.

There's likely a reason for empty fridge and cupboards. She decides that she will ask Joe about it, later.

A good snoop around someone's home always has to include seeing what's in the bathroom medicine cabinet. Hazel knows that she shouldn't but she cannot help herself but to slowly inch open the glass mirror on the cabinet door. She is alarmed to find that it's empty as well, except for one large item that sits on the bottom shelf. Hazel reaches out to grab it, so she can get a better look. She gasps upon realizing what it is that she now holds in her hand.

She first saw it weeks ago. It's the gold ring of the man who harassed Hazel one afternoon. He'd bragged about his wealth and how he could give Hazel anything that she wanted.

He'd been burned alive, while allegedly checking on his golf cart engine.

When Love Outweighs the Pain

Joe gets busy splitting wood for the fire. And, for the first time, in probably decades, he experiences a genuine feeling of peace and contentment. He attributes love as the magic ingredient for this salvation.

Paging through the story of his life, he comes to accept that any short-comings or downfalls that he's known for way too long are not necessarily of his doing. He did not ask that memories of child abuse stay with him. He's always wanted to ask for help in finding ways to get rid of those memories, but he also knows it means, first facing the pain. Maybe he's finally found the strength to do that.

Joe did not ask to be stricken with disease. Just as any person does not choose to live with diabetes or cancer, he didn't choose to live with the disease of alcoholism.

But, he did succumb to it. And, even through his worst moments, he was too proud to admit that. When help was available, he'd accept it for a while, until failure after failure at trying to stay sober was too much for him.

He wasn't strong enough to completely shed his childhood trauma, which caused so many problems later on in his life. When Joe was fully sober, he couldn't handle all of the detailed memories crashing back. Drinking is how he'd silence those old voices, by drowning them out with booze.

It's because he was scared. What is on the other side of that pain?

It is amazing to him how much physical abuse the body can endure. He should know, having done his fair share of excessive abuse of alcohol. But, emotional abuse, he thinks, leaves deeper scars. Some that never heal.

Pausing for a moment, Joe now knows, Hazel was always on that other side of the darkness where he'd been travelling. She'd been waiting for him, and now they finally found each other.

It is in this moment, that he counts his blessings. It's where he comes to understand that he hasn't been forsaken. Maybe Dust Man didn't take his life, as he's always believed, along with a feeling of scorn. Rather, maybe the Dark Angel changed the course of where he was heading.

Perhaps, it too, was somehow an act of love.

It saddens Joe to accept that what he's become happened due to a curse that cannot be removed. That curse is sad and painful memory. It isn't being turned into a vampire.

Regardless, he knows that if he wants to move forward, celebrating life with Hazel, those old wounds need to close. He must leave it behind. It's something that he's known for some time now, beginning with his long-ago and healthy practice of attending AA meetings. One of the important steps towards recovery in that program is to embrace forgiveness. Prominent in the AA literature are the words to a familiar litany, The Prayer of Saint Francis. Joe knows the significance of that prayer, and what it means.

Even more important than asking for God's forgiveness, Joe needs to forgive himself. Over the years, he's broken so many hearts because of his actions. No more. He's pretty sure that this is never what God wanted him to become.

While reminiscing about the threads of his life, Joe recites that prayer, inviting Divine intervention.

Make me a channel of your Peace.

I was born of strong roots, and a Mother who had the courage to overcome obstacles. She protected me and kept me safe. Some may suggest that a boy outgrows his attachment to his Mother. That never happened with me. Mom was the most important centre of my life, right up until the day she died.

Where there is hatred, let me bring your love.

No woman ever needs to live in fear, and have to wear sunglasses to hide bruises. Contrition. I stopped the spousal abuse because I could, even if killing is a sin. What I did, I did out of love.

Where there is injury, your pardon, Lord.

Mrs. Carter was a kind and gentle soul. She had lived in pain long enough. It was time for her to dance with her Royal again.

And where there's doubt, true faith in you.

Holly accepted that she was going to die, and did her best to do it with grace. I only hurried the process of something that was inevitable. I stopped her pain.

Where there's despair in life, let me bring hope.

Now that I know the teachings of Kohkum, I will carry on, and live as she has directed of my love, Hazel. I know, that if we do not accept our woundedness, it only festers, with the potential to poison, even cause death. But it means vulnerability, and that is courage, accepting our pain and shortcomings.

Where there is darkness, only light.

It is fire that cleanses, removing the stain of arrogance that threatens the safety of others. We were put on this earth to take care of each other, not bring each other down and cause harm. A woman like Hazel cannot be bought, damnation to anyone who thinks otherwise. It's my role to protect her.

And, where there's sadness, ever joy.

Joe recalls a Prayer of Confession. It was uttered during church services, years ago when he was a boy in church. It is as though being turned has somehow given him the ability of eidetic memory, where he remembers details from decades ago, in precise detail. The prayer asks:

Why are we always willing to descend into the worst areas life offers us?

Why can we stand on sin's shaky foundations, yet find it impossible to dance in joy?

Why are we so quick to trumpet hollow achievements, and do not seem to be able to hear whispers of hope for us?

Joe is grateful for the memory.

Oh, Master grant that I may never seek

I will stop hiding behind shadows, never again allowing fear to be my guide.

So much to be consoled as to console

When I see the opportunity to help, I will help. Providing food to the Community Fridge Project humbled me. Those people have dignity and are not too proud to ask for help. It's something we all need to do, to ask for helping hand when it's needed.

To be understood, as to understand

Those young longboarders were an inspiration. I'd been wallowing, waiting for something good to happen, instead of getting out and making it happen. I embraced that joyous movement then, and I'll do the same in other areas of my life.

To be loved as to love with all my soul.

When I looked in the mirror before, I'd see an image of someone scared, lost and forlorn. That image is now erased and I accept how I am destined to carry on.

In giving to ourselves that we receive

I am a disciple of Hazel, who helped to rid me of doubt and feelings of not being worthy. Love is just a word until someone gives it meaning. I have found it, and will protect it.

And in dying, that we're born to eternal life

I need to accept and acknowledge. I leave the bad memories that stopped me from moving forward, behind. With this, I ask for forgiveness.

Amen

No matter what he's become, Joe knows that he and Hazel were brought together by love, and that is a gift that comes from God. In some odd way, this leads to another thought, that Dust Man has given him a gift as well. In being turned into a vampire, not only was Joe able to stop drinking, but he was able to begin loving Hazel.

He decides that he needs to stop seeing what he's become as a curse.

Forgiveness is a powerful gift.

Joe lays his axe down on the ground and raises his hands to the sky. He is fully aware that drunkenness is one of the seven deadly sins, forbidden, because being a drunkard dishonours God. It is destructive to oneself, family and friends. It's a sin that he's committed too many times to count.

Still, it's never too late to hope.

Joe remembers the preamble to his Alcoholics Anonymous meetings, that alcohol is cunning, baffling and powerful, and that a person needs to be constantly on guard to avoid relapsing. He can't continue beating himself up because he couldn't stay the course. That's behind him now.

No more emotional relapsing because of a past, which he can't change.

He makes the Sign of the Cross, and makes a promise to accept whatever a new dawn might bring.

Night Moves

It's been an event-filled day for the both of them. And, even if they had thoughts of a long night filled with passion, it doesn't happen. Sitting beside the fire is peaceful. The air is still, and there are no sounds of seasonal residents partying in their backyards, tonight.

Hazel has already roasted two hot dogs, one for her and one for Saffy. She begins to nod off, and tells Joe,

"I hope you don't mind if I go in and just lay down for a few minutes. I had an early start this morning. And, I am tired." Joe reassures that she should feel comfortable in his home, and walks in with her to give her a kiss and cover her with a light blanket, as she lays down in Joe's bed. The dog follows, while Xavier sits out on the veranda observing. The cat's ears are turned back, like he's in a bad mood that his space is being invaded by newcomers.

Within about 30 seconds, Joe can hear Hazel begin to lightly snore. He knows that she is now out for the night. It is a deep sleep and a beauty rest for the woman he loves.

Joe was going to continue sitting by the fire for a bit, until the embers burn down, but he has hunger too.

He knows he's likely to find someone, out wandering in the night, trying to figure out where he parked his car, or even wandering aimlessly and wondering where he lives. And, there will be no killing tonight. Joe's in a good mood, and figures it's best for him to go back to the initial promise that he made to himself when he was turned. That he will not kill, he'll only feed.

Walking down towards the area where the bar is located, Joe is confronted. But, not by a man. Some grand-looking beast steps out from the shadows. He's half-man and half-elk, with a full rack of antlers.

And, like Joe's first meeting with Corbitt, the thing has a warning for Joe. But this Being goes further, also delivering an outright threat,

"You can't do this to Hazel," the Centaur says, "you are putting her in danger. Other Unnaturals will be attracted, and there is no way you can always protect her. Some of them are dangerous, wanting only to kill. And, you are no match for them. They will kill her to get to you."

The Being goes on to describe how, decades ago, he was faced with the same decision, and a similar dilemma. Whether to show himself and tell the truth, or continue to live in the shadows.

He was in love once, too.

Centaur talks about Hazel's Kohkum, and how he used to follow her while she was out berry-picking, when Kohkum was a young lady. He could sense her goodness and generosity, and wanted to make his acquaintance. But he never did, instead, just being present while she walked on the meadow, by herself, and making sure that she came to no harm. The best he could do was watch from a distance. That was his only job, to keep her safe but never to present himself. Centaur could smell the sage shampoo that the young Kohkum had used to wash her hair, and he always longed to touch her, to introduce himself. But, he knew it would be a violation to approach her. "That's just the way it is," he says, "humans live amongst us, but we are there only to watch and protect. Never to interact, it's forbidden."

Centaur describes a day that a group of coyotes were stalking and massing. He could sense their intention was to attack Kohkum. Maul her, kill her and eat her. So, he attacked first, kicking them hard, until the canines dispersed and ran away. No one had any idea that he was even there. No one heard a thing. Centaur had learned how to be invisible to humans. Kohkum had no idea that she'd just been saved from being eaten, except for the sharp safety of Centaur's antlers, and what he held for her in his heart.

He loved her, but could never show it.

Centaur still loves her today, and carries the memory of a sweet-smelling girl, who loved being out on the land. He tells Joe that he visits her grave site regularly, even now, especially during the Full Moon. That's when Centaur leaves a bouquet of wildflowers. They are the same ones that he watched the young Kohkum picking, all those years ago. He considers himself blessed to have been a part of it, even if the rest of his life means continuing to live in the shadows.

Unseen. Unheard. Unknown.

Centaur has felt love. He's known goodness, but that's as far as he dares travel. Being an observer, only. Centaur knows his role. He wants Joe to know his role as well, and it does not include being a husband.

"That's the law, Joe. The way us Unnaturals must travel. We can fall in love but we can only watch from a distance. To play with fire is to attract something unmentionable. You haven't yet met the ones who aren't so gentle. They live here, as well, taking without mercy or care. Break it off, Joe, and let Hazel live as she's meant to be living. With something that is not filled with darkness." Centaur sighs as he continues in the diatribe of advice, "Hazel is human, you are no longer. I don't have the stomach to come clean up the mess, again, if you don't stop. It can lead to nothing good. I know you love

her, but she deserves better. Think about it. More importantly, act on it. You are no longer human. That's just something
you'll have to accept and live with - without causing harm to
Hazel. The blood of Kohkum runs through Hazel's veins, and
I will protect her, even if it means, killing you. And I will kill
you, if you don't' heed my advice. But I won't kill you tonight.
I'll give you a chance. Go now, and break it off. There is no
other choice."

Centaur disappears into the shadows.

Joe finds himself stymied by this encounter. He did
transform, into ugly face, ears pointed and scary-looking
hands again, but he is grateful he didn't have to use force.
Centaur is so muscled, tall and strong, that Joe can't imagine
whether an actual battle would have resulted in his favour.

Joe doesn't want to make his acquaintance again,
and he wonders about the prophecy, about something that
Centaur said. That there are others who kill without mercy.
Centaur also threatened to kill Joe. In reality, he knows that is
more like a promise.

There can be no union, even if there is love.

Good Night Sweet Prince

Joe arrives back at his home that night, without having fed. And, since he's removed Hazel's fibroids, he can't even rely on that. Regardless, Joe finds that he feels exhausted. The encounter with Centaur took a lot out of him, and he's in dire need of rest.

Joe glances at the beauty of Hazel while she sleeps. He can't stop thinking about how much he's come to love her. Her love is the gift that he's always prayed for his entire life. Despite Centaur's warning, he won't give it up. He'll fight any Unnatural that comes around, and he'll lose his own life trying, if that's the way it's got to be.

Joe lays down beside Hazel, wanting to embrace her. But, he's got to push Saffy off the bed first.

Joe smells Hazel's hair. It holds the scent of homemade sage shampoo, just like Centaur had described. He runs his hands over the contours of her fit body, and then, he too, falls into a deep sleep.

It's close to dawn when Hazel awakens. She's feeling safe, with Joe's arms still in an embrace. But, she has to pee, so she gets up to head to the washroom.

The bright morning sun is just beginning to rise, and Hazel can't figure out why Joe covers up that light with heavy, darkened window shades. The window itself was left open last night, to let in the cool, night air. Hazel can hear morning doves cooing.

After relieving herself in the bathroom, she returns to Joe's bed.

She finds herself being terrified to notice that he has no reflection in the full-length mirror that's hanging on his closet door. She glances at her love, noticing that his hands are odd-shaped and unnatural. His ears are still pointed, and she sees fangs, instead of eye-teeth.

Hazel sobs, knowing what it is that Joe has become. Kohkum told her stories about this.

Every night when Hazel was a youth and planning to spend the summer evenings outdoors with her friends. "Never walk alone at night," Kohkum would advise, "and, if you hear something unusual in the bushes, or you feel like you are being followed, say a prayer to the Ancestors. They will help keep you safe. But, don't look back. You never know what you will find."

Joe never did let her in on his secret. But, Hazel knows what it is that she has to do. Her Kohkum told her about this. Hazel remembers stories about how mixing with those Unnaturals, that dwell amongst us, only leads to death and destruction. It leads to nothing that is good.

It breaks Hazel's heart to know, that her Joe is now one of them.

As wonderfully as he has treated her, it hurts Hazel to admit that somewhere, deep down in her intuition, she already knew that there was something, just not right about their union. She'd seen the signs, and to her detriment, she chose to ignore them.

Not all wishes come true, and if they do, they don't always last. In this case, their love story will not have a happy ending. It is a short story, meant to have a swift and sorrowful finale.

Joe never did tell her that he's one of the Unnaturals, but she can, physically, see it now.

She knows it can lead to things that are only evil, and Hazel begins to sob, remembering the words of Kokhum.

Bad medicine follows bad, follows bad, follows bad.
But you must never follow it.

Hazel loves Joe, and will act only out of love, for what she does next. She's to end Joe's suffering. And, to stop the suffering that both of them will surely encounter, promising to take each other as mates.

It is forbidden.

Hazel places the heart-shaped stone, that sits on the bedside table, in Joe's hand. It's the one she found by the lake all those days ago. She puts her emerald ring in his hand as well, crying while doing so. She loves Joe, but not enough for what she knows is destined to come, if they stay together.

Inviting pure evil.

Hazel prays to the Lord that what she's about to do is the right thing. She begs for forgiveness from God, for Joe and what he's become. As she glances at the rosary hanging from Joe's bedroom door knob, she hopes that Joe's Mom will be guiding her son as he embarks on this next journey. She asks for the blessing of Kohkum, as Hazel begins sobbing to the point of a wail. Her breathing becomes erratic, like she's on the verge of an anxiety attack.

Hazel bends to kiss Joe, just one last time. His lips are cold.

It is as though time has stopped, as she decides what to do next. Her hands are shaking as Hazel, ever so slowly, inches open Joe's heavy window covering. The first rays of the morning sun are gaining strength.

Hazel is so distraught that she's barely able to speak. Still, she whispers the words that she needs to say:

The pain in my heart does more than cry
I sense the Hand of God anigh
the morning sun is about to rise.